.45-CALIBER DESPERADO

W9-AXG-221

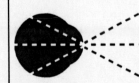

.45-CALIBER DESPERADO

PETER BRANDVOLD

WHEELER PUBLISHING
A part of Gale, Cengage Learning

GALE
CENGAGE Learning·

Detroit • New York • San Francisco • New Haven, Conn • Waterville, Maine • London

GALE
CENGAGE Learning·

Wheeler Publishing Large Print Western.
The text of this Large Print edition is unabridged.
Other aspects of the book may vary from the original edition.
Set in 16 pt. Plantin.

LIBRARY OF CONGRESS CATALOGING-IN-PUBLICATION DATA

Brandvold, Peter.
  .45-caliber desperado / by Peter Brandvold. — Large print ed.
    p. cm. — (Wheeler Publishing large print western)
  ISBN-13: 978-1-4104-4555-1 (softcover)
  ISBN-10: 1-4104-4555-0 (softcover)
  1. Large type books. 2. Outlaws—Fiction. 3. Gunfights—Fiction.
4. West (U.S.)—Fiction. I. Title. II. Title: Forty-five caliber desperado.
PS3552.R3236A61444 2012
813'.54—dc23   2011043539

Published in 2012 by arrangement with The Berkley Publishing Group,
a member of Penguin Group (USA) Inc.

Printed in the United States of America
    1 2 3 4 5   16 15 14 13 12

FD026

Once more, for Aunt LaVerne,
who loves chatting about the old days
as much as my mother did.

1

The bald giant's fist was a battering ram.

As it flew toward Cuno Massey's face, it grew as large as a wheel hub in the young freighter's eyes. It glowed like solid brass in the sunlight hammering the dusty prison yard. Black hair curled against the bulging knuckles. Grease and grime lay like mud chinking beneath the clamshell-thick thumbnail.

Cuno had feinted left when he should have feinted right, feet spread, hips pivoting. He was caught off balance. His father, who'd taught him to fight, would have clucked reprovingly.

The fist disappeared an eighth of a second after it had become all that Cuno could see. For a full second after that, the world went dark. It filled with the tolling of cracked bells. Beneath the ringing, there was an explosion. Beneath the explosion, Cuno could hear grinding sinew followed by the

racking agony of an Apache war lance rammed through his nose deep into his brain plate.

Warm blood oozed across his cheeks and dribbled into the corners of his mouth. It was thick as molasses, but it tasted like copper. He inhaled some of it, blew it out in a sneeze-like cough, brushing a fist across his mouth.

He shuffled a half-dozen feet straight back as he heard the prisoners yelling through the doors of their cells stacked in three tiers around him. Others, released from their cells for Fight Day to view the proceedings in the roped-off arena in the prison's main yard, were nearer the fight but were also being silently warned back by many guards wielding sawed-off shotguns.

Some of the crowd was cheering. Those who'd placed their bets on Cuno were booing. There were damn few of those, as the bald giant's reputation as a bare-knuckle fighter was second to none at the Arkansas River Federal Penitentiary outside Limon, Colorado Territory.

Somehow, though blood continued to dribble from his nostrils, and the yard with its buffeting American flag and roofed guard towers and three-tiered cell barracks pitched wildly around him, Cuno managed to set

his feet in the finely churned dust. He did not fall. The bald giant, with a mustache as large and sweeping as a raven's wing, narrowed his hawkish yellow eyes in amusement.

Amusement turned to resolve as, clenched fists raised, he grinned confidently and sidestepped forward, the muscles in his massive chest and belly ridging and writhing like snakes beneath sweat-slick skin tanned to the golden brown of a roasted chicken.

Like Cuno, Mule Zimmerman was clad in only the black-and-white prison pajama bottoms that dropped like knickers to just below his knees. His feet were bare.

"Ya should've gone down, kid. Should've gone down and stayed down." Zimmerman winked tauntingly, bobbing and weaving, moving his fists, poising himself for the final blow. Cuno could barely hear him above the roar of the crowd comprised of both reveling prisoners and armed guards. "Mighta gone easier for you if you'd just passed out. This way, see — since the warden's lookin' on an' all — I'm gonna have to kill ya."

He jabbed his left fist.

It was a weak punch meant only to drive Cuno's face into the big man's right. It didn't work. A red haze had bled down over Cuno's eyes when he realized the gravity of his situation and, flicking a glance to the second story of the barracks on his left, he saw the smugly smiling countenance of Warden Henry Castle flanked by two beefy guards in their tobacco-brown uniforms holding Henry repeaters up high across their chests.

In his straw boater, bow tie, and shiny black brogans, and holding a braided raw-hide quirt over the rail before him — he was leaning there like some tony cad admiring the girls as they passed in their summer-weight frocks — Castle resembled a smaller, dapper version of Mule Zimmerman. His face was waxy, his mustache polished to sharp ends that swept upward around and to either side of his pale, slender nose. His teeth were large and white beneath his curled upper lip.

Cuno set his jaws. His eyes dulled with a cornered animal's decisive fury as he stared at Zimmerman, who stood two inches taller than Cuno's five-ten, and a good thirty pounds heavier than his own lean two hundred. Just as the big man's fist flew toward Cuno's nose once more, his yellow eyes softening with shrewd confidence, Cuno ducked.

The fist made a sharp *whush!* as it slashed the air over Cuno's head.

Zimmerman grunted.

The roar of the crowd softened slightly. Cuno heaved up off his heels and, no slouch himself when it came to bare-knuckle savagery, hammered the big man's hard belly once with each fist. It was like pounding a muddy sandstone wall.

Zimmerman grunted again, voiced his indignation with a curse, and shuffled backward.

"Well," Cuno heard the warden say as he stood leaning over the balcony rail fronting his sandstone, bar-windowed office.

Zimmerman roared, narrowed his eyes, and bunched his lips. He started to raise his hands, but Cuno, swallowing the pain of his broken nose while aware that both eyes were swelling shut, used his quickness to his best advantage. He brought his own large fist up and hammered away at the big man's cheeks and jaws.

Zimmerman swayed, staggered, tried to raise his fists.

Cuno kept his own fists swinging, hearing his own grunts with each of the savage blows he brought up from his heels to smash against the big man's brick-thick skull. When he saw and felt the man's nose give and turn sideways against his face, he stepped back, feeling the warm spurt of the man's blood against his own bloody cheeks and chest.

He stepped in with his left foot, cocking his right arm back, but before he could release the jab, Zimmerman twisted around in a complete circle, stumbled, and fell on his back. Dust wafted around him.

The crowd fell almost deathly silent.

From one of the guard towers came the squawk of a Gatling gun being turned on its swivel base. This was a decisive time for the guards. In the wake of the weekly bareknuckle matches, almost always fought to the death on the warden's orders to temporarily relieve the man of the boredom of his lowly station at this remote federal outpost when he believed he was worthy of so much more, riots were always a threat.

Cuno stared down at Zimmerman.

The man was all blood, sweat, and dust. Only the top of his bald pate appeared unmarred and unstained. His blood-sodden mustache was stretched wide, showing yellow, crooked teeth also stained with blood dribbling down from his nose. His eyes were pinched down to little diamond chips of misery as he stared seemingly sightless up past Cuno toward the brassy Colorado sky.

His enormous chest expanded and contracted like a bellows.

In the sudden, funereal silence of the prison yard, the giant set his big hands palm down against the ground and lifted his head, trying to rise. He couldn't even lift his back. With a great, ragged sigh, he collapsed, causing more dust to waft up around him.

A soft snick sounded to Cuno's right.

He turned his battered head, rubbed blood and sweat from the corner of his right eye. The warden's bowie knife with its ivory-gripped handle protruded from the clay-colored dust at an angle. The glistening steel blade had been stropped to a razor edge. Cuno shifted his gaze to the balcony of the nearest brick barrack. The warden stood there, wrists and ankles casually crossed.

"Finish him," Castle said.

Cuno glanced at the big knife again, wondering how many throats that steel had slit here in the prison yard. So many, he knew, that the desert sand around this area of the yard was dark red with the spilled blood of fallen fighters. Some had likely had no business fighting; they hadn't been trained for it. Warden Castle didn't care. He chose his entertainment according to whim, like a perverted moron snickering as he chose which rats to feed to his pet diamond-back.

"I said finish him," Castle repeated, louder.

Cuno looked at Mule Zimmerman lying groaning at his feet and shook his head. "You want him dead, you come down here and finish him yourself."

Fire blazed in the warden's eyes as he scowled down at Cuno for a full fifteen seconds. The entire yard had fallen silent as a cellar at midnight. The only sounds were the blacksmith's hammer clanging down at the smithy's shop near the barns, stock pens, and other outbuildings that supported the prison.

Several of the guards, holding their shot-guns high, swung slow, ominous glances at Cuno, quirking their lips with the expectation of more entertainment.

Murmurs rose around the yard. Cuno held the warden's stare, but he could feel the Gatling guns boring hot spots into his sweating body, imagined the fingers of the eager guards twitching and drawing taut against triggers. They were likely flicking glances at the warden, awaiting Castle's deadly signal.

Cuno felt himself jerk with a start when the warden suddenly yelled, "Shackle him.

Shackle both of 'em and haul 'em down to the Pit!"

The murmuring around the yard grew, the other prisoners turning knowing glances at each other — some scowling, some grinning at the prospect of two of their brethren being sent to the warden's notorious Pit deep under the prison. Few men emerged alive from the place. When some did manage to keep breaths in their bodies, and make it out of that deep, stony, rat- and snake-infested hole, it was only to be led off to the prison gallows on the other side of the yard, beyond the three-deep cell barracks.

That was their last, long walk — the few feet from the heavy timbered door to the Pit on over to the gallows fifty yards away. Not all that long. But in the three months Cuno had been here, sentenced to life for killing four deputy U.S. marshals, he imagined quite a few lifetimes would pass during the walk.

Two guards handed their sawed-off shotguns to two other guards, then ran over to one of the stout wooden boxes arranged strategically around the yard. One unlocked the heavy padlock, threw the lid wide, and dragged out two sets of leg irons and manacles. Chains rattled and squawked as the two guards, one a Mexican, one a tall Englishman with a red spade beard and cold green eyes, came over and got busy throwing Cuno down on his belly and trussing both him and Zimmerman.

The big man appeared to have regained his senses, and now he just looked wary as he shuttled his gaze from the warden to Cuno and then to the two men brusquely shackling them both. Cuno met the giant's gaze, saw the fury there. The gaze told Cuno that Zimmerman would have preferred his throat been cut than to be sent to the Pit.

Most men would. Cuno, however, wasn't in the business of killing innocent men, even one who'd been forced by the whims of a blood-hungry warden into nearly killing Cuno himself. Cuno had killed the four marshals, all right, but only because they'd been intent on raping the girls Cuno had been leading to safety from an Indian raid across the Rawhide Mountains.

No, he wasn't in the business of killing, he thought as, glancing once more at the warden, he was brusquely hauled to his feet, pain pounding through his broken nose and sending shafts of fire through his brain. But killing would likely come much easier for him given another few days here in this death house masquerading as a federal penitentiary.

If he was alive in a few more days.

As if in response to Cuno's unspoken musings, the warden said, "Today, the Pit," as Cuno and Mule Zimmerman were led off across the yard, the Gatling guns squawking as they turned on their swivels to track the two bloody fighters. "Tomorrow," the warden added tightly, "they'll be hung with the others."

2

A soft scratching sounded, faint as fingertips brushing a rock wall. Cuno felt movement against his left thigh.

The sensations nudged him from the mercy of a light sleep. He lifted his head from his chest, opened his eyes and winced against the tightness of the swelling. Light was faint here in the Pit, sifting weakly down from airshafts along the high, timbered ceiling of what had once been the main shaft of a silver mine.

All Cuno could see were several blotchy brown blurs moving around him. He had heard the rats piping and scuttling when he and Zimmerman had been led down here at shotgun point, their wrists now shackled to chains hanging from iron stakes driven deep into the cold, pitted stone wall. Now, as if knowing he'd fallen asleep, they'd come out to sniff around for food. Or maybe to seek out his body warmth.

Something moved on his left, and he looked over to see a rat sitting on Mule Zimmerman's upraised left knee. It held its spidery front feet to its mouth, eating something. Cuno gave a repelled grunt and opened his mouth to yell but stopped when Zimmerman said, "Shhhh."

Cuno turned to the man shackled to the wall beside him, frowning. He'd thought Zimmerman had been asleep, but in the dimness he could see the giant's eyeballs gleaming faintly from between his swollen lids.

"Shhhh." Teeth shone beneath the ragged raven's wing of the bald man's mustache. "I'm growin' kinda fond o' this one here. Might make him my pet."

Cuno sighed and made an effort to suppress his innate revulsion. "Good thinkin'."

"He's kinda cute, you ask me."

"He's ugly as sin. I think your brain's swollen up like your nose, and you can't think straight."

Zimmerman groaned. As he pulled on the chains suspending his meaty arms above his head, the rat peeped and disappeared from his knee in a brown blur. "Shit," the big man said. "You're tougher than you look, kid — at least, from the neck up."

"Mule skinnin'."

"Freight?"

Cuno nodded.

"That'll build ya a set of shoulders. What kinda freight were you haulin' to get you thrown in here?"

Cuno merely scowled.

Thinking about the recent past only made him anxious not only about his own fate but about the fates of the three children and two young women he'd escorted in his freight wagon out of the mountains, fighting marauding Indians most of the way. He'd been wounded in the last attack, when his old partner, Serenity Parker, had been killed by the Ute pack trailing them toward Camp Collins. Cuno himself had turned himself over to Sheriff Dusty Mason, who'd been on his trail since finding his dead colleagues, in exchange for the sheriff making sure the three children and their attendant, Camilla, as well as Michelle Trent would be trailed to the safety of the fort.

Cuno was relatively certain that Michelle Trent and the Lassiter children had been given passage to relatives back East, but after he'd been taken into custody, he'd seen no more of Camilla. He worried about her now. Few good things came to young women alone on the frontier. Especially pretty young Mexican women alone on a remote military outpost, without friends or family.

And he'd found himself liking the girl more than a little . . .

In frustration, Cuno jerked on the chains holding his arms up high against the wall. More than anything, he wanted to lie down and sleep, but the chains made sure he remained upright, his shoulders bulging from their sockets.

"What's the point of these goddamn things?" he grunted, looking around the dingy, smelly environs. "It's not like we could get out of this hellhole without the chains."

"Torture."

The voice, high and almost feminine sounding, had come from the shadows on the other side of the dungeon. Cuno squinted and was finally able to make out three vague figures probably chained to the opposite wall as he and Zimmerman were chained to this one. He'd figured more men were down here, for he could smell the stench of sweat and human waste.

A while ago, he'd thought he'd heard something gurgling.

"Who's there?" Zimmerman called much louder than he needed to. In spite of his beat-up condition, he still had a good set of lungs. His voice echoed like thunder off the stone walls. "That you, Arguello?"

"Si, si." A pause, then the voice came more pinched and strained. "When'd you come, Mule?"

"I don't know — hour or two. Been catching up on some much needed shut-eye, I reckon. Good place for it, eh, Christiano?"

"Not much else to do," came the thin, defeated voice. "But come tomorrow, I won't have to worry about it any longer. Neither will Ralph and Moeller. I think Frank Skinner is down here somewhere, too, but I haven't seen him since the sun moved. Maybe he's gone to the saints."

"Not yet," someone grunted far off to Cuno's left, in another misty cell. "Can't believe I have to share a basement flat with a fuckin' bean eater. I hope they hang me sooner rather than later. As for the rats, Zim, try to catch one between your knees and rip its head off with your teeth. It's all your liable to get down here between now and your meetin' with St. Pete. The warden don't believe in feedin' the livin' dead. I just been sittin' over here prayin' St. Pete's got him a nice steak and a big baked potato waitin' on me. Maybe a side of garden greens covered with sweet butter and salt. And I sure wouldn't mind dancin' with his daughter, if he's got one that ain't too plain-faced."

"Shut up, Frank!" This from the Mexican, Arguello. "Don't antagonize the saints on the eve of your death, fool!"

Skinner chuckled. A couple of others laughed, as well, causing echoes to mingle and drown out for a time the tinny drip of water from an underground spring. The air was cool and damp, and Cuno yearned for the sun on his broken nose and aching eyes.

There was a long silence and then Skinner said in a desultory voice, "How'd you and Junior end up in here, anyway, Mule? I figured you for the warden's favorite bare knuckler."

"I was," Zimmerman said grudgingly. "Can you believe the shaver damn near beat the livin' shit out of me?" He sounded truly surprised and indignant. Cuno could feel the giant's exasperated eyes on him . . . as far as the big man could open them, that is.

"You best work on your footwork." Cuno hiked a shoulder slightly and winced at the pain it caused. "And don't get overly confident just because you're bigger than your opponent."

"Don't you get so damn big fer yur britches. You can't kill a man to save your own hide. All you did, bucko, was get us both in a helluva deep pit o' shit. I'd just as soon be dancin' with Ole Scratch as slummin' down here with Skinner and that Mex, smellin' their piss."

"Skinner's is the bad-smelling piss," Arguello said, and Cuno thought he could see a vague flash of teeth through a halfhearted smile. "Phew, he stinks like a Yaqui!"

"I wish I woulda cut your ears off when I had the chance, that night down in Juarez," Skinner growled.

A low eruption of laughter. Whoever had been gurgling continued to gurgle somewhere off in the shadows near Skinner. The man had likely been down here awhile and was half dead. Or he'd been half dead when they'd tossed him down here.

"I don't suppose," Cuno said, as the grimness of his situation suddenly swirled through the pain of his battered face to his consciousness, "that there's any way of bustin' outta here?"

Another eruption of wry laughter.

"I like him," Skinner said. "A kid who can beat the stuffing out of Mule Zimmerman and has a sense of humor to boot. Damn, kid, I wish I'd gotten to know you better up in the daylight."

"We'll shake hands tomorrow," Cuno said. "Just before they let us drop."

That had been an attempt to lighten his own mood. It hadn't worked. In fact, it had the opposite effect. A wriggly sensation flooded his bowels, and his chest grew heavy. Christ, he'd faced death many times in the few years since Rolf Anderson and Sammy Spoon had killed his stepmother and his father, and his young bride, July, had been killed by bounty hunters who'd come gunning for Cuno himself.

July and the baby she'd carried inside her, both dead. Murdered.

But he'd never been confronted by his own demise quite like this. Beat up and chained to a rock wall in a fetid, rat-infested, near-dark mine shaft. Had he always wanted to live this badly? You'd think, after all he'd been through — all the heartbreak and torment — he wouldn't mind dying so much.

Or maybe he just wanted to go out fighting. Not like this, trussed up like the fatted calf. But that's what was likely to happen. Even prisoners not sentenced to hang were hanged on the warden's whim. There was no proving they hadn't died trying to escape or from natural causes or even committed suicide, which happened every day, sometimes by twos and threes. He'd watched other prisoners led up from the Pit and over to the gallows, and they'd been chained so securely and guarded so closely that escape would have been impossible.

Cuno gave another furious tug on his chains, rattling them loudly.

"Forget it, kid." Zimmerman sneered. "Once you're thrown in here, there's nowhere to go except heaven or hell. You'd best put the rest of your time getting good with your Maker."

"Damned if I have one."

Skinner laughed. "Damned if ya don't!"

"Such sacrilege," muttered Arguello.

Cuno had never known a stretch of time to pass so slowly and miserably. Having his arms chained above his head, the blood draining out of them to pool in his shoulders, in addition to the pain of his broken nose, was exhausting.

It was also painful; he felt certain that his shoulders would pop from their sockets and hang by nerves and sinew.

For short periods, he could shove the pain into the back of his mind and doze, but that ability diminished as he weakened. The dripping of the spring seemed to grow louder and louder with every few drops until, when the sun had set and the pit was in total darkness, it sounded like the metronomic crashing of cymbals.

The night became so slow and agonizing, every second seeming like a long, torturous hour to be endured, that he found himself eagerly awaiting morning and his journey to the gallows. Death would be his only relief, and he looked forward to it like a dry desert traveler anticipates a drink of cool spring water.

Sometime in the night, he must have slept because his beloved young half-Indian bride, July, came to him, knelt, and softly kissed his battered nose. Then his eyes and finally his lips.

So real was the dream that he thought he could smell the girl's own unique aroma of chokecherry blossoms and sage mixed with two or three other fragrances he couldn't name.

He opened his eyes, half expecting to see her there but consciously knowing he would not. But he savored the smell of her, anyway. Until the dream, he realized that he'd forgotten what she'd smelled like. His heart swollen with the bitter heartbreak he'd managed to suppress until now, he silently wept with his chin hanging low against his chest, hearing a couple of the other condemned men crying softly as well as they endured their own individual torments that would find relief only in death.

When morning came, he nearly wept again with relief. The bits of light slanting through the airshafts revealed the men around him hanging from the spikes in the walls, only half alive. The half that still lived was praying for death.

Beside Cuno, Mule Zimmerman sat with his chin dipped low, slowly shaking his big, bald head in misery. He was making a low mewling sound that was probably as close as the giant could come to crying.

When the guards finally clattered down the stone steps, unlocking and opening the heavy timbered door, light spilled down from the morning sun above, revealing four men still alive — Cuno, Skinner, Zimmerman, and Arguello, who was out of his mind and muttering softly in Spanish for his beloved *Jesus* to fly down and waft him away on silken wings.

The other five men slumped against the walls, arms above their heads bowed low in death.

"Your brethren above is ready for their entertainment," the warden bellowed.

His laughter boomed throughout the mine shaft that had overnight become catacombs.

3

Chains clinked as the four weary prisoners stumbled up the stone steps of the pit.

The light was like spears impaling Cuno's eyes; it set up a vicious pounding in his already aching head. Connected to Arguello by a chain at the waist, he stumbled up the steps, stubbing his toes but barely registering that relatively minor pain below the other more severe misery in his head, face, and shoulders.

The Mexican was still muttering prayers as he shuffled barefoot up the cracked and pitted steps toward the grinning countenance of Warden Castle, who stood silhouetted in the open doorway at the top. Behind Cuno came Mule Zimmerman, half dragging Frank Skinner, who, Cuno had learned, had been in the Pit for three days. It was a wonder the man was still alive, if you could call his condition living. If the position you were chained in didn't kill you, the lack of food and water did. Skinner had survived, he'd indicated, by lapping up a rivulet of spring water tricking down the wall near where he'd been secured and killing a rat in the manner he'd instructed Zimmerman.

"Good morning, gentlemen," the warden said, clamping a hand on Arguello's shoulder in a mock gesture of brotherly love. "Did we all sleep well?"

The pain subsided in Cuno's eyes enough that he was able to hold a scowl on the man as he stumbled past him and out into the yard. Castle was grinning, his teeth white beneath his impeccable mustache. His eyes were like flint. Cuno hadn't wanted to kill someone so badly since he'd hunted the leader of the outlaw gang who'd killed his beloved July — Page Hudson.

Before that, Rolf Anderson and Sammy Spoon.

Now, if he could have managed the maneuver, he'd have lunged at the man and, with no other weapon handy, torn his throat out with his teeth. Castle turned his head to follow Cuno into the yard with his eyes, chuckling tauntingly as though reading the young man's mind.

"Warden, sir," Mule Zimmerman said behind Cuno, "kindly go fuck yourself. Lord

30

knows you likely haven't gotten it from anyone else in years."

"Oh, no — he's gotten it," Skinner said in a low, breathy growl that was all the voice he could conjure in his condition. "I think him and Dunlap been boning each other in the stables of a lazy summer afternoon." Skinner gave a droopy-eyed half grin.

Dunlap was one of the Pit guards coming up behind Skinner now. A man nearly the size of Mule Zimmerman, he raised a leg to kick Skinner, but Castle stepped forward to slap the man's shoulder with the back of his hand.

"Now, Sergeant — is that any way to treat our prisoners?" He pitched his voice with mocking admonishment. "Besides, if you kick him down, you'll likely have to carry him up the gallows steps. I don't think the poor man — the fierce train robber himself! — has an ounce of strength left in his wasted carcass."

"Like I said, Warden," Zimmerman said as the doomed procession was hazed eastward along the morning-bright prisoner yard, "kindly go fuck yourself, sir."

Just then, as he stumbled along behind Arguello, noting the other prisoners watching from their barrack cells or from out in the yard, he heard a sonorous voice begin singing "Bringing in the Sheaves." Cuno wasn't sure who was singing the hymn, as he was still too disoriented from the night in the Pit and from the fever in his brain to get his bearings in the bright yard, but at first he thought the singer, a former choirboy judging from the quality of the man's voice, was trying to add comfort to the condemned procession of shuffling, squinting, chain-rattling prisoners. But then a certain buoyancy in the voice and a few snickers rising around him, told him the man was only mocking.

Mocking the walking dead men. Cuno felt little acrimony toward the singer. He'd likely been here long enough to know the score. Every man here was one lost fight or one verbal misstep from the gallows himself.

As the guards led them around the barracks at the eastern side of the yard, the warden sauntering along to one side in his straw boater and flicking his quirt casually against his thigh as he strolled, Cuno was to the point that he just wanted to get it over with. He'd always found some comfort in believing, or at least hoping, that he'd see his pa and ma and stepmother and July and the baby again in some other world, and that prospect somewhat eased the fear in his shuddering heart.

The prisoners who'd been let out of their cells to watch the hanging moved as several loose groups around the yard, following the prisoners under the watchful eyes of the many shotgun-wielding guards. In the two guardhouses on the gallows' side of the yard, the Gatling guns swung on their pedestals as the guards, standing under the towers' peaked, shake-shingled roofs — two to each tower — kept the brass canisters with their six barrel spouts trained on the prisoners.

The gallows stood bathed in buttery morning sunshine rising over the southern Colorado desert of sage and bristly cedars. The log and pine board scaffold stood constantly rigged with nooses, so that all that needed to be done for a hanging was to lead the prisoners up the ten steps to the platform, drop the nooses around the con-demned men's necks, and trip the wooden lever that released the trapdoors beneath their feet. The oily musk of the creosote-slathered boards and logs made Cuno's eyes water.

There was never a preacher around, or even an executioner. Only the warden and his guards, all wearing their mocking, eager smiles.

Seeing that grin again on the warden's

face as he shuffled up the steps behind Arguello, Cuno knew one last blast of hot fury. He hoped he could return just once to this miserable world after he'd passed to haunt Henry Castle until the man died of a long, slow stroke that blew up his heart like a good portion of Magic Dynamite.

When Cuno and the other condemned prisoners had been released from their chains by the four guards who'd followed them onto the platform, the nooses were placed around their necks and the knots tightened. Cuno felt his pulse throb against the rope digging into his neck. Below him, on the floor of the prison yard, the warden turned and shouted for the singer to stop singing now, or he'd join the condemned on the platform.

The song broke off abruptly, mid-note.

The warden turned toward the condemned, flashed that smile again.

"Anyone have anything they'd like to say?"

Cuno had lots he'd like to have said, but he saw little point in it. Castle was only mocking him and the others again, as always. The other men must have realized that he was only trying to goad them into making fools of themselves. All, including big Mule Zimmerman standing slumped to Cuno's left, remained silent.

On the other side of Zimmerman, Frank Skinner, who must have been forty or older, stood with bent knees, silver-blond hair blowing around in the dry morning breeze. The Pit had finally almost gotten the train robber who had to be tough as whang leather to have survived as long as he had.

Now, like the others, he was just waiting for the relief of a quick death.

Cuno hoped the sandbags were weighted properly. Otherwise, he and the others would merely hang beneath the scaffold and choke to death, which is probably how Castle had planned it, anyway. Oh, well, the longest it had taken the other men he'd watched die was four minutes. One they had to hang a second time, but Cuno couldn't be that unlucky, could he?

Castle doffed his hat, twirled it on his finger. "Well, since you're all gonna be so grim about it, and it's already starting to get hot, I reckon we might as well get this show on the road."

Cuno saw a sudden quick movement in the guard tower on the prison's southeast corner. His mind barely registered the movement. He had other, more important matters at the moment. But then he heard the sudden chirp of a Gatling's swivel.

As Castle turned toward the man standing at the end of the gallows, whose hand was on the lever that would drop the trap-doors out beneath the condemned men's feet, there was a short burst of rapid fire that sounded like a hammer hitting an empty steel barrel four or five times very quickly. The bullets tore into the ground like giant raindrops, blowing up dust and horseshit. Cuno slid his glance to the mustached man with his hand on the trap-door lever, and now he saw a black splotch on the man's forehead. A thin stream of red sprayed out the back of his skull.

Warden Castle screamed.

Cuno turned his eyes forward to see the warden's knees buckle as he flung his left hand out behind him to grab the back of his left thigh. His white teeth shone beneath his impeccable mustache in an agonized grimace.

The guard who'd been about to pull the trapdoor lever dropped straight back to hit the ground without breaking his fall, a look of dumb awe making his heavy lower jaw sag. At the same time, all the other guards swung around toward the wounded guard, bringing rifles and shotguns to bear.

Bam-bam-bam-bam-bam-bam-bam-bam!

A line of four guards jerked as the bullets ripped through their uniform tunics, spraying blood into the dirt behind them.

The other guards, awestruck, froze. A couple jerked straight back, certain that they would be next to be beefed by the lunatic in the guard tower. Warden Castle, grunting and cursing and clutching the back of his left thigh, twisted around on his knees to peer toward the tower.

So much had happened so quickly that Cuno was still half expecting the trapdoor to open beneath his boots. He hadn't yet registered what was happening, though the echoes of the Gatling's rapidly fired shots were still echoing around in his head. Still, he had enough wits about him to be surprised at the girl's Spanish-accented voice yelling down from the tower, "Kindly have your guards toss their weapons away, Warden Castle, or the next round will blow the top of your head off!"

"How in the hell . . . ?"

The warden stared in agony and disbelief at the guard tower under the roof of which a girl in a red-striped serape and low-crowned straw sombrero crouched over the Gatling gun. Her long, dark brown hair dangled past her shoulders as she held steady aim on the warden. Beside her, a dark gent with long sideburns and a thick brown mustache aimed a Henry repeating rifle from one knee, sliding the rifle about the general vicinity of the warden. He, too, wore a Sonora hat — a black one with elaborate silver stitching.

Cuno's cheeks bunched, puzzled. "Mexicans?"

The girl grinned over the down-canted brass canister of the Gatling gun. "You shouldn't put on such an entertaining circus show, Warden!" she mocked. "Your guards become so distracted that they lose track of what's happening outside the prison walls!"

One of the guards lay on his back, head, shoulders, and arms dangling off the tower's wooden platform. Blood shone thickly across his paunch.

"In case you're wondering," the girl said, lifting her head cockily, "your other towers have also had a changing of the guards!"

Castle looked around from where he slumped on the ground. A spate of fire erupted from the guard tower in the fort's southwest corner, blowing up dust around the fallen warden. In turn, the other two towers fired several loud, dusty bursts, as well, leaving the warden slumped forward with his head on the ground, arms up as if they could protect him from .45-caliber bullets.

"Now, Warden!" the girl shouted gutturally, as though to further prove she meant business. "Order your guards to drop their guns. The ones on the gallows will please lift the nooses from the prisoners' heads and free them from their chains. Any foolishness, and me and my amigos in the other towers will turn you and your men into bloody heaps! Now! Quick! My finger is eager to make this wonderful contraption roar so loudly again . . . and kill so easily!"

"You'll kill us anyway!"

"Maybe," the girl returned. "But you'll die in one more second if you don't give the order, *mi* amigo!"

The warden stared back at the girl for two more beats then threw an arm up suddenly. "Do as she says! Throw your guns down!" He shook his head, overcome with emotion. His voice turned thick and crackly as he added, "Release the prisoners!"

That seemed to be just the order the two guards flanking Cuno and the other prisoners were waiting for. The platform creaked and clattered as they bolted forward and began loosening the knots and lifting the nooses off Cuno's and the other condemned men's heads. When all four were free of the ropes, the guards began unlocking the cuffs and padlocked chains. Their hands were shaking. Cuno could almost smell their fear lacing their rancid sweat, and it lifted his spirits though he still had no idea who in the hell had ordered him freed.

He suspected that Skinner's men had come to their notorious gang leader's rescue. Or maybe it was Zimmerman's men, though Cuno didn't know what the giant's profession had been before prison.

No, since they were Mexicans, they were more likely aligned with Arguello, though when he glanced at the wiry Mex beside him, the man looked as befuddled as the others.

When the chains were removed from Arguello's wrists, he fell hard on his rump to the gallows floor. Cuno turned to him as his own chains fell away, and dropped to one knee beside him.

The Mexican bandit, whose face was long, bony, haggard, and framed by lice-flecked locks of wavy, curly black hair, looked as though he'd have preferred the hanging to the confusion around him now. His cracked and swollen lips moved as he muttered incoherently beneath his breath.

The girl had shouted some new orders though Cuno hadn't heard them above the clanking of the chains, but now he saw movement near the front gates on his right, fifty yards away. The unarmed, blue-

40

uniformed guards with the red stripes on the legs of their wool slacks were busy removing the locking bar from the steel brackets on either side of the arched, timbered doors.

In moments, the doors were drawn wide and at least a dozen riders charged into the yard on sweat-lathered horses. They dispersed at once to gallop around the yard between the barracks, bearing down on the guards, who threw their hands up and backed quickly against the barrack walls.

The prisoners, too, moved away from the riders, most of whom were Mexicans but with several Anglos in the group, as well. They all wielded Winchesters or Henry repeaters, with sidearms showing in several holsters per man, knives protruding from high-topped, mule-eared boots. They were a rough-looking lot in grubby, dusty trail clothes, and whatever their purpose here was, they went about it with the boldness of seasoned renegades.

Now, Cuno thought as he knelt beside Arguello, they'll start looking for the man or men they'd come to free, take him, and ride the hell out of here. The reflection had no sooner swept across his brain than he shot his angry gaze toward the warden, slumped in a twisted heap before the gallows, blood

41

dribbling into the dust beneath his bent left leg.

Cuno was free of his chains. He could grab one of the rifles or shotguns the guards had tossed away and kill the man. Blow his savage head off. Then he'd bolt out through the open doors. He doubted he'd make it far in his battered condition, but what the hell? It was worth a shot. Here, he'd die for sure.

His heart thudded with grim purpose. He'd just poised himself to drop over the side of the gallows when a rider galloped toward him from the gaping prison doors. The rider was trailing a saddled horse by its reins. As the rider reached the gallows, he turned his own horse sharply, giving the reins of his second horse a toss.

They landed on the gallows near Cuno, who froze as he stared, lower jaw slack, at the beautiful skewbald paint stallion that had stopped before him in a twisting broil of sand-colored dust. The paint shook its head and twitched its ears, stomping one rear hoof in the dirt and blowing.

Cuno blinked, certain that Zimmerman had given his brain such a pounding he was only seeing what he wanted to see. His own horse, his own prized stallion, couldn't be standing here before him.

"Renegade . . . ?"

Another horse, a chestnut bay, galloped toward him. This one carried the Mexican girl who'd been in the guard tower. She drew up before the gallows, and dimpled her cheeks in a grin. Wisps of dark-brown hair clung to her tanned, dusty, pretty face.

"You just gonna stare at that horse, gringo?" said Camilla, jerking her shoulders back and thrusting her breasts out as she canted her head toward the open gates. "Or you gonna ride that cayuse the hell out of here?"

4

Cuno shuttled his befuddled gaze between the horse and the girl once more, vaguely wondering if the Pit had driven him mad.

But then before he realized it, he'd grabbed the reins and bolted off his heels and into the saddle that felt familiar and comfortable beneath him. His old saddle. His horse . . . the skewbald paint he'd bought after he'd sold his father's business and lit out on the vengeance trail after Anderson and Spoon.

He and the horse had dusted many trails together, chasing or being chased. The cavalry had confiscated Renegade at Camp Collins, when Cuno had been taken into custody under the watchful eye of Sheriff Dusty Mason, and that had been the last he'd seen of Michelle Trent, the Lassiter children, and Camilla (had she ever told him her last name?) . . . until now.

Cuno reined the horse toward the girl,

who watched him a little skeptically, no doubt a little repelled by his swollen and purpled nose and eyes. He blinked, frowned. "You came for me?"

She smiled a little sadly. "I am sorry it took so long."

Cuno looked around at the men of her gang milling on horseback, dust rising in the morning sunshine around their pintos, bays, mixed Arabians, and paint mustangs, the guards standing against the barracks walls holding their hands high above their heads. Rifles thundered as several of the guards were shot, sent bouncing off the barrack walls or, in one case, flying into the large stone water trough in the center of the yard. A few of the prisoners were killed, as well.

It appeared to be payback time all around for Camilla's men.

The warden continued to grunt and groan as he stared up at Cuno and Camilla, fury in his eyes.

"You can run," he seethed through his dusty mustache, pewter-gray hair flopping down above his left eye. He shuttled his glare from Cuno to Camilla. "But the army will hunt you like the Mexican dogs you are."

Camilla carried a Schofield .44 in a black

shoulder holster. As more rifles cracked around her, she drew the big hogleg, rocked the hammer back, and brought it to bear on the warden, whose eyes suddenly lost their bravado.

"Hold on." Cuno swung gingerly but quickly out of his saddle, walked over, and used his bare right foot to kick the warden onto his back. He stared down at the man, fists tightly clenched at his sides. "I want the honors."

"No," the warden mewled, grinding the heels of dusty brogans into the dirt and trying to crawl away backward. "Please, I . . . I'm only doin' my job."

"I don't think so."

Cuno leaned down, threw the right flap of the man's gray serge jacket back, and slid the big bowie from its sheath. It was the only weapon he carried, and he didn't mind using it willy-nilly, his armed men backing his cowardly play.

"Go ahead," Camilla said when she saw that Cuno was hesitating. "Cut the pig's throat. Many men have died worse than pigs under his command. Down along the border, he was a scalp hunter under the guise of a cavalry lieutenant."

"*Chiquita*'s right. Go ahead, kid." This from Mule Zimmerman, whose shadow angled across the warden's shoes as he stood at the edge of the gallows, looking straight-backed and damn near healthy aside from his swollen face. He grinned with menace as he smashed a fist into the palm of his ham-sized other hand. "Less'n you'd like me to do it."

Frank Skinner sat near Zimmerman, legs hanging down over the front of the gallows, slump-shouldered and weak, but grinning.

A pistol roared close by. Cuno jerked with a start. The warden screamed and raised his right leg, wrapping both hands around his bloody knee.

The pistol roared again and the tip of the warden's nose disappeared in a blood spray, leaving a blunt, ragged red nub. He released his knee to clutch his face, throwing himself belly down in the dirt and mewling like a gut-shot javelina.

Hooves thudded. Cuno turned to see the dark man he'd seen in the guard tower with Camilla gallop toward him on a tall black Arabian steed with two white front socks and a white star on its face. He had a thick mustache, and his brick-red cheeks were unshaven. It was a broad, savage, thick-lipped face with large, fervid brown eyes.

"How you like that, Warden?" the man

intoned as he brought the steed to a dusty halt.

Leaping out of the saddle, he stepped in front of Cuno. He removed his black, salt-stained Sonora hat and crouched in the dirt beside the warden. He pointed at the hairless top of his own head that was so badly knotted with pink and white scars that Cuno felt himself wince as he took a step away from the man. He'd seen healed scalping cuts before, and this man's looked like a particular nasty job.

"How you like this, uh, Warden?" he shouted in heavily accented Spanish, spittle flying from his broad, dark-pink mouth. "This what your men do to me on the border summer before last. You like, uh?"

The broad-faced Mexican jerked the warden's own head up by his hair, and with his other hand he slipped a horn-gripped knife from a sheath attached to the double cartridge belts crossed on his waist.

"Maybe you like a haircut like mine, uh?"

Cuno turned away as the man lowered the knife to the warden's head. The warden's scream was high-pitched and long-lived.

"I think I keep this one here," shouted the Mexican, straightening and holding the bloody scalp aloft. "Think I'll dry it and hang it from my cartridge belt the way your men did with mine and those of my *compañeros* you corralled in Yaqui Canyon . . . snuck up on us like a bunch of dirty coyotes!"

He twisted his face with yellow fury, holding the bloody scalp high above his head, his eyes and jaws wide as he glared down at the howling warden. "You were after Apaches — oh, but you didn't care! All Mexicans were half Apache, you said as your men hacked away at me! But I'm no Apache, Warden. Uh-uhhh!" He laughed suddenly — mad laughter that rose to drown out the warden's howls. "No, I'm Yaqui, and that's even worse!"

He lowered the scalp but lifted his chin, sending guffaws careening toward the bright blue sky over the prison.

Cuno turned to Camilla. Her face was expressionless, but she was keeping her eyes off the warden, who continued to scream, cry, and curse so shrilly that Cuno thought his eardrums would burst.

Good lord, who were these savage saviors of his, anyway? And why was Camilla riding with them? He'd known her to be a far meeker creature than the one he'd seen manning the Gatling gun — a girl who'd been brought north from Mexico by an American confidence man, then dumped.

She'd done what she could to survive, including playing nursemaid to the three children of a Colorado rancher.

"Finish him, Mateo," the girl said impatiently, reining her horse around in a tight circle, holding the ribbons up close to her chest. "We've wasted enough time here with this gringo. Umberto and Xavier have destroyed the Gatling guns. Let's ride, Brother!"

Cuno looked through the wafting dust at Mateo. *Brother?*

"I will leave him as he left me," said Mateo. "Wounded and dying and howling like a gut-shot cur!" He turned to the riders milling around him. "No one kill him! Anyone kills the warden will answer to Mateo de Cava!"

Mateo cleaned his knife on the warden's coat then swung up into the saddle. He turned toward the gallows, scowled first at Skinner and then at Mule Zimmerman and Arguello. "Those of you who Warden Castle condemned to die are welcome to ride with us. We have extra horses waiting. If you cannot keep up, however, we will not leave you to mark our trail. We will shoot you and hide your bodies so that only the panthers will find you!"

Zimmerman glanced at Cuno and

grinned. "Think I'll take my chances on my own."

Frank Skinner said, "Hell, I'll ride with any man who saves me from the gallows."

Mateo looked at an American in a pinto vest sitting a steeldust stallion nearby and jerked his head at Skinner. The man on the steeldust rode over to the gallows, and Skinner stepped gingerly onto the back of the man's horse.

Cuno looked at Zimmerman. "You sure?"

Zimmerman looked at Mateo and several of the other Mexicans with barely concealed disdain and shook his head. "I'm sure."

Cuno switched his gaze to Arguello, who sat at the edge of the gallows staring off through the prison's open gates, moving his lips and muttering soundlessly. "Christiano," Cuno said, riding over. "You wanna ride with us?"

The Mexican prisoner said nothing. He continued staring through the open gates, at the sun-blasted sage flats beyond the prison, and moved his lips as though speaking only to himself. Brusquely, Cuno grabbed the man's hand and drew him onto Renegade's back, behind the cantle of his saddle.

He wasn't sure why he felt the urge to bring the young Mexican along, but there was something so heartbreakingly vulnerable in the young man's eyes that he couldn't leave him. They were roughly the same age, twenty-two, and their surviving the Pit together, as well as the gallows, had sort of made them brothers. Cuno wanted to make sure Arguello had a fighting chance to survive.

As Mateo gigged his horse toward the open gates and threw up his arm, loosing a shrill summoning whistle to his other riders, Cuno glanced at Camilla. She returned his look with a dubious one of her one. "He won't make it."

"He'll be all right once we get some food and water into him," Cuno said.

Camilla smiled halfheartedly and reined her own horse into the dust of the other riders pounding on past the guards standing at their posts with their hands extended high above their heads, and on out the prison's gaping doors.

Hearing the warden's bone-splintering shrieks, Cuno touched his bare heels to Renegade's flanks, and the horse responded instantly, giving an eager whinny — maybe a whinny of relief that he was back under his old master's rein once more — and they galloped on out the gates and onto the sage flat. Camilla and the other riders spread out across the two-track wagon trail that connected the prison to Limon on the other side of the Arkansas River. Likely, the lawmen there had heard the shooting at the prison and were forming a posse.

A half mile from the town, Mateo lead his men off the trail's left side, heading for a southern curve of the Arkansas that was sheathed in dull green cottonwoods, willows, and grama grass. The water beckoned to Cuno though he could see only intermittent flashes of it through the screen of heat haze and the dust being kicked up ahead of him.

Behind him, Arguello was clinging loosely to his waist. Cuno felt the man's head flopping against his shoulder.

He could smell the young bandito's sour sweat and other sundry fetors from the Pit. Doubtless Cuno smelled as bad. He hoped the group stopped long enough at the river for him to throw himself into the cool, beckoning water. He hadn't had a bath, except the occasional sponge bath, in months.

Camilla rode just ahead of Cuno. He stared at her slender back, the dark brown hair bouncing across her red-striped serape. He wondered again how she had come to be riding with this band of Mexican cut-throats.

Mateo was her brother, and that was another question. How had such a sweet, innocent girl — at least, the girl he'd known back in the mountains, when they were on the run from the marauding Utes — come to have a brother like Mateo de Cava?

As though she were reading his mind, Camilla glanced back at him and quirked the corners of her mouth slightly, telling him silently that in due time he'd have the answers to all his questions.

The river grew brighter before him, the dusty cottonwoods looming larger and larger. A breeze rattled their branches. Behind Cuno, Arguello groaned and leaned more of his weight against the young freighter's broad back and shoulders.

"Hold on, Christiano," Cuno urged. "We'll get you a cold drink of water soon."

A cracking sound rose in the distance ahead of Cuno. It sounded like branches being broken over a knee. Then louder pops sounded, as well, as someone at the head of the outlaw pack screamed.

Another man shouted.

A horse whinnied shrilly.

Cuno squinted to peer over the heads of the other riders. Several of the lead riders

were checking down their mounts and raising rifles.

Amidst the trees along the river, smoke
puffed on the heels of the spattering gunfire.

Cuno's heart thudded, and his lips
mouthed the dreaded word.

Ambush!

5

Ahead of Cuno, a couple of de Cava riders flew off their horses. One horse tumbled headfirst in the dust, turned a ragged, screaming somersault, and got up shakily, its saddle and bloody rider hanging down its side.

Mateo pumped his rifle and one fist in the air and shouted something in Spanish. The other men spread out around and behind him, and they lifted a howling din, like a pack of moon-crazed, flesh-hungry lobos. They galloped toward the river from which more pistols and rifles popped, smoke puffing to mark the shooters' positions in the trees.

Cuno checked Renegade down, looking around wildly, confused. He had no weapon, but he sure as hell didn't want to sit out here on the flat like a duck on a millpond. *Christ,* he thought. *Out of the frying pan and into the fire . . .*

"Cuno!"

He looked to his right. Camilla had stopped her horse and squinted through the dust at him. "In your right saddlebag!"

It took him a moment to realize what she'd said, as the shouting and gunfire had almost drowned her out.

"Reach into your right saddlebag!" she repeated, yelling above the din.

Cuno leaned back past Arguello, who'd awakened now at the savage popping of guns along the river. Cuno dipped a hand into the pouch and rummaged around in his cooking supplies until his hand closed around a gun handle. Instantly, before he even saw it, he knew what he was holding, and his heart quickened eagerly.

He pulled out the old, familiar gun — the .45-caliber Colt Peacemaker that his old friend and former gunslinger, Charlie Dodge, had given him when he'd first started out after the men who'd killed his father and stepmother. Ivory-handled, silver-chased, and factory-scrolled, the Great Equalizer was a beautiful gun. Cuno had thought for sure that when he'd turned the pistol over to the sheriff who'd arrested him that he'd lost the prized gun forever.

He looked at Camilla, whose eyes blazed as, turning toward the river, she shouted,

"It's loaded. Come on — Mateo's rushing the bushwhackers!"

She drew her own Schofield from the soft leather holster she wore for the cross draw under her left arm, and buried her spurs into the flanks of her handsome chestnut bay whose rump was speckled cream. Cuno glanced behind at Arguello, who sat with his back straight now, staring anxiously toward the river.

"Hold on, Christiano!"

The young freighter batted his heels against Renegade's flanks, and the horse bounded forward off its rear feet. Into the sifting dust, horse and riders galloped, Camilla several yards ahead, the other riders now entering the brush and trees bordering the river, whooping and hollering and triggering pistols and rifles.

Pop! Pop! Pop-Pop! Boom!

The din sounded like a mini war being waged along the banks of the Arkansas.

Christiano grabbed Cuno tightly around the waist. Cuno stared straight ahead, where the outlaw gang was returning the fire of the ambushers, sometimes from nearly point-blank range.

A couple of the desperadoes were shot out of their saddles. A couple more crouched as though they'd been wounded. But they clearly had gained the upper hand against the bushwhackers, who were falling by twos and threes, some taking off running toward the river where they were cut down as they splashed across the rocky ford.

Cuno followed Camilla into the trees, her big chestnut leaping deadfalls and blow-downs, the girl riding lightly, rump rising and falling in her saddle. She held her pistol up high as she rode, looking around warily.

Cuno had just put Renegade over a blow-down when a pistol cracked to his right. The bullet screeched past his face to tear into a cottonwood. Instinctively, he brought the .45 to bear, saw a man peering over the top of a tree stump, a smoking pistol extended in his right fist. He had blue eyes, a gray mustache, and a mole on the nub of his left cheek.

Cuno didn't see the tin star pinned to his brown wool vest until the Colt had already bucked in his hand, drilling a neat, round hole through the center of the lawman's forehead. The man's blue eyes rolled back into his head. His chin lifted. His right hand opened, releasing the .44 Remington, and he sagged straight backward until he'd disappeared behind the stump.

Cuno's lower jaw sagged as he continued holding the .45 straight out from his shoulder. His belly tightened, and a fist wrapped itself around his heart, squeezing.

As he lowered the smoking Colt to his side, suddenly no longer hearing the shouts and shooting and hoof thuds around him, he put Renegade around the tree stump and looked down.

The man lay on his back, his legs clad in brown-checked trousers curled beneath him. His head was turned slightly to one side, eyes open, blood leaking from the wound to dribble down across his forehead to the ground. The tin star that read LIMON CITY MARSHAL burned like a brand into Cuno's retinas.

A whooping laugh sounded, and Cuno turned to see Mateo de Cava staring down at the dead lawman, dark eyes brightly jubilant. "Nice shot, *mi* gringo amigo! That's some really nice shooting!"

Slowly lowering the .45, Cuno turned his gaze back to the dead lawman.

"Come on!" the bandito leader shouted, beckoning. "Time to head for hills and some fresh horses!"

Cuno ripped his gaze from the dead lawman to look around the trees. Several riders, posse men from town, were galloping back toward Limon that sweltered on the shimmering plain to the northwest. Several banditos were triggering shots at them, though most were headed on across the river. Whooping raucously, Mateo headed that way, too, his black sombrero tumbling down his back to hang by a horsehair thong, his grisly pink pate glistening in the sun, as his black Arab high-stepped across the rocky ford, spraying up water around its legs.

Seven or eight men, including the lawman, lay dead in the trees and along the shore of the stream. One man in a brown suit lay with his head in the water as though he'd dropped down there for a drink. His brown derby hat hung by a branch extending from the bank several feet into the stream, and the water around his head was pink.

"Cuno!"

He turned to see Camilla sitting her chestnut in the middle of the ford, the Arkansas glimmering around her. She beckoned.

The other riders were galloping up the opposite bank beyond her and heading out across the dun and lime-green southern plain from which a heat haze rose as though from distant wildfires. Their whoops and howls and the thuds of their horses' hooves were quickly dwindling, so that all Cuno could now hear was the quiet voice of the river washing over the rocks. The breeze made a *whush*ing sound in the tops of the fragrant cottonwoods.

Camilla frowned at him impatiently, throwing up one arm, beckoning.

"He would have killed you," she called. *"Vamonos!"*

Cuno lowered the .45. "Hold on, Christiano," he muttered, not looking at the dead lawman again but batting his heels against Renegade's flanks and heading on into the stream.

He realized after he'd ridden a mile from the Arkansas, following the dust strings of Mateo's gang that looked to be comprised of twenty or so riders, that he hadn't stopped at the river for water. They stopped for a small remuda of extra horses, placed there in case they lost any at the prison, and to give Arguello and Frank Skinner their own saddled mounts.

But as soon as the young Mexican and the train robber were seated, they were off again, riding hard across the sage- and greasewood-crusted hogbacks.

Cuno was parched. He'd fallen back to keep an eye on Arguello, who seemed to ride well enough on his own but whose lips continued to move as he prayed. Occasionally, he shook his head violently as if to clear of it. They rode hard, and it soon became obvious to Cuno that Arguello wouldn't make it on his own.

"Forget him," Camilla told the young freighter, as she held her chestnut to Renegade's loping pace. "If he drops back, the posse will find him and give him water."

Cuno glanced once more at Christiano Arguello, who was falling a good fifty yards back behind him now, and more.

Cuno cursed and slowed Renegade to a walk, throwing out his hand to reach for Arguello's reins as the young Mexican's paint pony caught up to him. One of the riders from the main pack was riding back toward Cuno and Camilla, a burly American whom Cuno had heard someone call Brouschard.

He was dressed in sweaty buckskins with a green silk neckerchief flopping down his chest and a Sharps rifle snugged down in a beaded saddle scabbard. As he approached Arguello's paint, he shucked a big, pearl-gripped Colt from a shoulder holster, and pointed the barrel up as he thumbed the hammer back.

"No!" Cuno bit out.

Too late. The revolver roared. Christiano Arguello's head snapped straight back on his shoulders. It sagged there for a second, and then the young bandito fell straight back against the paint's rump before rolling down the left stirrup fender and piling up in the dust. The paint whinnied and buck-kicked, and Camilla reached out to snatch its reins before it could run off.

Cuno glared at the burly American, who aimed his smoking pistol at Cuno and narrowed one eye. "No slackers. They slow up the whole damn bunch. Now, let's get a move on, you two, or" — he glanced at Camilla — "your boyfriend's gonna get the same thing, *chiquita*."

He turned back to Cuno, and his eyes flicked to the .45 that the young freighter held against his stout right thigh. Cuno looked back at him, nostrils flaring. Silently, with only his eyes, he told the man that he'd kill him if he ever aimed a pistol at him again.

The big man seemed to understand. A faint splotch rose into his yellow-bearded, sun-seared cheeks, and he depressed his own weapon's hammer, returned it to its holster, and galloped up the trail.

Cuno swung out of his saddle. He did not look at Camilla staring apprehensively at him as he said, "I'll be along in a minute."

"We have to hurry, Cuno. There are several lawmen in Limon. They'll throw in with the prison guards, and there'll be a helluva posse after us."

Cuno's eyes flared as he turned to her quickly and flung his arm out. "Go on! Git outta here!"

The girl shook her head slowly. "He would have died. One way or the other. He's better off this way. You can't take the time to bury him."

He leaned down and dragged Christiano up with one arm, then bent his knees as he slung the dead man over his naked back. Shifting the young man's light load on his shoulders, he glanced up at the girl staring at him, her pretty face taut with impatience.

"Who the hell are you?" he asked.

She pursed her lips, drew a breath, and flared her nostrils. "The girl that saved you from the hangman!"

She tossed the reins of Christiano's horse down. She whipped her own horse around and ground her spurs into its flanks.

As she galloped off, Cuno walked over to a patch of thick brush and lay the dead man between two boulders. He straightened, stared grimly down at the inert form half wasted by a year in Castle's pen, then crouched over the body once more and crossed the young man's hands on his belly. If he wasn't going to bury him, he could at least arrange him decently.

Christiano stared up at Cuno, glassy-eyed, lips forming a wry smile, as though he knew as well as Cuno did that the carrion eaters would be on him soon, and crossing his hands wasn't going to mean a tinker's damn when they came.

"Sorry, amigo."

Cuno glanced back the way he and his savage saviors had come. In the far distance he saw a slender dust plume. Beneath it, half a dozen or so riders, little more than brown blotches from this distance, were galloping toward him.

For a moment, he felt torn. He could take his horse and his gun and go his own way, or he could follow the men and the girl who'd saved him from the gallows and who'd probably figured out an escape route.

With the outlaws — cold-blooded killers, all — he had a chance. Without the outlaws, he was probably finished. Besides, having killed the Limon marshal, he was for all intents and purposes one of them now, anyway. Maybe it would have been better if he'd been hanged . . .

He'd felt his shell belt in the same saddlebag in which Camilla had placed his gun. Now he retrieved it from the pouch, wrapped it around his waist, dropped his prized .45 into the holster, and fastened the keeper thong over the hammer.

He had a gun. Now he needed a hat and clothes. The sun was branding his face and naked torso.

Swinging up into the saddle, he grabbed the reins of Christiano's horse, and led it off after the others, all of whom, including Camilla, had disappeared over a hill. She was waiting for him on the other side, a worried look in her eyes. Cuno remembered seeing the same look in the eyes of his young half-breed wife, July, a long time ago, just after he'd finished off Anderson and Spoon.

The look bit him hard, caused a stone to drop in his belly.

Christ, the world was crazy. His life was crazy. He kept reliving the same horrors, over and over. He'd always hoped he'd be able to find a safe place in which to hole up quietly and live well, but here he was running for his life with a passel of kill-happy outlaws, and all because he'd saved this girl waiting for him now from a passel of rogue lawmen intent on raping her.

"Come on," she said when he rode up beside her. "We stop soon, get good water, a good meal in our bellies." Her eyes flicked across his broad, hairless chest with its flat ridges of hard muscle on which sweat glistened like honey. "Get you some clothes." Her mouth corners quirked again. "Maybe even do something about your nose."

Cuno nodded slowly, thoughtfully. He was alive and free. And he had a pretty girl who obviously wanted him. He may not know who she was exactly, but all in all he supposed he had little to complain about.

He nodded again, chewing his lower lip. "Let's ride."

She began to turn her chestnut.

"Wait," he said, holding up a hand. "Where the hell are we going, anyway?"

She turned back to him, hiked a shoulder. Her long hair was blowing across her tan, heart-shaped, chocolate-eyed face shaded by the broad, bending brim of her straw sombrero. "I don't know. Only Mateo knows. Probably Mexico in the end. Does it really matter?"

Cuno glanced behind him, saw only the top of the hill and beyond that the far horizon against which the riders were coming. He faced her again, gave a wry snort. "No, I reckon it doesn't."

"Come on, then. You save my life, I save yours, huh?"

"Okay," he said, nodding — what choice did he have? — and put Renegade into a run beside her.

6

They rode wild and unfettered as the prairie wind, following the network of creases between the low buttes pocked with bits of dried brown buckbrush, needlegrass, sage, and cactus.

It was obvious that Mateo de Cava had run from his share of posses; he had it down to a system, vamoosing hard and fast and maneuvering over the best ground possible for leaving little trace — namely, meandering, rocky watercourses.

And they were moving through some of the driest, emptiest country in south-central Colorado, staying well clear of traveled roads and trails, steering wide of the few, broadly spaced ranch headquarters out there. And though their course was a zigzagging one, there was no hesitation, as though Mateo had a clear destination in mind. One that, apparently, he did not share with the others.

No one, including his sister, seemed to know where he was going. He likely didn't share that information in case, amongst his horde of ragged lobos, he had a traitor in his midst, which was always the risk when you ran in a pack this large. Some lawmen, Pinkerton agents, and Wells Fargo trouble-shooters were good at infiltrating unwieldy bands of desperadoes and bringing them down from the inside or alerting others of their ilk to block the planned escape route and set up a bloody ambush.

No, Mateo knew his business right down to setting up his own little network of temporary hideouts, for that's what they reached about an hour and a half after leaving the bloody skirmish along the Arkansas. It was a row of spindly cottonwoods along a winding creek just south of a weather-beaten jackleg ranch headquarters from which rose the smell of cow and chicken shit and from where the lazy spinning of dry windmill blades could be heard like a couple of golden eagles quarreling.

In the trees, a picket line had been strung. There was a low fire and two butchered deer — young bucks with small racks still attached to their heads — hung upside down, rear legs splayed to show gaping, red cavities, from a stout cottonwood branch. Mateo reined up in the trees near the picket line and swung down from his mount, looking around as he instantly set about unsaddling his black Arab. Cuno checked Renegade down at the camp's perimeter and looked around as the other men swarmed around him on their hot, sweat-silvery, blowing and snorting horses.

From the direction of the gray ranch headquarters — consisting of a log cabin with a pole corral connecting it to a small shed — came the sound of a screen door slamming, and Cuno turned to see a man with long black hair step out of the cabin, thumbing suspenders up his shoulders clad in a faded, red plaid work shirt. The suspenders were attached to threadbare canvas trousers.

He turned his head to one side as two more people came out of the shack behind him — one an older woman with the same Indian features as the man, and a young redheaded pale-skinned woman in a work shirt and pleated gray skirt.

There was a buckboard wagon hitched to a mule standing out front of the shack, and the man and the two women climbed aboard and began moving at a brisk trot toward the outlaws who'd all gotten busy unsaddling their horses near the fire. Cuno glanced at

Camilla, who did not meet his gaze but only stared toward the approaching wagon and then at two men, wounded in the dustup at the Arkansas, who were being helped down from their horses by other members of the bunch.

"What do we have there?" Mateo asked one of the wounded — a small Mexican who wore his hair in a tight braid down his back. "How are you doing, Ignacio?"

"I'm all right," said Ignacio in Spanish, holding his bloody right arm tight against his body and crawling awkwardly down from his saddle while another man held his horse for him. He spoke again in Spanish, which Cuno mentally translated: "I just need a drink of water, and I'll be fine."

"Let me see." Mateo rose up on the balls of his feet to inspect the wound in the Mexican's right arm about halfway between his elbow and shoulder. The outlaw leader pulled the arm away from the man's body, and Ignacio sucked a sharp breath through the gap of his missing front teeth.

"Sure, sure," Mateo said in English, for the benefit of the Americans, which made a good half of his pack. "You'll be fine." He glanced meaningfully toward the burly, yellow-bearded Wayne Brouschard and canted his head toward Ignacio who stood leaning against his horse. "Brouschard will take you over to the creek, *mi* amigo. Get you some water, help you clean the wound, make it all better."

"Water," Ignacio said, lifting his chin and glancing eagerly toward the stream. "*Si, si* — I could really use some water, Mateo."

As Brouschard came over and began turning Ignacio by one arm, Mateo looked at the other man who'd just ridden in and who had dismounted his palomino gelding to stand beside the horse, eyes closed, using one hand to support himself against the saddle.

A tall half-breed with roached brown hair and one pale eye and one cobalt blue one, he swooned a little, as though drunk. He wore a ragged frock coat over crisscrossed bandoliers and three big pistols bristled on his hips and from a cross-draw holster half hidden by the coat. He wore salmon-colored checked pants, both knees patched with green ducking.

"White-Eye — how you doin' over there?" Mateo walked around Ignacio's horse, heading toward the half-breed. "You don't look so good."

White-Eye looked at Mateo, his milky eye dull and lifeless, the blue one sharp and

73

anxious. "What's that, Brother? I'm all right."

"You took a bullet back at the river, no?"

"Oh, it's just a scratch." The half-breed chuckled, stepping away from his horse and lowering his arms to his sides as if to prove how well he was despite the blood glistening on the low left side of his dust-powdered black frock. "Shit, I've been hurt worse tussling with whores. Them fingernails can get mighty sharp across a man's back when you pleasure 'em just right!"

He laughed woodenly, the blue eye crinkling at the corner as he watched Mateo approach him.

The outlaw grinned broadly at the half-breed. "That's so, Brother!" He looked down at the man's waist. "Where you hit, huh? Don't tell me they gutted you, Brother. Huh? They gut you?"

Quickly, he reached out and flipped the flap of White-Eye's coat away from his side, revealing a broad patch of thick blood on the man's shabby white shirt that was ruffled down the front, like the shirt of some fancy tinhorn gambler or southern plantation owner.

"Oh, shit," Mateo clucked, frowning and shaking his head. "White-Eye, they got you good, eh?"

"What? You mean that?" White-Eye laughed a little desperately. "Looks much worse than it is, Mateo. Really. The bullet just clipped my side there, went all the way through."

Cuno stood tensely beside Renegade and near Camilla as he watched Mateo's expression slowly change from a bemused smile to a baleful stare. White-Eye stared at the outlaw leader, and fear blazed in his blue eye. "Mateo. My brother," the man said, groveling and taking a step back. "It's just a flesh wound. Really. I won't slow us down — I promise. Shit, I can't wait to eat some of the deer and get back in the saddle again!"

He laughed again but there was only desperation in it. His blue eye watered as he continued to laugh, his mouth stretching and twisting bizarrely, making a terrified mask of his large, brown, unshaven face. "Mateo, goddamnit!" he yelled suddenly, the blue eye flashing with rage, the other one rolling unmoored in its socket.

"You know the rules," the outlaw leader said reasonably. "We all agreed to the rules before our first ride. Right, White-Eye? Right, Wade?" he asked a gringo rider who was slowly, distractedly unsaddling his buckskin.

"That's right," the stocky Wade agreed, nodding, his fleshy, shaven face somber as he turned away from the two men who had become the focus of everyone's attention. "We all agreed, White-Eye. I seen that fella shoot you from three, four feet away. Preacher with a white collar." He shook his head at the irony of White-Eye's fate. "If that don't beat all," he muttered and walked away toward the trees with his saddle on a shoulder.

"But I killed him good, didn't I?" White-Eye called after Wade, who did not look back at him. "I got that sky pilot good — didn't I, Wade?"

"Let's take a walk," Mateo said to White-Eye.

"No."

"Come on, my brother. Let's don't make this hard."

"No!" White-Eye took another step back and shucked a long-barreled, black-handled Russian from his shoulder holster. He hadn't gotten the barrel pointed forward yet before Mateo grabbed it out of his hand and smacked him hard across the face with it.

White-Eye screamed and staggered.

"Don't you ever pull a pistol on me, you half-breed son of a bitch!"

Mateo drew one of his own pistols, shoved the barrel against the bloody stain on White-Eye's coat. The gun's roar was muffled slightly by the half-breed's gangly body. The man screamed shrilly as his shirt around the fresh wound burst into flame. As he staggered backward and sideways, grabbing for another pistol, Mateo shot him twice in the chest.

He hit the ground and lay shuddering.

Silence except for the warily nickering horses.

Cuno stared down at the dead man, feeling a curious lack of emotion.

"No!" a voice screamed along the creek.

Cuno turned, as did the others in the group, toward where Ignacio was breaking brush toward a heavy thicket of cottonwoods. Behind him, Brouschard aimed a long-barreled pistol. The gun whanged. Red licked from the barrel, smoke rising.

Ignacio dove forward as blood and brains spewed from his forehead. He hit the ground, rolled, spraying rocks and gravel, and lay still against a fallen branch.

"Hey, Ignacio was just my size." This from Frank Skinner, standing next to the horse he'd just unsaddled — a beefy bay.

Cuno had lost sight of his fellow escapee amongst the group. Skinner was still dressed

— or undressed, as it were — like Cuno. Just the striped prison pajama bottoms and nothing else. He was staring off toward where Brouschard was holstering his big pistol and walking back toward the group, Ignacio lying dead behind him.

"Help yourself," Mateo growled, grinning hatefully down at White Eye. He glanced at Cuno as he gave the dead man before him a savage kick in the ribs. "Go ahead, *mi* gringo amigo. Help yourself to his boots, clothes, anything. He might have spares in his saddlebags. The only thing you cannot help yourselves to, you and Senor Skinner, is the loot we acquired from our last job."

He glanced at one of the other men, jerking his head toward the horses of the two dead men standing to his left. "Divide it up, equal shares for everyone except the two newest members of our party."

He looked at Cuno and Skinner, who was walking tenderly on bare feet toward Ignacio but glancing over his shoulder at the outlaw leader. "They will have to earn their keep soon."

He narrowed a black-irised eye at Cuno. "Very soon."

The man driving the ranch wagon had stopped a good ways from the outlaw gang when he'd seen the confrontations with the two wounded men. After the shooting, he'd come on with his cargo of two women — a pretty but sullen young redhead and his Indian wife.

The man's name, Cuno learned, was Romer Gaffney. A half-breed who wore an old rag around his forehead under a weathered canvas hat, he'd been in cahoots with Mateo de Cava for years, supplying the man with horses, shelter, and quick meals whenever the bandito shuffled his operations north of his usual stomping grounds and into Colorado Territory.

Gaffney, Cuno learned as both deer were quickly spitted by the women and coffee brewed, was a dealer in stolen horses and cattle — a fairly easy trade this far off the beaten track. He occasionally sold whiskey. But mostly he provided succor to outlaws on the run, and, while he did not seem to be making an exceptionally good living at it, judging by the squalidness of his ranch headquarters, he seemed a carefree, happy man who took great pleasure in palavering with outlaws like Mateo and smoking his corncob while ordering his wife, Matilda, and his pretty redheaded niece, Wanda, around.

While the outlaws talked and relaxed

around the fire, drinking coffee spiked with Gaffney's whiskey and ogling Wanda, Cuno dressed in the rough trail clothes he gleaned from White-Eye's saddlebags — fringed deerskin trousers, calico shirt, red neckerchief, and horsehide vest with a torn pocket.

The duds were none too clean, and they smelled sour, but they'd do until he could find a mercantile. He donned the man's undershot boots and his straw sombrero, both of which were a tad on the small side but would do now in this pinch he was in.

"Now you only need a dead eye," said Camilla, sitting against a tree before him, the creek gurgling nearby. The others, including Frank Skinner, who looked much better now dressed and with food and whiskey in his belly, were a good fifty or sixty yards away. "A blond half-breed — that's what you look like. One that gets into fights."

Cuno finished adjusting the sombrero on his head, letting the rawhide thong dangle down his chest, and touched his tender nose. He didn't think it was a bad break. He'd had worse. He could breathe through it well enough. His eyes were still half swollen, however. Physically, he was miserable — tired and hungry and sunburned and wracked with the grinding pain in his face.

But at least he was out of the Pit and still alive, and he knew he had Camilla to thank for that.

"I'll look almost human in a few days," he said, lowering his hand from his nose.

"That will be good. I almost did not recognize you up there on that gallows."

"How did you know I was about to hang?"

She smiled coquettishly, small white teeth flashing beneath her rich upper lip. "A woman must not give up her secrets."

Cuno frowned at her, puzzled.

She relented. "Mateo paid off one of the guards to inform us of the happenings at the prison. Especially about what was happening with you. The man was paid well, and he spoke with two of Mateo's men at a saloon in Limon nightly. We have been a few weeks setting it up."

"My god . . ." Cuno stared at her, puzzled by all the work she and her brother had gone to in setting him free. They'd become lovers on the trail out of the Rawhides, but he'd had no idea she'd felt so strongly about him. He felt a little guilty that he hadn't felt as strongly about her; but, after all, with the Utes hounding their trail, he hadn't had much time for falling in love.

She smiled at him, her brown eyes warm and inviting.

Cuno felt his cheeks warm, still a little uncomfortable around females. He'd been married a very short time, and before that his experience had been limited by an innate bashfulness around members of the opposite sex.

Changing the subject, he tried to whistle but because of his nose it came out low and stilted. "Well, I reckon that was about as close as I'll ever cut it. I was beginning to feel the devil reaching up out of the burning pits of hell to tickle my bare feet."

Camilla got up from the tree and walked over to him. Her brown eyes bored lovingly into his, causing his cheeks to burn. "You would not have gone down there. Up there is where you belong."

With a gloved finger, she pointed toward the sky. "After all you did for me and the Trent girl and the Lassiter children. You are a good man, Cuno. My heart broke when you gave yourself up to that Sheriff Mason." Slowly, keeping her eyes on his, she shook her head. "All so he would make sure we made it safely to the fort. You are a saint, I would say."

"Far from that. Any halfways decent soul would have done the same, especially if he was wounded and needed doctorin' himself."

"That is not true. Though I am only eighteen years old, I have seen much of this world, Cuno. It is a bad place, filled with bad men. But not you. You are a good man. And . . ." She let her voice trail off, wrinkling the skin above her nose as though not sure how to continue. "And . . . you must know how I fee—"

She cut herself off, color rising in her cheeks. He was glad she'd stopped when she did, as he was also feeling snakes of nervous embarrassment coiling and uncoiling in his legs and shoulders.

She dropped her eyes toward the ground then reached out for his hand. "Enough of that. I know what you must think of me . . . out here with my bandito brother. *Half brother.* Mateo's mother was a Yaqui from southern Sonora. We will talk later. For now, let's go eat. Knowing Mateo, he will want us to saddle up and ride soon."

"Ride where?" Cuno asked the girl as she led him over to the fire. She was holding his hand. "You have any idea at all?"

"No. Like I said, only Mateo knows. He will probably tell us soon."

Several of Mateo's men cast furtive, dark glances at the pair approaching the fire hand in hand. Obviously, several of the bunch wanted their leader's comely sister for their own. Feelings of resentment toward Cuno were building. He could feel the animosity; apprehension plucked at his spine like a guitar string.

He'd have to take care to never give these men his back, unless he wanted a knife in it.

7

Deputy U.S. Marshal Spurr Morgan drew his buckskin to a halt in a chokecherry thicket near which a muddy creek trickled and shucked his 1866-model, brass-framed Winchester repeater from his saddle boot. Gently, he racked a round into the old but familiar weapon's chamber, then lowered the oiled hammer to half cock.

He stared through the tangle of shrubs and cedars and past a falling-down privy toward the back of the three-story roadhouse that looked so sun-blistered and rickety that the next strong breeze would likely obliterate it and muttered, "There's three of 'em, and I've been after them rancid polecats' hides for nigh on two months now. Let's not muck this up, shall we, Sheriff?"

To his left, Sheriff Dusty Mason out of Willow City, Wyoming Territory, slid his own, much newer rifle from his saddle boot and gave the older Spurr, who was pushing sixty though he himself was not sure of his own age, a condescending look. "You should have had him in Wheaton."

Spurr felt anger surge up from deep in his loins. Making it all the hotter was the humiliation that came with it. Indeed, he should have taken down Wes Leggett, Christopher Fancy, and Marvin "the Maiden Killer" Candles back in Mason's county in Wyoming Territory.

Three things had gotten in Spurr's way — a bad ticker, a comely, big-bosomed whore half his age, and one of his notorious benders. Leggett, Fancy, and Candles had indeed been holed up just outside of town, at a little outlaw ranch owned by an Irishman and stage relay station manager, Burton P. Murphy, while Fancy had been sparking the Irishman's blond daughter, Lucy.

Spurr hadn't known that at the time, however. He'd thought they'd ridden on to Deadwood. But he'd been fairly deep in his cups by then, and he hadn't bothered to check the authenticity of his information.

So here he was now, riding with the tinhorn county sheriff whose father he was damn near old enough to be and whom he'd been ordered to ride with by Chief Marshal Henry Brackett in Denver as a sort of punishment for his misstep in Wheaton, and having to take load after load of subtle and not-so-subtle shit from the arrogant bastard who obviously thought Spurr had ridden roughshod after owlhoots way longer than he should have.

Spurr didn't like the man's mustache or the liquid cobalt-blueness of his eyes. He also didn't like the fact that Mason was a Texan. Spurr didn't like Texans for too many reasons to go into, but the main one being that they thought they owned the whole fuckin' frontier — cow, wagon, six-gun, and doxie . . .

"You ever make a mistake, Dusty?" Spurr asked the county sheriff now. "Ah, never mind. You think on it hard. Chew your mustache over it and get back to me later. For now, let's go get them three fork-tailed critters and haul 'em back to Cheyenne for hangin'."

"I'm for that."

Mason swung easily out of his saddle, hiking his right leg up high with a flourish, even making his spur rowel trill as it cut the air. Spurr glowered at the tall, rangy lawman, almost twenty years Spurr's junior, setting himself lightly on the ground beside his tall strawberry. He often thought the man tried to look healthier, faster, and lighter on his feet for the sole purpose of getting Spurr's goat, which he'd gotten over two weeks ago now, even before they'd picked up the trail of the three killers in southern Dakota.

Spurr looped the reins of his big roan, Cochise, over a chokecherry branch. The back windows of the roadhouse had flour-sack curtains drawn over them. When gold and silver was still being hauled out of the nearby hills, the place had done double and triple time as a mercantile and brothel. Spurr had done some skirt chasing here himself not all that long ago.

He remembered that the whores here had taken pride in the place and had even planted flowers around it. Now, however, the placed seemed nearly as rickety as the outhouse that flanked it, and there was nothing left of the flowers but wiry bits of brush nearly sunken into the ground.

"Well, I reckon you're in charge since you're federal," Mason snorted. "How you wanna play this, Spurr?" He spat a wad of chew onto a flat-topped rock and, holding his rifle up high across his chest, crouched as he stared across the sage-stippled flat and past the two-hole privy that was missing most of its vertical boards, at the roadhouse. "We could call 'em all outta there. But maybe we oughta wait till dark when they're all three sheets to the wind."

"I see no reason to get fancy," Spurr said and began walking toward the roadhouse, holding his old Winchester down low by his side. "I'll go in the front while you go in the back. They either throw down iron and come along sweet as cherry pie, or we dust a few hides."

"Spurr!" Mason called, keeping his voice low and jerking an anxious look at the sagging, sun-blistered building toward which the older lawman was strolling like he was merely heading uptown for a leisurely lunch and perhaps a game of euchre.

Spurr threw an arm up, beckoning, and tramped down the well-born path curving from the building's back door to the privy. From the ammoniac smell and the dead brown leaves of the sage shrubs just outside the back door, most of the place's customers didn't bother with the extra hundred-foot hike to the dilapidated privy.

Spurr veered left of the path and walked along the east side of the place and past split cordwood stacked against the wall, to the sagging front gallery. Stopping and glancing back the way he'd come, he watched Dusty Mason run at a low crouch across the backyard, his face around his dragoon-style mustache mottled red with anxiety. The sheriff disappeared behind the building as he made a dash to the back door.

Spurr chuckled and shook his head. It was not to his credit, as his late mother used to say, that he loved it when he could get the otherwise cool son of a bitch's own goat and stretch the younger man's nerves taut as piano wire.

"Teach him to ride with this old mossy horn," the older lawman muttered, swiping a sleeve across his sweat-damp, salt-and-pepper mustache. "This old bull buff rides alone from now on, or he don't ride at all! Specially with no local sheriff who thinks he's the next Bat Masterson . . ."

But then, he'd been entertaining the idea of retirement in Mexico for a long time, and nothing had come of it. Truth was, if he wasn't lawdogging, he'd likely grow so bored with himself that he'd blow his own head off inside of two weeks.

He gave Mason time to calm his nerves and enter the roadhouse, then make his way to the roadhouse's main front drinking hall. Then he mounted the creaky, splintered porch steps from which a coat of green paint had long since dulled to a sun-bleached gray and turned toward the batwing doors shaded by the low brush roof.

A wind gusted suddenly, and Spurr turned

90

to see a screen of dust lift from the adobe-colored street and fly toward him, flecked with bits of hay and straw and ground horse shit. The breeze peppered his face and blew his hat off his head. Before he could grab it, it had drifted under the batwing doors and tumbled on into the saloon. Spurr crouched to swipe it out of the air.

As he did, a thunderous boom sounded, making the porch boards jump beneath his boots.

For half a confused second, Spurr thought the wind had blown in a thunderstorm despite the plainly sunny sky. But then he felt a mad spray of slivers across his back and shoulders. He raised his gaze to see that both tops of the now madly swinging batwings had been blown clear away. They lay in slivers around the worn, high-topped moccasins he'd preferred since his Indian-fighting days when he'd often needed to walk a distance quietly.

He spun to his left, slamming his shoulder against the front of the building.

Kabooommm!

The porch floor leapt again beneath Spurr's moccasins. The rest of what had remained of the batwing doors after the first blast now blew out past the aging lawman, across the gallery, and into the broad trail beyond. Only a few bits of wood remained, jerking back and forth on the spring hinges.

The echo of the second blast had not died before Spurr gave a raucous yell and threw himself through the dark, smoky opening, instantly smelling cordite as he thumbed his Winchester's hammer back to full cock.

He hit the floor on his creaky right shoulder and hip, trying to ignore the hammering pain that lanced through both and making a vague mental note that he was getting too old for such maneuvers. He blinked against the misty shadows inside the saloon, saw an uncertain man shape before him, the light from the doorway behind him glinting on the black iron bores of a double-barreled shotgun.

He fired once, twice, three times before he'd even stopped sliding on his hip and shoulder, and heard the man with the shotgun scream as he flew straight backward over a table. Spurr's old eyes were slow to adjust to the gloom shot through with the glare of two long windows on the room's left side, so all he saw were jostling, man-shaped shadows before two guns flashed simultaneously.

The slugs hammered the front of a bar to his right, just above his sprawled, buckskin-clad body.

"Kill the old, nasty son of a bitch!" some-one shouted.

More guns popped, bullets chewing table legs and ceiling posts in front of Spurr, and the front of the bar to his right. Quickly, lying prone, elbows on the floor, he racked another live round into his rifle's breech, took quick aim at the shadow before which one of the guns flashed, and fired. His target yelped and disappeared.

He aimed at two more figures as they triggered revolvers while moving around the tables, and watched as he blew one of the yellow-toothed demons out one of the long windows, the man screaming and triggering his pistol into the ceiling and then disappearing through the shattering glass and out into the yard.

More men screamed and shouted — many more than the three he was after — and triggered more lead, the gunfire in the close confines sounding like many blacksmith's hammers rapping on empty tin washtubs.

Spurr was low enough that several tables and chairs offered rudimentary cover, but he was glad to see a stout heating stove just ahead of him, in the middle of the room. It was flanked by a stout wood box with high side panels.

He triggered two more rounds, then rolled

to his left, wincing as several slugs hammered the floor around him, pricking his face with slivers. Two more screeched raucously off the woodstove as he piled up behind it, a man shouting, "He's behind the stove — get him. I want that lawbringer *beefed!*"

"Hey, who is that?" Spurr shouted, hunkering low against the floor and thumbing fresh cartridges from his shell belt into his Winchester's receiver. "I think I recognize that voice . . . just can't recollect the name!"

"It's Ludlow Walsh!" A bullet clanged loudly against the stove simultaneously with a revolver's bark. "Take that, you dirty, badge-totin', privy-suckin' dog!"

"Lud Walsh?" Spurr chuckled. "Hell, I wasn't after you, Lud!"

A figure moved to his right — a man trying to work around him toward the bar. Spurr whipped his repeater around and fired, but the man ducked behind an awning post, and the bullet hammered a ceiling joist behind him, shattering a hurricane lantern.

"Hell, I didn't think you was!" Walsh called from the far side of the room. "But I vowed I'd perforate your big, ugly hide first chance I got, Spurr. No way you're walkin' out of this waterin' hole alive, lawdog. No

94

way at all. Too many against you in here!"

"That's how it sounds," Spurr called. "I just hope the three fork-tailed devils I came special for are here! Wes Leggett, Chris Fancy, and Marvin 'the Maiden Killer' Candles — you boys in here, I hope?"

"Oh, we're here all right," came a raucous, laughing voice from ahead and to Spurr's right.

It was followed by four pistol blasts, all four bullets hammering the woodstove and setting up the clanging of cracked bells in Spurr's ears.

"Behind you, Fancy!" shouted the familiar voice of Spurr's partner. "Sheriff Dusty Mason! You boys are surrounded, so give yourselves up and live to die another day!"

"Fuck!" one of the outlaws cried.

There was the thumping of boots and the bark of a chair across the crude puncheon floor. A rifle thundered at the back of the room. That'd be Mason, Spurr figured. About time he showed. The older lawman was beginning think his young partner was standing in a back room, dribbling down his leg.

As a man screamed and another shouted curses and a rapid volley of shots rose, making dust sift from the rafters, Spurr rose to a knee and picked out movement through the gun smoke webbing through the brown air.

He fired his Winchester and sent another man flying out a window. He fired again and saw another figure in a derby hat spin around and clutch his left shoulder with his right hand that was holding a big LeMat pistol. As the man turned back toward Spurr, loosing a string of German-accented English epithets — that would be Rutger Von Muelssen, Spurr absently considered, recognizing the voice — Spurr drilled him again, causing dust to puff from the dead center of the big German's chest, slamming him back against the wall.

The shooting stopped abruptly. Somewhere in the thick shadows and webbing smoke, a man was groaning. Then two more shots sounded from the top of a stairs at the back of the room. A gun flashed from behind a table at the bottom of the staircase, and then boots thumped at the top of the stairs.

"That was Candles!" Dusty Mason shouted. "I'm goin' after him!"

"Hold on, goddamn — !" Spurr, slowly rising, felt a sudden heavy pain in his chest, and he dropped back down to both knees. His left arm stiffened up. He clutched it hard against his side, set his smoking Winchester onto the floor, and reached into his breast pocket for the little rawhide pouch he kept there. His hands shook.

Upstairs, boots thumped loudly, making the ceiling above Spurr's head creak and groan. Dusty Mason shouted, "Hold it, Candles!"

A girl screamed.

Candles's voice thundered in the ceiling. "Drop the gun, lawdog, or this pretty little gal's gonna look right funny without her head!"

Shakily, using his teeth, Spurr opened the drawstring on the hide sack. He dribbled a little gold tablet into the palm of his right hand and popped the pill under his tongue. It tasted like iron, but almost instantly he felt a relaxing of the colicky iron crab in his chest that was firing off pain spasms into his left shoulder and into his neck.

Upstairs, the sheriff and Candles were shouting, and the girl was sobbing.

"Mason!" Spurr rasped, unable to raise his voice loudly enough for the young deputy to hear. "Wait for me, goddamnit!"

Spurr stuffed the hide sack back into his shirt pocket, picked up his rifle, and climbed to his feet.

"I mean it, lawdog!" Candles yelled. "You don't drop that pistol, I'mma cut this little bitch's head clear off!"

"I don't think so, Candles!" the deputy returned though Spurr could hear the slightest hesitation in the man's voice. "That knife goes any closer to her neck, you're gonna be the one missin' his thinker box!"

Breathing heavily through gritted teeth, Spurr looked around. Smoke webbed. Bodies lay everywhere, some atop overturned tables or chairs.

A hot breeze blew through the two broken windows. He heard a slight groan behind him and wheeled, pressing his back against a support post and bringing the Winchester to bear on a fat-faced gent in an apron standing behind the bar. The man raised his pudgy hands in the air. His dark eyes flashed. He had big ears and fleshy, pitted cheeks.

"No, no!" the man cried, waving his hands. "I own dis place, senor. These men . . . I am no part of, senor!"

Still hearing the din on the second story and wanting to get up there to help Mason, as Spurr knew Marvin 'the Maiden Killer' Candles's reputation for extreme deviltry, but not wanting to give his back to the main saloon hall until he was sure he wouldn't take a bullet between the shoulder blades, the old marshal gestured with the Winchester.

"Come out from behind there and keep those hands in the air. Go on outside and stand in the middle of the yard, but you keep those hands high, you hear me? If I look out and you ain't there grabbing for clouds, I'm gonna be mad!"

He'd known more than one lawman sent to his reward in bloody pieces by aprons wielding double-barreled shotguns.

"*Si, si*, senor!" the barman cried, waddling out from behind the bar and on out the gap where the batwings used to be. "*Si, si,* senor!" he yelled, running into the yard, his broad ass jiggling like a croaker sack filled with straw. "Don't shoot me, *por favor!*"

8

When Spurr saw that the fat Mexican barman was safely out in the yard and holding his arms high above his head, he turned to the stairs. Things had gotten too quiet upstairs, and his weak old ticker was thudding heavily. He still felt the heaviness in his left shoulder and arm, but that fractious crab in his chest had loosened, and he was able to breathe relatively freely.

Thank god for the nitroglycerin. A doctor had given him the pills up in Buffaloville, Wyoming Territory, and they'd saved his life more than once, sort of setting off a mini-explosion in his heart that kept the old raisin ticking.

He took the steps one at a time, hauling himself up by his left hand, holding his Winchester's butt taut against his double shell belts over his right hip, hammer cocked. He heard Mason's voice in the second story. It was grim with authority.

Candles was grunting replies. Meanwhile, the two men were moving around, as the ceiling continued to creak.

Spurr gained the mouth of the second-story hall. About halfway down, a girl stood there, facing the open door of a room on the hall's right side. She was naked — a slender blonde with mussed hair and full breasts — and she was aiming a long-barreled, black-handled pistol through the open door with both hands.

Spurr's eye widened. "Hold it, girl!" He spread his feet and snugged the Winchester's stock against his right cheek, lining up the sights on the girl's head. The gun in her hands roared, the smoke and blue-red flames stabbing into the room on the right side of the hall. Turning toward Spurr, she screamed and raised the pistol once more.

Spurr held the sights steady on the girl's head, drew a dreadful breath, and squeezed the Winchester's trigger. The girl's head snapped violently back. She jerked the big pistol in her hands straight up, fired a round into the ceiling, flew back several feet, and hit the floor with a slapping thud on her naked back.

Spurr lowered the Winchester slightly, staring wide-eyed through his own powder smoke. Slowly, he lowered the Winchester's cocking lever, ejecting the spent casing, which clattered onto the floor around his boots, then slid a fresh shell into the chamber. A head appeared in the open doorway, wearing Mason's hat. Automatically, Spurr aimed the rifle at the man. The head turned toward the girl lying naked on the floor, a quarter-sized hole in her forehead, then Mason showed his face as he turned to look at Spurr.

The young marshal's eyes were saucer-round, and his mouth was open, forming a small, dark circle as he stepped slowly into the hall. He held his rifle in his right hand. He was holding his left hand to his ear. Blood oozed from between his fingers.

Wicked laughter sounded from the open doorway behind him.

Mason stepped over the girl, holding his rifle on the open doorway but staring down at the girl's pale body. Heart chugging slowly in his chest and his arm and shoulder feeling heavy and tingly but not as sore as before, Spurr walked slowly down the hall toward Mason and the girl, his moccasins snicking softly on the scarred puncheons.

Neither he nor Mason said anything for a long time. The smoke in the hall settled. Beyond the open door, Marvin 'the Maiden Killer Candles' lay naked on his belly, pale, hairy ass in the air. His wrists were cuffed behind his back. His body spasmed as he laughed, holding his chin off the floor. Tears dribbled down his cheeks.

Spurr looked at Mason, who was staring stone-faced at the girl. "I told you he was holed up with a girl back in Wheaton. Lucy Murphy."

Mason swallowed. "This here's Lucy . . . ?"

"He sparks 'em. Sorta mesmerizes 'em like what diamondbacks do to cats . . . before he kills 'em. He's a goddamn sick son of a bitch, Sheriff. I done told you that."

Mason brushed sweat from his forehead and mustache with his shirtsleeve. "Well, you killed her deader'n hell, didn't you, Spurr?" He stepped over the dead girl's body, brushed past the federal lawman, and walked into the room where Candles was laughing as though at the funniest joke he'd ever heard.

"Wouldn't have to, if you hadn't left that crazy bastard's pistol out in the hall."

"What's done is done," the sheriff muttered, not looking at Spurr.

Candles continued to laugh hysterically, eyes pinched shut.

Spurr glowered at the lanky outlaw, whose neck was so sunburned in contrast to the rest of his flour-white body that he appeared to be wearing a red neckerchief. His hair was thin, showing his scalp.

"You think that's funny, do you?" Spurr seethed.

"Oh, it's real funny, Spurr. I think it's damn funny. Only wish you'd left her for me to finish. Woulda gotten around to it when she'd finished pleasin' me. For havin' such an upstandin' ole pa back home in Wheaton, she sure knew how to —" Candles cut himself off as he widened his eyes in terror. "Hey!"

Spurr rammed his forehead with the butt of his Winchester. It made a strangely pleasing sound after the man's bizarre laughter and oddly high-pitched, raspy voice. Candles's head dropped to the floor, jerking a short time before the Maiden Killer lay still, breathing softly, openmouthed, against a sour-smelling hemp scatter rug.

Spurr stepped back, both hands shaking now. Mason looked at him, drawing the corners of his mouth down, his blue eyes dark as the high-altitude sky. He didn't say anything, just shouldered his rifle and began digging into a pocket of his wool shirt for a half-smoked cheroot.

As he lit it, hooves thudded in the yard outside the roadhouse. Spurr walked over

to a window, saw the Mexican apron standing in the yard, still holding his hands above
his head as he faced three men riding in
from the east. All three wore dusters, and
Spurr thought he saw badges flashing
amidst the billowing dust as they drew up
in front of the fat bartender, who regarded
them desperately, as though hoping they
would tell him he could lower his hands.

"What now?" Spurr growled.

"What is it?" Sheriff Mason asked, puffing
the cheroot as he rolled it between his lips,
holding his rifle down low under his right
arm.

Spurr stepped over Candles's still form
and out into the hall. Stepping over dead
Lucy Murphy, keeping his gaze from the
girl's tender, parted lips and pale breasts,
her eyes staring at the ceiling in shock at
her own too-early annihilation — he headed
on down the hall and then down the stairs.
As he crossed the main saloon hall, which
was growing thick with buzzing flies amidst
the coppery smell of spilled blood and vis-
cera, he tramped on out through the missing batwings and onto the roadhouse's front
gallery.

The three newcomers held their jumpy,
sweaty horses on short reins as they turned
toward Spurr. The man with the handlebar

mustache was Sheriff Walter McQueen from Holyoke, the county seat about forty miles east of here. He furled bleached-yellow brows at the federal lawman. "What in the hell brings you way out here, Spurr?"

"Lookin' for a barn dance." Shouldering his rifle, Spurr flexed his left hand and squinted into the sunlit yard. "What're you doin' here, Walt? I was told the last whore left this place nigh on a year ago now. Keep my ear to the rail on such matters."

"You ain't heard?"

"Heard what?"

McQueen shook his head darkly and spat a long wad of chew into the dust at the Mexican's feet. "Got the message over the telegraph 'bout an hour ago. The federal prison over at Limon." He jerked his chin to indicate west. "Been a break. A big one. And all them howlin' devils is runnin' wild for the hills."

Trouble broke out amongst the outlaws when someone finally gave into their lust and ripped the blouse of Romer Gaffney's sullen, redheaded niece, Wanda, off her freckled shoulder, exposing one entire breast. Gaffney got shouting mad.

The niece appeared as though she'd been in this position before and was relatively unruffled by it, though she held her torn blouse up over her breast and glared at her attacker. De Cava got mad then, too, because he'd promised Gaffney that his men would leave the half-breed rancher's women alone, and he was a man of his word. Also, Cuno figured, the ranch was a valuable relay stop when de Cava was on the run, which he almost always was. The outlaw leader backhanded the culprit savagely, splitting the man's lip, and made him apologize not only to the eternally sullen Wanda but to Gaffney, as well.

Then he ordered everyone to stow their gear, saddle their horses grazing by the creek, and head on up the trail.

Cuno rode somewhere in the middle of the pack, near Camilla, who kept looking over at him as though gauging his mood. The food and water at the ranch had made him feel better, but after the pummeling he'd taken from Mule Zimmerman, and his night in the Pit without food or water, and with a broken nose, he tired quickly.

The clothes he'd taken from White-Eye's stash made the ride in the hot sun more bearable, however, despite their stench of whiskey sweat. He kept the sombrero tipped low on his forehead, and gave Renegade his head, letting the skewbald paint follow along with the others as they traced dry watercourses on a generally southwestern course across southern Colorado, possibly northern New Mexico by now.

In the west, the Sangre de Cristos grew tall above the plain, the sun shifting across the high, snow-mantled ridges, making it appear a different range altogether each time Cuno glanced at it.

He was glad when they stopped in the late afternoon and holed up in a badland area just beyond the ruins of an abandoned military outpost.

"You know where we're headin', kid?" Frank Skinner asked him as they unsaddled their horses in a deep, gravel-floored canyon with a series of notch caves showing darkly in the canyon's chalky western wall.

"Can't say as I do."

"Well, just the same, I appreciate your friends."

"They're not my friends," Cuno said, as he set his saddle on a rock and glanced at the other tired, dusty, sun-reddened riders unrigging their horses, a few joking and laughing and breaking out whiskey bottles. "Just the girl."

"*Bonita* senorita."

Cuno gave the train robber an icy look. "Easy, Frank."

Skinner laughed as he ripped up some dry grass and began to rub his sweaty horse's back with it. "Don't worry about me, kid. I ain't one to mess with Mateo de Cava's little sis." He narrowed a deep-set, red-rheumy eye at the young freighter. "No, it ain't me you got to worry about. It's de Cava's other men. I'd sleep light tonight, if I was you. And I'd check regular for rattlesnakes in my bedroll."

Cuno began rubbing Renegade down with a scrap of burlap he found in his saddlebags. "Thanks for the advice."

"Don't mention it."

Suddenly, as though to validate the train robber's warning, de Cava's voice broke above the general din. "Hey, Senor Massey!"

Cuno looked at de Cava's grinning, bearded countenance regarding him over the back of his black Arabian stallion. The outlaw leader jerked a thumb at the big Yank, Wayne Brouschard, who stood beside de Cava, grinning through his yellow-blond beard at Cuno. He stood a good four inches above Mateo, who himself was a good six feet tall. The west-falling sun angled under the brim of his sombrero and made his eyes glow demonically.

"*Mi* amigo here wants to fight you for the affections of my sister," the outlaw leader said. "What do you say, huh? It is a tradition in Mexico to fight with knives with a five-foot length of rawhide clamped in the opponents' jaws."

Brouschard stepped out from behind his coyote dun mustang, shucked a horn-handled bowie knife from a sheath strapped low on his left thigh, and tossed the blade straight up, flipping it slowly above his head. Catching it by its handle, he stared at Cuno as he touched a thumb to the blade and gave a mock wince. "Ouch!"

Mateo was absently rubbing his horse down with a feed sack. "Brouschard has killed many an unfortunate Rurale with that blade. Cut their heads off in about two swipes."

"You gotta keep 'em sharp and well oiled," said the big Yankee, who had a west Texas accent. Probably from the Big Bend down close to the border.

Cuno glanced at Camilla, who was staring over the back of her own horse at her brother. Her lips were white with fury. Stepping out to face the big Texan, Cuno set his feet wide apart and hiked a shoulder. Canting his head toward Camilla and thumbing his chest, he said, "The girl's mine. But the .45's all I have."

From ahead and right, a blade flashed in

the air. The knife landed at his feet. Another big bowie with a hand-carved wooden handle wrapped with rawhide. The blade was rust-spotted, with dried blood crusted to the rust. Cuno glanced at the man who'd thrown it. The man smiled — a short, beefy American with a shabby brown bowler hat and two silver eyeteeth. Cuno had seen him hanging around close to Brouschard. His name was Eldon Wald.

Cuno leaned down and picked up the knife. He flipped it in the air, caught it by its handle, and stepped forward. As the other outlaws began closing a circle around the two challengers, Camilla tramped out from behind her horse, brushed past Cuno, and stopped in front of Brouschard, who towered over the petite senorita.

Instantly, she cut loose with a string of Spanish, rising up on the toes of her stockmen's boots, her face red and eyes spitting fire.

Cuno had a pretty good understanding of Spanish, but she was speaking so quickly that he couldn't make out much more than the frequent curses, but he was relatively certain that she was denouncing not only the Texan in no uncertain terms, but several generations of his family, as well. She ended her tirade, which rocked the big man back

111

on his undershot heels while evoking laughter from the others, by gesturing with one hand at Brouschard's crotch, holding her other hand up in front of his face, and spreading her thumb and index finger about two inches apart. Casting an admiring glance at Cuno, she held both hands up in front of Brouschard once more and spread them about two feet apart, palms facing each other.

She curled her upper lip at the big man disdainfully and crossed her arms on her breasts.

Brouschard's face turned as red an Arizona sunset.

Mateo and the other men roared.

Brouschard looked so exasperated and embarrassed that Cuno couldn't help laughing, as well. He'd been around such men as these enough to know he couldn't allow the senorita to defend him without showing some of his own spleen. After what he'd been through, he had little strength for his next move, but from somewhere deep in his bones he summoned a last reserve. Bounding toward the girl, laughing, he pulled her around to face him, crouched, and slung her over his shoulder like a fifty-pound sack of cracked corn.

Camilla screamed as he spun twice

around, laughing like a victor holding up his trophy.

While the other men except for Brouschard laughed and hollered and clapped, Cuno hauled Camilla down a twisting corridor in the rocks and down a slight grade toward where a spring bubbled around sand and gravel and bits of green grass.

"Okay, cowboy," Camilla said, when the men were out of sight behind a stone scarp behind her and Cuno, "you can put me down now. I think they get the drift, as you gringos say."

He stopped by the spring, set the girl down before him. He kept his arms around her. His blood surged hotly in his veins, dulling the pain in other parts of his body.

She stared up at him, her brown eyes darkening. Her cheeks flushed and her bosom swelled behind her calico blouse. Pulling her brusquely toward him, Cuno swept her hair back from her face, nudged her chin up, and kissed her.

He hadn't had a woman in a long time. His loins warmed.

She tasted good.

9

"Feels like Sunday around here," said Sheriff Walt McQueen, glancing at Spurr, who rode off McQueen's left stirrup. "Don't it feel just like Sunday?"

"It ain't Sunday," said Sheriff Dusty Mason, who was leading the horse on which Marvin Candles rode, hands tied to the saddle horn. "Think it might be Tuesday."

"I ain't sayin' it *is* Sunday," McQueen said testily. "I'm sayin' it feels like Sunday."

Spurr was looking around the buildings lining Limon's main street, which was all but deserted except for small groups of horses standing at hitchracks fronting saloons. The only sound was the wind and the ticking of windblown dust against the sides of buildings.

The wind had picked up early that morning, not long after the five lawmen had left the roadhouse where they'd captured the Maiden Killer, and had pelted them raw with dirt and sand the entire four-hour ride to Limon. No, there was another sound. Spurr heard it beneath the eerily moaning wind. The sound of pounding.

It seemed to be coming from Jurgens's Undertaking Parlor, a long, low building that sat just ahead and on the left side of the street. It was flanked by a large cottonwood that was nearly doubled over by the wind.

A man's shout rose from behind the two large sliding doors on the building's east side. The doors were open a foot, and in this crack a dog suddenly appeared. The little, weed-colored, long-nosed cur bolted out the gap with a short-topped stockman's boot in its jaws. The dog's eyes sparked with deviltry. Spurr's roan spooked, rearing slightly, as the dog dashed past him and shot straight across the street with its tail between its legs.

Behind the sliding doors, the man shouted again. Spurr and the other lawmen, including McQueen and his two deputies from Holyoke, drew their mounts to a halt as a man poked his broad, wrinkled, mustached face out between the doors, snarling like a rabid cur himself.

"That dog!" he shouted, shouldering out between the doors and raising a double-barreled shotgun to his shoulder. "The god-damn Widow Wallace's dog stole the mar-shal's boot. I told her . . . I told her if I saw him again — !"

Kaboom!

The buckshot blew up dust in the street just behind the cur's back legs as the dog dashed into a narrow break between two buildings on the street's north side. The report echoed briefly before the thunder was swallowed by the wind.

"I told her I'd kill the damn mutt and throw him through her goddamn front window!" the man cried through gritted teeth, lowering the barn blaster and shaking his fist at the break into which the dog had disappeared.

"Marshal's boot?" Spurr said. "You mean the marshal of Limon?"

The man who was apparently Jurgens, the undertaker, nodded as he turned to Spurr and then to the other badge wearers around him. "Sure enough," he said with a faint German accent, lifting his voice to be heard above the wind. "Killed him deader'n last night's supper, that gang did. Over there by the Arkansas, between town and the prison."

He nodded to indicate the far side of Li-mon and beyond, where the prison sat a mile away like some sprawling medieval

116

castle misplaced here on the windblown prairie.

Spurr looked toward where the cur had disappeared, and glowered. He'd known the Limon town marshal, Willard Overcast, from his old hide-hunting days. Another lawman dead. And a mangy mutt had run off with the boot Overcast had intended to be buried in.

It was a damn cruel world, the old marshal absently reflected, the image of the dead blonde, Lucy Murphy, still clear in his head.

"Who's in charge?" Dusty Mason wanted to know.

"James T. Vernon," said the undertaker, canting his head toward the stone jailhouse at the west edge of town. "We appointed him constable in an emergency town meeting last night. Older'n them hills yonder, but he's the only one who'd take it. That breakout at the prison, leaving six citizens dead and a whole bunch of prison guards and the warden without his nose and topknot, has got everyone around here feelin' owly."

Spurr looked out at the prison obscured by windblown dust, and asked, "Who's in charge at the pen?"

"Army group from Fort Sewald. Overcast sent a telegram as soon as he heard them

Gatlings barking over to the prison. Then he formed a posse and they laid low at the creek, waiting for the break the sheriff figured was comin'."

The undertaker clucked and shook his head. "Well, if you fellas will excuse me, I got a load of business all sudden-like. Still makin' coffins. Funerals start tomorrow." He looked toward a small cemetery topping a low, brushy rise north of town, where two men were busy digging. "The gravedigger had to hire on a local boy to help."

Spurr glanced at McQueen. "I'm gonna stow my prisoner in the hoosegow yonder, under the guard of James T. Vernon. Then we'll ride out to the prison, see what's what."

"Like hell you are!" the Maiden Killer yelled. "You can't leave me under lock and key in this jerkwater town, with some old man who's likely so senile he'll forget to feed me!"

"Shut up, Marvin," Spurr and McQueen said in unison as they and the three other lawmen gigged their horses on up the street.

"Scalped him," Major Pike Donleavy said, blowing cigar smoke out the warden's open office door. "Blew a hole in his leg, another in his knee. Crippled the poor man for life.

Then Mateo de Cava blew his nose off. Or the end of it, anyways. Don't know how in the hell you get a good breath without a nose but he seems to be managing good enough through his mouth. Between screams, that is."

The paunchy, round-faced, high-cheekboned major from Fort Sewald shook his head and tapped ashes off the end of his cigar. "He's down in the infirmary. The prison doctor's lookin' after him. Keeps him drunk on ether and laudanum, but he was screamin' all night, I'm told. My men and I didn't arrive until just a couple hours ago. Rode all night after we got the telegram from Overcast."

"Is the warden gonna make it?" Spurr asked.

He walked from where he'd sat on a visitor's chair in front of the warden's desk and stood beside the major. Both men stared outside where order was finally being reestablished in the blood-splattered prison yard, the bodies of the dead prisoners and guards being hauled off by surviving guards and the major's men in cavalry blues.

"Doubt it," said the major. "If the blood loss alone doesn't kill him, gangrene'll set in. Usually does. Seen enough men taken by it during the war."

"I'd sure like to know how in the hell he let this happen. This is a maximum-security federal prison, for chrissakes."

Spurr fired a match and turned to regard two of the roofed guard towers as he touched the flame to his cheroot, an indulgence proscribed by his doctor in Buffalo-ville. "Four Gatling guns and thirty guards. With a good half mile of open ground in all directions. How does a group of twenty or so just ride in and sack the place?"

"Good question," Major Donleavy said, turning his head as three soldiers rode through the prison's open front gates, leading three bedraggled, barefoot men in prison stripes by riatas looped around their waists. The escapees looked ready to drop. "Ah, three more. Likely, after my reinforcements have arrived from Camp Collins, we'll have all those prisoners who hightailed it after the break safely back behind bars. Except, probably, those who managed to grab some horses from some woodcutters on a creek just north of here."

"Who'd they come for, Major? Mateo de Cava's gang. Who'd they break out?"

"When the warden was still coherent he said they — meaning de Cava as well as a Mexican girl identified as his sister — came for . . . for . . ." The major turned and

120

started walking toward the warden's desk, where he'd left a sheet of notes he'd scribbled during his interview of the warden.

McQueen was standing by the desk, as the other lawmen had taken up the rest of the visitor chairs. The Holyoke sheriff looked down at the paper, jabbing a finger at it and scowling. "Cuno Massey."

"Yes, Massey," the major said, turning back to the open door. "An unusual name. You'd think I'd remember it. Cuno Massey." He enunciated each word clearly, separately then poked his cigar into his mouth, and puffed. "A gringo. Odd for a gang led by a notorious Mexican desperado to —"

"Cuno Massey?" This from Sheriff Mason, perched on a corner of the warden's desk, a stove match protruding from a corner of his mouth. "I know that name."

Spurr and the other men in the room looked at him.

"Matter of fact, I arrested him," Mason said. "He killed a trio of territorial marshals in the Rawhides last winter. They caught him runnin' rifles to the Utes."

"Gun runner," Spurr said, the disdain plain in his voice. There were few men more diabolical than those who provided Indians with rifles with which they could wreak havoc on the people of the men who'd armed them purely for money. "Figures he'd be aligned with de Cava. Heard he ran rifles along the Arizona border."

"Who else did they take out, Major?" Mason asked.

"An old train robber named Frank Skinner. A Mex named Arguello, but my men found him dead a few hours ago. Likely wounded in the skirmish with the townsmen on the Arkansas."

The old marshal turned to Donleavy. "I take it you have men tracking them killers?"

Donleavy shook his head. "I came with only twenty men. There's been an outbreak of typhoid at Fort Sewald. At the moment, we're badly under-garrisoned. I'm hoping that Camp Collins is sending enough men that they can leave some to help out here and some to send after de Cava."

"How long till they get here?" asked Mason, his blood up. The name Massey had lit a fire inside him. "De Cava's probably headed for the border."

"Another twenty-four hours by train." The major blew a smoke plume through the open door and looked at Spurr. "By now, every lawman in Colorado, New Mexico, and Utah has heard what happened here. Thank god for the telegraph. Those lawmen will be keeping a close eye out for de Cava. I'm betting the gang won't make it as far as Albuquerque."

"I wouldn't count on that, Major."

Spurr stuck his cheroot between his teeth and walked over to a cherry table that sat beneath a large, framed, flyspecked map of Colorado Territory. On the table were four decanters of different colors and sizes. He turned a goblet right side up and poured a liberal jigger of what looked like brandy. He held the glass up and looked at the amber liquid, swirling it between his dirty, blunt fingers.

"De Cava is a killing machine. Every man ridin' with him is mean enough to shoot his own mother for overcookin' his eggs. There ain't no local lawmen anywhere on the frontier ready to deal with a herd of wildcats like this bunch."

"What are you suggesting, Deputy?" The major looked piqued. "I have five men out chasing escaped prisoners. The rest I need here to keep the other monkeys in their barrel. I'd suggest forming a posse from Limon, but Overcast already tried that, and the undertaker there is making enough money to buy a stake and move to Sherman Avenue in Denver."

"I ain't suggestin' nothin'," Spurr said,

throwing back half the brandy. "I'm sayin' someone's gotta go after 'em now. While their trail's still warm." He threw back the rest of the shot and slammed the glass down on the table. "I reckon that means us, fellas," he said raspily, the brandy searing his tonsils as he shuttled his glance to the four other lawmen in the room.

McQueen and his two deputies, both in their early twenties, regarded him skeptically. He knew what they were thinking. Could the old man make it? They'd likely seen him struggle to get mounted this morning, in the wake of the mule kick to the chest he'd endured in the roadhouse the day before.

He poked his cigar between his teeth, shouldered his rifle, and brushed past Donleavy on his way out the door.

"Hold on, hold on," yelled Dusty Mason, quickly pouring himself a shot of the warden's brandy, throwing it back, and choking on it. He'd arrested Massey, and he, by god, would make damn sure the lawman-killing younker whose fresh face belied his obviously black heart would pay for his sins.

"Wait for me, damnit, Spurr!"

10

It felt good, being free.

Even better than he'd thought it would when he'd fantasized about it all those long months in the prison, figuring he'd spend the rest of his life there, brawling for the warden's amusement, fighting for every drop of water, every bite of rancid food.

But now that he was out he took special note of the grass and the sage and the hat-shaped bluffs and sand-colored cliffs cropping up around him here east of the mountains that loomed like a perpetual storm. He loved the sky here. It was all around, and clouds didn't so much slide across it as pile up on top of him so that he had to stretch his neck back to get a look at those big, gray, billowy thunderheads.

It was monsoon season, and the storms were spilling down off the mountains and filling the washes out here on the prairie. It was good-tasting water. The best Cuno had ever tasted. Lightning crackled and flashed like witches' fingers poking the lime-green tableland. Thunder sounded like gods tossing boulders.

He and the de Cava gang rode hard for three days after the prison break. Cuno wasn't sure where in the hell they were going; he was beginning to wonder if Mateo even knew. They headed west toward the mountains, and just as they began make the climb into them, heading toward the passes, they swung hard east again and holed up in another isolated badlands.

They headed out before sunrise the next morning, angling northeast.

Cuno didn't much care, as long as he didn't have to push Renegade too hard and ruin him. He didn't care where they were going, because he had nowhere to go now that he was a fugitive. A desperado.

In fact, riding was as good a thing for him to do now as anything. The gang, unheeled as a pack of rabid wolves, provided safety in its numbers. The air and the sun were balms to his battered body, and now, after three days, the swelling around his nose and eyes was going down.

As they rode, Cuno often glanced at Camilla riding beside him. She glanced back at him, her hair flying out behind her shoulders, her blouse billowing forward then pulling back taut against her breasts as she rode.

It was exhilarating, riding hard and looking at her and then stealing off with her alone at night and enjoying the delights of her supple, dusky body. He liked how, just as he brought her to fulfillment, she snarled like a bobcat and sunk her teeth into his shoulder. And she'd said only Mateo was part Yaqui! He'd lain with her before in the Rawhides, but she'd seemed so much quieter then. Demure.

Now there was a wild carnality, a hunger about her that thrilled him. Maybe because it matched his own savagery, which he'd felt growing in him gradually behind the prison walls, then burgeoning suddenly as soon as he rode through those prison gates and knew that he could never go back to the old life he'd had before.

Not after killing that town marshal.

Not that he'd been so damn civilized before. In fact, he'd killed many men. But at least he'd tried to settle down and live the life of a good citizen, until he and Sheriff Dusty Mason had made the deal that had likely saved the lives of Michelle Trent and the Lassiter kids, not to mention Camilla herself. A tough deal, because Cuno hadn't killed those marshals in cold blood. And unlike what Mason had thought, he and his old partner, Serenity Parker, hadn't been running rifles to the Utes.

They had been running rifles, all right. Against their wishes, they'd hauled several crates of Winchesters to the Trent ranch, though Cuno had thought they'd just been hauling supplies, not finding out till they reached the ranch that Trent had double-crossed him and had arranged for rifles and gunpowder to be hidden in their freight wagons, to be used by Trent's ranch hands against the marauding Utes themselves.

That was all past now. All water under a high bridge.

Now he had a gang and a woman and his old horse and the .45 that Charlie Dodge had given him back in Nebraska. He had the damp breeze spiced with sage and cedar in his face.

And he had a good, albeit wild, Mexican filly who reminded him, bittersweetly, of his dead wife, July. And maybe best of all was not knowing or caring where in the hell Mateo de Cava was leading him, because he had nowhere to go and he'd come from nowhere . . .

In the late afternoon, the falling sun behind him, Cuno watched a settlement of sorts rise from a broad, shallow bowl in the prairie, surrounded by low bluffs. Shiny silver rails stretched toward the village from the east and ended a little ways south, where graders and drays were parked around large gravel mounds, and fresh rails were stacked, ready to be laid in the bed that twenty or so men were building with picks, shovels, grading pies, and horse-drawn winches.

Coffee fires burned, sending up smoke. Mule teams stood tied to picket lines. There was the hum of the men's raucous working conversation, and the clinks of hammered rail spikes.

North of where the new rails were being laid, the village sprouted — a shabby oasis consisting of both simple and elaborate frame buildings surrounded by tents of all shapes and sizes. One faint wagon trail led there, and Cuno and Camilla followed the rest of the gang onto the trail and into the railroad supply camp.

Judging by its two sturdy saloons, so new that the resin from their whipsawed planks made the whole area smell like a pine forest, and a gaudy, two-story building on the second-story balcony of which several young women milled like willowy birds of plumage, the camp had ambitions toward becoming a town.

Dogs ran out from alley mouths to bark at the large group of dusty newcomers astraddle their sweat-frothy mounts. Chickens scattered. A white horse hitched to a small, black buggy reared and whinnied.

Mateo's men whooped and hollered as they thundered on up to the brothel, which was not yet identified by a sign but which could only be a whorehouse, with all the painted girls dancing and smoking and drinking on the second-floor balcony. The girls answered the men's mating calls in kind, leaning over the wrought-iron rails, shaking out their hair, and letting their wraps and gowns billow out from their bosoms.

"Good lord," shouted Brouschard. "I do believe we done died and flew to heaven, amigo!"

Mateo covered his chest with his black sombrero as he halted his big, black steed and regarded the fluttering birds on the balcony with a caballero-like grin. He didn't appear at all self-conscious of the ugly scalping scars.

"Good afternoon, lovely ladies," the gang leader said in his heavily accented Spanish, giving a courtly bow, then raking the women staring down at him with his eager gaze. "Are you open for business or just getting some air?"

Several of the girls looked at each other, vaguely puzzled. A couple were speaking in some foreign tongue Cuno didn't recognize — French? German? — and then a big blonde stepped forward and lowered both straps of her sheer, purple gown, and let her giant breasts adorned with double strings of fake pearls spill forth.

That was answer enough for the outlaws. Mateo and the other gang members gave another volley of jubilant yowls, leapt out of their saddles, dashed across the broad front, wraparound gallery, and bulled through the brothel's open double doors.

Suddenly, Cuno and Camilla were surrounded by over a dozen riderless horses. Inside the brothel, a din rose, echoing, as the men went looking for the women, some of whom remained on the balcony. Others disappeared, heading for their cribs.

A little redhead remained, clad in a pink corset and gauzy black wrap. Her eyes were rimmed in seductive black that nicely complimented the burnished red of her hair. She rested an arm on the rail and arched a brow as she regarded Cuno still sitting Renegade in the middle of the broad street. He let his gaze stray to the twin mounds of creamy, freckled flesh pushing up from the top of her corset, and felt a surge of heat in his loins.

Camilla put her horse up hard against his, leaned toward him, and wrapped a slender, strong arm around his neck. She mashed her mouth against his, held the kiss for a good five seconds, then pulled away and turned to the redhead, who was about her age. Curling her upper lip, she said, "Why would he buy a cow when he gets all the milk he wants for free?"

Lines cut into the whore's forehead.

Camilla hooked a thumb at a hotel up the chaotically laid-out street and winked at Cuno. "Let's go pound the mattress sack, *mi amore.*"

"I got a better idea."

As they'd ridden in, Cuno had seen the creek angling along the northern outskirts of the town. Now he turned to Renegade, pinched his hat brim to the incredulous whore, and booted the skewbald paint through a broad gap between a hardware tent and a bathhouse and down a slight grade beyond.

Ahead lay the creek in its shallow ravine sheathed in tall, brown grass, alders, and the ubiquitous cottonwood. Clear water shimmered in the late light, chuckled over rocks. Cuno put Renegade up to a deep pool that back-eddied into a break caused when one of the large cottonwoods had blown down, wrenching its roots out of the earth. Only the roots remained; the rest of the tree had likely been used in the building of the unnamed encampment.

Cuno's boots hit the ground. He looked over Renegade's back. Camilla's chestnut bay lunged down the grade, hoofs thudding, the girl's rump bouncing against her saddle. Her cheeks, brushed by her flying hair, were flushed.

Cuno held her cool gaze as he quickly unbuckled Renegade's latigo. She lifted her mouth corners, and a darker color rose in her cheeks as she swung down from her saddle and went to work unrigging her own horse. She had her back to Cuno now, but as she worked she tossed him several luminous glances over her shoulder, coyly tucking her lower lip under her upper front teeth.

Cuno tossed his gear on the ground. As Renegade trotted off, then dropped and rolled, kicking up dust and weeds, Cuno kicked out of his boots and then quickly shucked out of his clothes. Shedding the dead man's duds was like shedding extra layers of heavy, smelly grime, and when he'd tossed his underwear over a sage shrub, he threw his shoulders back and scratched his chest then ran his fingers through his longish, blond, sweat-damp hair.

"Damn, that feels good!"

Camilla turned to him. Her breasts jostled and sloped toward the ground as she leaned forward to slide her pantaloons down her cinnamon-colored legs. Her eyes roved across him, lingering below his belly, where his desire had made itself obvious, and then she turned away to pile her own clothes on her gear. Her rump was round and smooth and the same dark tan as the rest of her — two taut mounds of ripe, womanly flesh. Cuno walked to her, placed his hands on her hips as he pressed his chest against her back and nuzzled her neck.

Her buttocks were cool and supple against his thighs.

She drew a sharp breath and wrapped an arm around his neck from behind, turning her head. Squeezing her eyes closed, she kissed him, entangling her tongue with his.

He wrapped his arms around her, cupped her breasts in his hands, felt the soft nipples pebble. Continuing to kiss him, she twisted around to face him, and he lowered his hands down the long, tapering angle of her back to her rump, squeezed her buttocks and felt his heart thud harder. Her rump was heavy and inviting in his callused hands.

He pulled his mouth away from hers. He leaned down, grabbed her around her back and knees, and hoisted her up. She was light, easy in his arms, and she smelled dusty and warm and of horses and sage and of something else that could only be her own special female fragrance and which he'd come to know so well in the past few days and remembered from before, in the Rawhides.

She screamed and wrapped her arms around his neck, laughing and kicking, flattening a tender breast against his chest.

"No!"

He stumbled over to the creek, peeled her hands from his neck, and against her protestations, threw her into the deep, cool, dark pool, then jumped in after her.

"Bastardo!" she cried, laughing and rubbing water from her eyes.

He grabbed her and held her close and pushed her back against the bank. He looked at her seriously. She returned the gaze. She wrapped her legs around him, pressing her heels hard against the small of his back.

Placing her hands flat against his ears, she closed her hungry mouth over his as he took her. When they finished spasming together, groaning and sighing and clutching, Cuno pulled back away from her but froze when a gun clicked behind him.

Camilla snapped her eyes wide, looking over his shoulder, and gasped.

11

"Holy shit, Stewart — look at the tits on that little Mex girl!" said one of the two riders sitting at the edge of the bank.

They'd come in so quietly that Cuno hadn't heard the hoof thuds above his and Camilla's love cries and the chuckling of the creek around their naked bodies. He'd whipped around to face the men now — two unshaven hombres in dusters and sweat-stained hats. Both had two pistols on their hips and oiled carbines in their saddle boots. The lather on their horses told they'd been ridden hard.

The man on the right held a pistol on Cuno. He had dark eyes, and the middle of his face bulged out as though pressed by an unseen fist behind his beak-like nose. He squinted one eye now as he centered his sights on Cuno's dripping chest. The other man lounged forward in his saddle, hands on the horn, a smug smile on his face covered in beard stubble the color of iron filings. His eyes were pale blue and seedy.

"This is a private party," Cuno said, holding Camilla behind him as they both stood belly deep in the creek. "Kindly move along."

"You ain't the one givin' the orders, feller," said the man with the cocked and aimed pistol. "Tell your girlfriend to get on up here. We want a better look at her."

"I told you," Cuno said, a low whistle starting up in his ears. "It's a private party." He put some steel in his voice — manufactured steel, as he was not only unarmed but without a stitch of clothing. As was his girl, whose fingers pressed into his arms from behind, just above his elbows. "You move on, I'll forget the interruption."

Both men chuckled.

"You will, will you?" said the man sitting easily in his saddle, atop a rangy sorrel with a bite out of its left ear. "Well, guess what, boy? We don't give a shit if you forget it or not. We want your girl. And if she don't come up here right now, my friend H. D. is gonna blow a hole through your heart. Now, he'd hate to do that. Seein's how you're ridin' with the de Cava gang, you likely have a rather large bounty on your head. But me an' H. D.'s right randy after that long ride, and we're wantin' your girl. We'll be right quick about it, and then you can have her back."

Camilla's fingers dug deeper into Cuno's arms. "There's plenty of willing girls in the camp yonder. Take your pick."

"We don't want a whore." Hatchet-faced H. D. spoke slowly, menacingly, showing large yellow teeth between his cracked, pink lips. "We want your girl. We seen you two, and we want her. Yeah, she'll do just fine."

"Well, you can't have her. I do apologize."

H. D. with the cocked gun hardened his jaws.

The other man slid a .36 Remington from its holster, and clicked the hammer back.

"Wait!" Camilla tried to move out from behind Cuno, but he pushed her back behind him.

"Come on outta there, *chiquita.* Or we'll shoot your boyfriend."

"Who the hell are you?" Cuno said, keeping the girl behind him.

"The worst dream you ever had, she don't come willin' like. With me first. Off in the brush yonder while H.D. keeps you here." The man with the cocked .36 grinned and slitted his eyes as he swung down from his horse, the other man following suit and stepping forward. They were both enjoying this — terrorizing two naked lovers fresh from the carnal throes. "Then it's H. D.'s turn. Then we're through, and you two can go about your business."

H. D. laughed.

The other man stopped at the creek's edge. His eyes sparked between narrowed lids, and he slowly spread his lips back from his teeth, showing several gaps.

Cuno clenched his fists, felt a burning fill his head. "I'll kill you for this, you depraved sons o' bitches."

Camilla caught him off guard and lurched around him. He grabbed for her. She jerked her arm away from him and waded toward the bank.

"It's all right, Cuno," she said, her voice low and hard with fury as she kept her eyes on the two men watching her lustily. "If it will make these two dogs feel like men, to take a girl by force, then let's see how much man they really are!"

H. D. said, "I like her already!"

The other man grabbed Camilla's arm, pulled her up out of the water, and turned her into the trees and brush along the shore. Cuno strode forward.

"That's far enough, bucko," H. D. said.

Cuno continued forward, fists clenched at his sides. The man with the gun backed up, flushing anxiously, keeping the gun aimed at Cuno's chest. Cuno came on up the bank, slipping a little in the mud and wet grass. He had to make a play. He wouldn't let them take Camilla. He'd stop them or die.

H. D. didn't want to shoot him. He wanted Cuno to hear what went on in the brush. He'd kill Cuno later. Sadist was the word for such men as him and his partner. They had the look and smell and armaments of bounty hunters. H. D. stepped back, keeping a good ten feet between him and Cuno, grinning.

Cuno followed Camilla's slender, brown back with his eyes. The other man was following her slowly, thumbs hooked behind his cartridge belts. Camilla glanced back at Cuno, her eyes wide and dark. The man behind her pushed her forward hard, and she stumbled, dropping to her knees with a sharp curse. The man laughed.

Cuno had just turned to the man in front of him when a rifle barked. There was a cracking thud and a grunt.

In the corner of his eye, Cuno saw the man following Camilla jerk his head as though he'd been socked in the ear. The man ahead of Cuno turned to look in his partner's direction, and Cuno bounded across the break between them. He grabbed the gun as H. D. swung his head back toward Cuno, and just then Cuno grabbed the gun in both his large hands and raised it.

H. D. jerked the trigger. The gun's roar was a miniature lance through Cuno's ears, making them ring. Holding the gun around H. D.'s hands, Cuno pushed the hachet-faced man straight back against a broad tree trunk.

H. D. cursed and spit like a riled bobcat, bunching his lips and trying to push the gun down and away from him and aim it at Cuno. He was strong. Cuno was stronger. H. D. sucked a breath through his teeth as Cuno pried one of the man's hands away from the back of the gun and clicked the hammer back. At the same time, using steady pressure, Cuno snugged the pistol's barrel up against the soft skin beneath H. D.'s chin.

He lifted his head, gritting his teeth, all the blood running out of his face. "Ah, *shit!*"

Cuno pulled down on H. D.'s trigger finger.

Pop!

Cuno released the man's head and stepped back, warm blood spashing his face, neck, and shoulders. H. D.'s knees buckled, and he dropped as though a trapdoor had been opened beneath him. He lay quivering on his side at the base of the trunk.

Cuno held the bloody gun in his hand and looked around. Mateo de Cava was striding toward him, his fringed deerskin leggings jostling about his slightly bowed legs, the spurs on his black boots trilling. His eyes were large, his black-bearded face expressionless. Camilla looked down at the man her brother had shot. She cursed and gave him a savage kick with her bare foot, then turned to Mateo.

"Cover your eyes, fool! I'm naked!"

Mateo flashed a relieved smile. "I see that, my beautiful sister." He turned to Cuno, standing naked and bloody and holding the bloody gun in his clenched fist, his broad chest rising and falling heavily with rage. He wanted to kill the man slumped and quivering at his bare feet again and again.

No matter how foul he was, a man could only die once. It didn't seem fair.

Mateo came over and stood near Cuno, staring down at the dead man whose limbs were finally settling. "H. D. Harold." His voice was low, grim. He walked past Camilla, who was pulling on her clothes, and stopped over the man he'd shot with his carbine. He'd apparently come alone, as

Cuno saw no one else around. "Dwight Tevis," he said, prodding the other man's black leather holster with his boot toe. A tarnished, silver star had been sewn into it. "Used to be a lawman. Took the star with him when he quit to start on a more lucrative career."

"Bounty hunter?" Cuno was looking around, wondering if there were any more man hunters where these two had come from.

Mateo sighed and shouldered his Winchester, looking around. "This pair of carrion-eating lobos have been following us for two days."

Cuno looked at the outlaw leader. He didn't care that he was still naked and wearing a pint of blood and brain matter on his face and shoulders. Prison had a way of hardening your spleen and stripping away your modesty. "You knew."

Now he felt foolish for not only letting these men sneak up on him while he and Camilla were rutting but for not knowing they'd been sniffing his and the gang's trail for days.

"Si, si."

"Why didn't you say something?" Camilla asked her brother. She scowled at Mateo as she pulled her blouse on over a threadbare camisole.

Mateo spoke in Spanish, purposely excluding Cuno to let the young freighter know he still had much to prove if he was to be considered a bona fide member of the gang. He said something along the lines of: "I told those who needed to know. Since there were only two, we were not worried."

In English, he said, "But from the window of the whorehouse, I saw them riding down here." His voice was cool and teeming with disapproval. "If you're going to ask for my sister's hand in holy matrimony, *mi* gringo amigo, you're gonna have to prove you can protect her. And that you're not dumber than a cartload of stove wood."

He swung around and began taking long, rolling strides — the Spanish cock of the walk — back toward the brothel, his spurs trilling. When he was gone, Cuno turned to Camilla. He didn't know what to say so he brushed past her and into the creek.

She turned her head, following him with her eyes. "What's wrong?"

Cuno waded into the creek and began angrily splashing water up to wash his head and shoulders. "Your brother's right. I damn near got you killed."

"It wasn't your fault. I should have heard them coming myself. We were preoccupied."

"None of the other men in the gang have women riding with them. Now I reckon I know why."

She swung around to face him squarely, planted her fists on her hips. "Well, you don't have much choice, do you?"

Cuno turned to look at her over his shoulder. Her brown face was dappled with golden sunshine tumbling through the leaves. He splashed more water onto his chest, walked up the bank, and stood over her.

His heart felt swollen, tender. He'd known such harrowing loneliness even before prison that he couldn't conceive of being without this girl who apparently loved him to her own detriment.

Slowly, she lifted her hands to the hard, swollen slabs of his chest. He leaned down and kissed her.

"No, I reckon I don't have much choice."

"Do you wish you did?"

He shook his head. "But I need to work on this desperado stuff. Up to now, I've been the one doin' the hunting, not the one bein' hunted."

"We could leave — you and I. We could head south together."

"Leave the gang?"

"Sure. Neither of us really belongs with

Mateo. I did at one time, back in Mejico, after our father died and I had no one else. But I could give up this crazy bandito life . . . if you wanted."

Cuno studied her, but half his thoughts were elsewhere. He looked off toward the brothel. Mateo was halfway between him and the camp, the late light gilding his black-clad shoulders. A low din of drunken revelry rose on the breeze, emanating from the brothel.

The bandito leader had saved Cuno's and Camilla's lives. In this new world he'd suddenly found himself in — the world of a fugitive — there was safety in numbers.

"What else do we have?" he asked Camilla.

She lifted her hands from his chest, brushed her fingertips across his cheeks. She closed her eyes very lightly, rose onto the toes of her boots, and kissed him gently. "Each other," she whispered.

12

To distract himself from the young Murphy girl he'd recently drilled while saving Mason's worthless hide, Spurr was thinking about a whore he knew, known simply as Abilene from up Wyoming way, and whom when drunk he often considered marrying, though he wasn't drunk now, and there was no question that what had just screeched past his face and over his horse's head, abruptly snuffing all thoughts of Abilene and her buxom, raspy-voiced allure, was a bullet.

Likely a large-caliber bullet. It hammered the ground to his right and ahead about six feet with a heavy *whump!* and twangy *yip!* that echoed across the broad bowl he and the other lawmen were crossing, on the trail of the Mateo de Cava gang.

The thunder of the heavy gun reached Spurr's old ears a half second later, and it drowned the ricochet's echo.

"What in god's name?" cried Sheriff McQueen, jerking back on his horse's reins and whipping his head toward the low hill from which the shot had been fired.

"Everyone down!" Spurr shouted, reaching for his Winchester. "Take cover!"

When he had the Winchester out of its scabbard, he dropped clumsily out of his saddle. The roan shied from the bark of another shot before the old marshal had gotten his left boot clear, and the movement tripped him up and threw him. He hit the ground on his left shoulder and hip and sucked a breath as his old bones seemed to clank together like rocks in an ore car. The padding between his rickety joints had long since turned to scrap leather torn and bleached by a thousand suns and winds.

"Goddamn you, Cochise!" he cried, rising heavily and groaning with the effort.

"Spurr, for chrissakes!" Sheriff Dusty Mason admonished, shaking his head.

The sheriff was already off his strawberry, of course, and on one knee behind a rock that didn't offer much cover at all. He cast a quick, disgusted look at the older man just now raising his own rifle to his shoulder, then snugged his cheek up against his own rifle's rear stock, and triggered a return shot toward the hill from which the large-caliber

149

bullets had been fired. Spurr followed the younger lawman's gaze but saw nothing but medium-sized boulders strewn about the top of the knoll.

"Where is the pot-shootin' son of a bitch?"

"In them rocks up there! Can't you see?"

Spurr ignored the insult and triggered three quick rounds, vaguely proud of himself for landing the shots where he'd wanted them, watching dust and stone slivers puff from the rocks. But he saw no sign of the shooter. If he was up there, he'd dropped back down out of sight.

"Jason!" someone cried behind him.

As he ejected a spent cartridge from his brass-framed Winchester, he glanced back to see McQueen and his two deputies still sitting their fiddle-footing horses. One of the young deputies was flopping back in his saddle, blood bibbing on his pin-striped shirt near where one suspender climbed his shoulder. He held his reins high, and his eyes were wide and white-ringed, lips bunched. He looked like he was about to go under water and was holding his breath for it.

His hat was gone. Beside him, Sheriff McQueen's mouth gaped. Blood from the deputy's shoulder and chest had splashed across McQueen's own left arm, and his sun-leathery cheek above his silver mustache was splattered, as well. Blood continued to well from the young deputy's chest.

"McQueen!" Spurr shouted. "Get that man the hell out of here! We'll cover you!"

As McQueen reached stiffly out to grab the reins of the wounded deputy's sorrel, Spurr and Mason pelted the rocks topping the knoll with .44 slugs, kicking up dust and bits of sage and yucca. When the sheriff and his two deputies had galloped out of sight, heading toward three cone-shaped bluffs in the western distance, Spurr raised his left hand. Mason held fire.

"You drop back. Get into that trough back there." The federal lawman glanced at the slight depression twenty yards behind him — a shallow gully that carried runoff during the wet times. "I'll cover you."

"I haven't seen him. I think he's gone."

"Just do as I say, Sheriff," Spurr said, seating a fresh round and staring tensely down the brass-framed rifle's smoking barrel at the rocky mound. The bushwhacker had likely been firing a Sharps. Possibly a Big Fifty.

A buffalo gun like that could blow a fist-sized hole in a man, tear an arm or a leg clean off.

"All right," Mason called when he'd

reached the trough.

Spurr stayed where he was. The iron crab in his chest was tightening up on him but it wasn't hurting too bad. His leaky heart was thudding slowly, stubbornly. Keeping his rifle trained on the knoll, he used his left hand to pluck cartridges from his shell belt and to slide them, one after another, into his Winchester's receiver.

"Like I said, Spurr — that bastard's gone," said Mason with an impatient air.

Just then a silhouetted, hatted head appeared above and between two rocks atop the knoll. The man swung the big gun down. "Oh, he is, is he?" Spurr snarled as black smoke puffed up from amongst the rocks and a stone-sized chunk of lead hammered the ground two feet in front of him, spraying dirt and grass up across his thighs.

The big gun thundered like a fast-approaching prairie storm.

To himself, he muttered, "Mason, you're so damn full o' shit . . ." as he triggered three more quick rounds and watched the slugs blow up dirt and rock atop the knoll. The silhouetted head had dropped back down behind the rocks.

Spurr ejected a smoking brass casing and seated another fresh one as he cursed sharply through gritted teeth. "Come on out if you wanna play, you chicken-livered son of a bitch!"

"You best get back down here, Spurr!" Mason called from the gully.

"Bullshit!" Spurr looked to his left, then to his right. He saw a hummock there that would offer cover of sorts if the dry-gulcher opened up again with his cannon. "Cover me, Mason. I'm gonna get around that bastard."

He planted a fist on his thigh and heaved himself to his feet much more slowly than he'd intended. His knees popped and cracked, and pain from his recent tumble hammered through his shoulder and hip. His heart chugged like an old locomotive and took a while to get thumping in earnest as the old marshal rambled along the edge of the hummock, heading south through a slight crease in the prairie.

Behind him, Mason opened up with his Winchester. The rifle cracked. Bullets spanged.

Running hard, moccasin-clad ankles twisting between bulky clumps of bear grass and cactus, he made a path partway around the base of the rocky-crested knoll. Another rise humped south and east of it. Spurr gained it, dropped behind a two-foot-high shelf of eroded rock sheathed in greasewood, and watched the tail end of a prairie rattler slither into a crack in the rock two feet away from him, the snake's three-inch rattle quivering and sounding like a shaken, sand-filled gourd.

"No offense taken, viper," Spurr rasped, trying to catch his breath as he knelt behind the low escarpment. "I didn't wanna shake your hand, neither."

Looking north, he saw the dry-gulcher breaking brush down the knoll, heading toward a horse tethered to a lone tree about a hundred yards east. He was a big man in a blue shirt, buckskin pants, and a black, bullet-crowned hat, with a long gray ponytail flopping down his back in a hide-wrapped braid. He ran with a hitch in his step, bespeaking age or gimpiness.

Spurr bore down on him with the Winchester and squeezed the trigger.

Dust puffed just beyond the man, on the side of another knoll. He whipped around suddenly, wide-eyed.

"There you go," Spurr chuckled savagely, ejecting the spent brass and seating fresh. "How'd you like them apples, you curly fuckin' wolf?"

The dry-gulcher swung around and ran limping off behind a boulder only a little larger than the man himself. Spurr fired again, hammering the face of the boulder and causing the ambusher to jerk back, shake his head against the ringing in his ears, and finger dust from his eyes.

As he raised the big, octagonal-barreled rifle, Spurr drew a bead on the man's forehead, allowing for the distance, elevation, and breeze. It was seventy yards — not a hard shot for a practiced rifleman like Spurr, who'd been using the same rifle now for nearly fifteen years of snipe hunting.

He squeezed the trigger.

The bushwhacker nodded as if responding to a question posed by someone behind him. Then he disappeared.

Spurr ejected the spent brass, seated fresh, and waited. He looked around.

There was nothing out here but low knolls peppered with the occasional boulder, cactus, and sage. A hawk hunted to the south, and a jackrabbit leapt from one rock to another before hunkering low in a shade patch.

The breeze rustled gently.

Finally, Spurr rose creakily and, holding his rifle up high across his chest and continuing to rake his gaze around cautiously, traversed the space between himself and the bushwhacker. The big man lay stretched out on his back behind his covering rock. His

155

hat lay nearby. He had a big, rawbone, pitted face with about three days' worth of pewter-brown beard stubble. His eyes were half open, lips parted, showing the uneven edges of his upper front teeth which were yellow as clamshells.

"Miserable bastard," Spurr said. "Why in the holy hell were you pot-shooting us?"

Movement caught his eye, and he swung abruptly around, but then let the rifle sag in his hands. Mason was tramping over the hill behind which they'd been ambushed. He carried his rifle low in his right hand, and dust puffed up around the long-legged Texas bastard's boots as he walked in that long, straight stride of his and which Spurr had once had himself, a few years ago.

But Spurr had never had the young sheriff's unearned cockiness — an arrogance which the man still had even after he'd caused Spurr to kill a mixed-up young woman who'd fallen prey to the charms of Marvin the Maiden Killer, though she probably hadn't been aware of that devil's nickname or reputation.

"You get him?" the sheriff asked.

Spurr grumbled and returned his gaze to the dead man, whose foul body odor nearly made Spurr's eyes water. "The question is," the marshal said, "where'd he come from?

And who's he with?"

As if in answer to his question, Spurr spied a dust plume rising in the southeast beyond several hills. He stared at the dust for a time. Could be a stage or drovers hazing cattle to a shipping center.

Could also be where this smelly dead man came from . . .

"I'm gonna check that out," he said as Mason walked up, stonily regarding the dead man. Spurr stuck two fingers into his mouth and whistled. "You go see about McQueen and his men. I'll be along shortly."

"You sure you oughta ride over there alone?" Mason had turned his attention to the dust plumes. "That's enough dust for a passel of others of this man's stripe."

"You do as you're told, Sheriff."

"Pullin' that federal business on me, eh, Spurr?" Mason tilted his head back and looked smugly out from beneath drooping eyelids. "Well, go ahead. Get your old ass shot off. I couldn't care less."

"Don't worry," Spurr said, watching Cochise gallop toward him, the roan's trailing reins bouncing and flipping along the ground. "I don't expect you to sing at my funeral, Mason." He tightened his latigo then swung into the saddle.

"Hey, Spurr."

The marshal jerked back on Cochise's reins and turned to where Mason stood holding his rifle across his thighs. The sheriff brushed a gloved hand across his nose. "Sorry about the girl."

The apology had come out of nowhere. Spurr felt as though a mule had kicked him. He didn't know what to say to that, so he grumbled as he swung Cochise around, flipped his rein ends against the big roan's hip, and galloped off toward the rising dust.

A half hour later, he was hunkered behind several poplars and ash trees, adjusting the army field glasses he was holding to his craggy face. He was on the side of a bluff, looking into a broad valley through which half a dozen large wagons, like army ambulances, were passing from west to east, quartering gradually southward.

Only the men driving the wagons and leading them and following on horseback were not wearing army blues.

They were dressed in buckskins or denim, or duck or checked wool trousers, calico shirts, brush jackets, and shabby hats. They were bearded and long-haired. One outrider wore an eye patch under the brim of a sugar-loaf sombrero adorned with grizzly claws. Several others wore tattoos on their sun-bronzed, heavily muscled arms laid bare to the sun.

Spurr scrubbed his jaw as he lowered the glasses, a prickling dread climbing his spine. A mix of whites and Indians, these men. Half-breeds and every other kind of breed. Some with Mexican blood. Granite-faced desperadoes of the foulest sort. A good dozen in all.

Spurr raised the glasses again, shuttled the two spheres of magnified vision back and forth between the wagons.

In the wagon boxes, at least a half dozen per wagon, were children of varying ages. Young boys as well as girls. Most of the children rode sullenly, eyes downcast, heads rolling with the wagons' pitch and sway. They were dusty and sunburned and appeared to be in shock.

One little girl with bright yellow hair was bawling and reaching over the tailgate of the last wagon in the line, toward a man with dark red hair riding a brown-and-white pinto behind the girl's wagon. The man road lazily, chin dipped to his chest — asleep and oblivious to the girl's desperate cries.

Spurr lowered the glasses, bunching his cheeks in a pained look, and cursed. His

weary heart hiccupped.
  Slave traders.

13

"I like this one," Camilla said.

"Which one?"

"The tan one. It looks the best."

They were in a hardware/clothing tent near the boxlike depot on the as yet unnamed railroad encampment's southern perimeter. It was their third day in the camp, and Camilla had thought it was time for Cuno to acquire some new clothes and shed the smelly ones he'd garnered from White-Eye. Cuno was trying on hats in the cracked mirror hanging from a nail in the tent's center post, shelves of dry goods heaped on tables around him.

The muscular young freighter set the cream Stetson he'd been trying on back onto a stack of other such hats and took the tan one from Camilla. "I used to have a tan one . . . before the warden took it, along with my rifle and everything else I own. Sure am glad you got Renegade."

He leaned down and kissed her lips grate-
fully before sweeping his hair back and
snugging the tan hat down tight on his
head. He looked in the mirror. The hat was
broad-brimmed, good for sunny country,
with a medium-high crown banded with
braided rawhide.

"It fits." He turned once more to Camilla.
"You like it?"

"It's the best one."

"All right, then . . ."

He let his voice trail off as movement out
the tent's open flap caught his attention. A
small-combination spur train had pulled up
to the train station a short time ago, when
he'd been picking out denim pants and a
simple blue work shirt. Several people had
detrained — salesmen and whores looking
for a new place to ply their trades, mostly.

But now the door of a stock car opened,
and several men were leading their horses
down the loading ramp, the shod hooves
clomping noisily. The men had shaggy, hard
looks about them. Rifles jutted from the
boots of their saddled horses.

"What is it?" Camilla asked, turning to
look out the tent flap.

"A whole passel of riders."

He watched more men lead horses down
the ramp and gather in a large group before

the stock car. An ugly, dapper little man in a brown suit and derby hat stood before them. The man who appeared to be the leader of the bunch was talking to the man in the derby, who stood a good head shorter than the group leader, the tips of his fingers buried in his vest pockets. He bounced nervously on the toes of his brown leather shoes.

"*Si,*" Camilla said, frowning.

Still wearing the tan hat, as well as the denims and shirt he'd picked out, though he was still in his stocking feet, having not yet decided on a new pair of boots, Cuno began moving toward the door. Behind him, the bald, aproned proprietor cleared his throat.

"That'll . . . uh . . . that'll be one dollar and fifty cents extra for the hat. Handmade by John B. Stetson himself, of course."

Cuno glanced over his shoulder at the man, who stood behind his plankboard counter, grinning unctuously.

"Don't worry," Camilla growled. "You'll get your money, senor. We don't rob hardware stores."

"Of course, of course," the man responded quickly. "I only thought you might be curious is all."

Cuno stood in the open tent door. The

newcomers and horses were gathered for a time around the derby-hatted man, who jerked his thumb toward the heart of the encampment, and then the leader turned to a couple of his other men, his mustached mouth moving as he spoke. One of the others nodded, and the leader led his horse away from the derby-hatted gent and began walking past the hardware/clothing tent toward the hotels and saloons on the other side of the hamlet.

A Colt pistol poked up from a holster tied low on his right, chap-clad thigh. Another jutted from a cross-draw holster on his other side. He wasn't wearing a badge, but that didn't mean these men weren't lawmen.

If not lawmen, who were they? And what were they doing here in this unnamed little railroad stop so heavily armed and looking so grimly intent?

Cuno turned and walked in his stocking feet back to where he'd left his boots. "Tally the total for everything," he told the proprietor, a witch's cold fingers of apprehension raking the back of his neck.

He stooped to pull one of White-Eye's right boots back on his foot, grunting with the effort and feeling the pain of the too-small boot shooting up his leg. "Shit!" He tossed the boot aside and went over to a shelf holding new ones.

Camilla turned from the open tent flap. "Lawmen, you think?"

Cuno was picking through the boots, looking for his size. "They don't look like it. Maybe bounty hunters. Possibly Pinkertons, but I don't see how they'd know we were here. It ain't like Mateo cables ahead."

The shopkeeper had gone over to the open tent flap and was staring up the street, where the newcomers had gone, leading their horses, the derby-hatted man walking along to one side of the leader and thumbing his round-framed spectacles up his crooked nose.

"You recognize those fellas?" Cuno asked the proprietor, picking up a pair of plain brown Justin boots.

"Me?" the man said, turning his bald head sharply, his eyes suddenly bright with nerves. "Never seen 'em before. Likely game hunters for the railroad, here to feed the crews layin' rails farther west. Yeah, that's who they are. No doubt about it."

Cuno liked that explanation. But as he pulled on both boots to test the fit, he wondered why the railroad would send that many hunters to feed a rail-laying crew of undoubtedly less than thirty men . . . His heart began to beat insistently. When he looked up, Camilla was staring at him, her eyes edgy.

"I got a bad feeling, Cuno."

"Pay for my gear," Cuno told her. "I'll pay you back soon as we hit a bank or somethin'." He couldn't believe he was saying that, but how else was he going to make money from now on, riding with Mateo's bunch, unless he stole it?

Sheriff Mason and Warden Castle hadn't left him much choice.

"I'm gonna take these boots, too." To the proprietor, Cuno said, "Mister, I'll take that Winchester carbine over there, and two boxes of cartridges, if you throw in these suspenders." He held up the leather galluses, which he preferred to a regular belt, knowing he'd likely have to wear one or two cartridge belts around his waist from now on.

The proprietor looked at the 1876-model saddle-ring carbine hanging on the wall behind the counter. He seemed to hesitate, and the back of his neck turned pink. He pointed with a shaky hand. "That one there?"

Cuno frowned, annoyance mixing with his apprehension. "That's the only one up there, amigo."

"Oh, yes. Of course. That one is twelve

dollars. The cartridges are a dollar a box."

"Camilla, you have that much?"

She nodded as she dug a wad of green-backs out of a back pocket. "*Mierda!* You are an expensive boyfriend."

"Yeah, but I'm worth it," Cuno said with a chuckle despite his growing nervousness, thumbing the second suspender up over his shoulder and then walking in his squeaky new boots over to the counter, behind which the proprietor was reaching for the new rifle.

The man took his time totaling up the bill. As he did, Cuno stood in the open tent flap, staring up the street and thumbing fresh cartridges into his carbine's breech. "Come on, come on," he said, warm and jittery as he looked over his shoulder at the bald proprietor still penciling figures on a pad.

Camilla looked at Cuno, flushed and rolling her eyes.

Cuno ran back to the counter, peeled a bunch of bills off Camilla's roll, and tossed them onto the counter. Then he grabbed his second box of .44 shells and took Camilla's arm, swinging her toward the front of the place. "Keep the change, mister."

"Hold on there, sonny," the proprietor called when Cuno and Camilla were halfway to the tent flap.

Cuno turned back around, then rammed his left shoulder hard against Camilla, throwing both the girl and himself to the floor. At the same time, the shotgun that the proprietor had produced out of seemingly nowhere went off like a hundred-pound keg of black powder.

"Cristos!" Camilla cried, squirming around under Cuno.

Awkwardly, he rolled off the girl, rose to a knee, and levered a cartridge into the Winchester's breech. He kept his head down beneath the level of a table between him and the hardware proprietor. He could hear the man sort of groaning and wheezing fearfully as he shuffled around, likely maneuvering for another shot.

"Mister!" Cuno shouted, "you're one dead son of a bitch!"

"Not yet, you young devil!" the man returned, his voice quaking. "There's gotta be a bounty on your head, and I aim to get it!"

Cuno jerked his head up above the table. The man had moved out from behind his counter and was ducking under some deer-skin leggings hanging from a rope. He jerked his head toward Cuno, eyes wide and glassy. Grinding his teeth, he slid the double-bore shotgun toward his target.

Cuno quickly drew a new bead on the man and triggered the Winchester. He fired twice more until three blood-pumping holes shone in the center of the man's aproned chest, forming a triangle pattern. The man shot a hole in his floor with the barn blaster, twisting around and staggering backward before falling behind a table strewn with miscellaneous hardware including tin pots and pans. He hit the floor with a heavy thud and a liquid sigh.

"Madre Maria!" Camilla said, gaining her feet and looking at the smoking carbine in Cuno's hands. "You should never shoot a man with his own gun. It is very bad luck."

Cuno reached down for the box of cartridges he'd dropped. "It's not his anymore. You bought it from him, remember?"

"Oh, *si!*" Camilla ran around the tables to the counter, swept her pile of wrinkled greenbacks off the pine boards, and stuffed them down her shirt. "He doesn't need them anymore, right?"

Cuno laughed again from nerves and the excitement of this new life he'd suddenly, unexpectedly found himself in. "Come on!"

He ran to the tent's open flap, the canvas around it torn by the proprietor's shotgun blast, and looked up the street in the direction the gunmen had gone. There was only the churned dust of their passing. Boots thumped behind him, and then Camilla was beside him, anxiously flushed and staring up the street.

"Clear so far."

Cuno moved on out of the tent and headed up the street. It wasn't much more than a trail, twisting amongst the tent shacks and a few timber dwellings that had been placed willy-nilly though generally along the spur-line tracks. The smell of latrines, chickens, and horses was heavy on the warm air.

"We have to warn Mateo," Camilla whispered.

Cuno nodded. He was about to tell the girl they'd work around to the back of the hotel, but just then they rounded a broad beer tent — empty now but likely patronized by the track layers after hours — and Cuno could see the brothel. It was easily one of the two or three largest, most permanent structures in town.

Headed back away from it and toward him and Camilla were three men carrying rifles.

Cuno recognized the three from the group that had gotten off the train. They'd come back to check out the gunfire. The others were positioning themselves around the hotel while one led the horses on up the street and out of the line of imminent fire.

Cuno pushed Camilla back behind a stock pen in which goats milled, staring at the pair through the ocotillo slats. A man shouted. Cuno gritted his teeth and, levering a round into the Winchester, bolted out from behind the pen. He dropped to one knee as he pressed the rifle's butt against his right shoulder.

The three men walking toward him stopped suddenly, jerked their own rifles up. Behind him, Camilla screamed in Spanish, "Mateo! *Emboscada,* Mateo! *Emboscada!*"

Ambush!

Firing and levering, Cuno dispatched two of the riflemen before they could get a shot off. One sent a round screeching just over the crown of Cuno's new hat before Cuno drilled the man in his lower belly and sent him stumbling dustily backward, lowering his head and shaking it fiercely and yowling as his rolling-block repeater tumbled into the street at his boots.

From the direction of the hotel came the screech of breaking glass and then a raucous scream, like that of a moon-crazed lobo. A man on the street shouted. A rifle boomed. Then there was more breaking glass and men shouting in Spanish and English.

Cuno could see dust puffing in the brothel's windows, heard girls screaming, saw bullets hammering the brothel's walls as others plunked into the street and sent the riflemen scattering.

One ambusher clutched his upper right leg and dropped to a knee. Another bullet silenced his wails as it snapped his head violently sideways and tore his hat from his head. He crumpled, his duster forming a shroud, and lay still in the street.

One of the gunmen who was sidled up to a tent shack on the street's left side triggered a rifle toward Cuno. As Camilla returned the man's fire, Cuno wheeled and dove back behind the goat pen. Camilla bolted around a corner of the building as several rounds hit the ocotillo slats of the pen and dropped to a knee beside Cuno.

"Shit!" she cried. "I told Mateo we shouldn't stay here so long!"

"The whores yonder must be right talented. Makes me wish I'd have checked 'em out myself."

Ignoring the quip, Camilla said, "What are we going to do? They're trying to surround the whorehouse! They'll have us surrounded soon, too!" She cursed and punched her thigh as she looked around the front of the goat pen toward the brothel. "My crazy brother is getting careless. He's been a lucky bandito for too long!"

A savage fusillade rose from the direction of the brothel. It sounded like all-out war. Men shouting and screaming. Bullets hammering wood and lifting angry whines as they ricocheted.

There was a shrill cry and then the loud smashing thud of what was probably one of the outlaws being shot out of a window of the brothel. From the south side of the street, one of the ambushers raised a victorious cry.

Cuno ran crouching toward the other end of the pen in which the goats were bleating and running in tight, frantic circles. He edged a look around the pen, saw the brothel with smoke puffing from its broken windows on both floors. The man who'd fallen out of the window lay stretched in the street before the place, ankles crossed. He was clad in only his socks and neckerchief. Blood pooled in the dust beneath his head. A rifle lay nearby.

On the south side of the street, to Cuno's left, the ambushers had taken up positions behind rain barrels fronting the timber and canvas shacks. Some were stretched out prone on rooftops. Others were shooting from the gaps between the buildings. Some had fallen dead where they'd been shooting.

Cuno's stomach heaved. It was already a bloodbath and it was fast getting bloodier. He was only vaguely surprised to feel such a strong alliance with Mateo and the other outlaws. They were all he had now. Somehow, he had to help them get out of the brothel and over to the stable where their horses waited.

If he could work around behind the ambushers, he might be able to take down enough of them that the others would get discouraged and call a retreat. At the very least, he could thin their ranks, though he could hear by the intermittent yowls and screams that Mateo's men, despite the bender they'd been on, were holding their own.

He turned and ran back toward the other side of the goat pen. He stopped suddenly, jaw falling slack. Camilla was sitting back against a lower slat of the pen, clutching her upper right arm and wincing, breathing hard.

"What the hell'd you do?" Cumo admonished the girl.

"It's just a nip."

"Nick," he corrected her, not so sure.

Cuno saw the bullet hole in the slat near her arm, heard several more thumps as the ambushers, knowing part of the gang was here by the pen, triggered lead in Cuno's and Camilla's direction. Soon, a couple would peel away from the main bunch and work around them. So much for Cuno's idea. They had to get out of here fast.

Cuno ripped off his neckerchief and quickly tied it around the girl's arm.

"Ouch! Not so tight!"

"Shut up."

"You're mad at me, damn you!" She gave him a petulant look as he lifted her to her feet.

"I get that way when girls I like get themselves shot."

He'd said it before he'd realized that he was voicing his fear of losing another woman he'd fallen in love with. She studied him curiously as he steadied her, then handed over her rifle, which she'd leaned against the pen.

"Never mind," he said. "Come on."

Glancing over his shoulder to make sure none of the ambushers was closing on them, Cuno ran east, keeping the goat pen between him and the riflemen. He and Camilla passed behind the hardware tent, saw Renegade and Camilla's mount standing outside the timber, shake-roofed box that was the town's only café.

They'd left the horses there after they'd had breakfast a little over an hour ago. The café's long-haired half-breed cook was hunkered down behind a rain barrel on the little front stoop, hands clamped over the side of the barrel as he stared toward the sounds of battle, wearing an expression much like that of the horses.

Cuno stopped, remembering the cartridge boxes he'd seen lined up in the hardware tent. "You go on over and fetch the horses. I'm going back for more ammo. Didn't realize we'd be going through it this fast."

Camilla nodded, her face tight with pain, and jogged on over to where the horses waited, stretching wary looks behind them and flapping their tails.

Cuno ran around to the front of the tent and dashed inside. He grabbed four boxes of cartridges off one of the cluttered shelves behind the counter, stuffed them into his pockets, then leapt back over the counter and ran to the front of the tent.

He looked westward along the winding street. A bearded man in a gray hat was running toward him, crouching under the awning of a half-built saloon. Spying Cuno, he ducked down behind a supply wagon filled with lumber and snaked his rifle out around the side.

Cuno dropped to his knees as the rifle roared, puffing smoke. The bullet tore into a tent post, splitting it. As the front of the tent began to sag, Cuno returned fire on the man behind the wagon, but the man ducked behind the cargo, and Cuno's .44 slugs blew slivers from the raw green boards piled in the back.

"Cuno!" Camilla shouted.

He turned to see the girl sitting her chestnut farther up the street, partly shielded from the west by the train depot around which two railroaders stood, owl-eyed and putting their backs to the train still panting along the new tracks. The locomotive was taking on water, and black coal smoke was billowing from its large, diamond-shaped stack.

The ramp of the stock car was still down.

Cuno fired two more shots at the bearded man still hunkered behind the lumber dray, then bolted out from the hardware tent and sprinted on up the street. Camilla covered him with her pistol, squinting down the barrel as she fired several shots toward the dray. As the bearded ambusher shouted something toward his bethren still assaulting the brothel which Cuno couldn't hear above the locomotive's chugging thunder and the rush of water from the tower trough into its massive, black boiler, Cuno climbed onto Renegade's back.

"Let's get the hell out of here!" Camilla shouted, triggering one more shot toward the man behind the lumber dray.

"What about Mateo?"

"My brother is a fool! Let's ride, Cuno!"

Cuno looked at the stock car. A moment ago, he'd gotten a crazy idea. He switched his gaze to the girl. Blood oozed around the bandanna he'd wrapped around the wound, but it indeed appeared only a flesh wound. Tending it could wait.

He swung back down out of his saddle and tossed his reins to Camilla. "Lead the horses onto the car!"

"What?"

"Hurry, goddamnit. We don't have all day!"

Cuno turned toward the depot agent and the two beefy engineers clad in watch caps and striped coveralls, standing around near the locomotive and the water tower. He aimed his Winchester straight out from his right hip and put some hard-case steel into his voice as he ordered, "You two climb into the engine. Vamoose! We're goin' for a ride . . ."

14

Cuno assumed the men in the striped coveralls were the fireman and engineer. As he moved toward them wagging his new Winchester, they reached for the sky as though they were bank tellers being held up by the James gang. Their mustached faces were stony, but their eyes were sharp with fright.

He said, "Get this thing moving. Now. Or I'll drill ya both!"

"Moving?" said the man on the right, whose long, thick gray hair dropped from his black watch cap. He had a face like the wall of a dilapidated train station. "Move where? We're fillin' with water, and we . . ."

Cuno only hardened his jaws at the man and pressed the Winchester's barrel up snug against his broad chest. The man swallowed and let his heavy lower jaw sag as the blood ran out of his face.

The man to his right elbowed him. "I

reckon we got enough water, eh, Earl?"

"I reckon we do at that, Chub."

"Why don't I chuck some wood in the stove, then?"

Cuno said tightly, "That'd be a good idea, Chub."

As the fireman and the engineer climbed heavily but anxiously up into the locomotive's pilothouse, Cuno heard the clacking of a telegraph key inside the cracker-box depot building. He stepped onto the new pine platform upon which the building sat and jerked the screen door open.

There was a small waiting area outfitted with simple pine benches to the left. On the right was a grilled partition adorned with a wall clock with a gold pendulum that woodenly ticked away the seconds. Behind the partition, a little man in a green eyeshade sat tapping away at a telegraph device.

"Letter home, old-timer?"

The oldster jerked around, widening his eyes beneath the cottony tufts of his silver brows. He saw Cuno's cocked Winchester and raised his withered hands, palms out. Cuno slid the barrel toward the telegraph key and pumped two steel-jacketed slugs through it, sending the pendulum, weights, springs, and thumb and finger pieces flying in all directions.

The oldster groaned and flapped his hands as though at pestering flies.

Cuno went back outside to see black smoke thickening as it swooped up and out of the diamond stack. The man filling the boiler from the scaffold supporting the tank was swinging the trough away from the locomotive and eyeing Cuno nervously. He wasn't too nervous to yell, "Your gang's done for, kid. That's the Ed Joseph bunch of bounty hunters swappin' lead with your bunch in the whorehouse yonder." The waterman shook his head. "Ain't been no owl-hoots yet who outrun Joseph's bunch."

"Who brought 'em in?" Cuno asked the man as he climbed the ladder alongside the locomotive's pilothouse.

"Why, T-Bone, of course. Town constable."

"T-Bone's the little man in the suit I seen out here?"

The waterman nodded as he hooked the heavy leather watering trough back into its brackets beside the wooden water tank. "That'd be him. Railroad-appointed."

"Why don't you give him Grimley's street address while you're at it, Norman?" This from the engineer poking his gray head out of the pilothouse.

Cuno climbed into the locomotive where the fireman was busily chunking split pine

181

and oak logs from the tinder car into the open door of the firebox. He was sweating and breathing heavily and eyeing Cuno's Winchester.

"You just do as you're told," Cuno said, "and you won't have to worry about my long gun."

"That's the one over at Hoyt Wilson's hardware store, ain't it?"

"So what?"

"That's the one I had my eye on," grunted the fireman as he chunked two more sticks into the firebox.

Cuno looked at the engineer. "Get this thing moving straight ahead, fast as you can get it to go."

"It'll take me a minute. Still buildin' up pressure."

Cuno cursed as he stared off toward the brothel. Rifles and pistols continued to pop, and men continued to scream and shout. Smoke rose from the brothel's far side. Cuno cursed again. A bullet had likely knocked over a lit lamp. The lumber in the building was still green, but it wouldn't last long after flames started chewing at it.

Cuno climbed down off the locomotive and ran back to the stock car. Camilla had the horses inside the car but was having trouble pulling the heavy, plankboard ramp up. Cuno helped her get the ramp into the car then dropped back down to the ground. "Stay here!"

"What the hell are you doing?" she called out the stock car's open door, both horses fidgeting behind her.

"Gonna drive this straight up the track, flank them bushwhackers and cover Mateo till he's out of the brothel. Then we'll head back and pick him up east, after he's gathered his horses."

Camilla dropped her jaw. "You're as crazy as he is," she said. But as he ran up toward the locomotive, she climbed gingerly down from the stock car, wincing against the pain in her arm, slid the door closed with a grunt, and ran up behind him. "I'm coming with you!"

Cuno helped Camilla mount the ladder into the pilothouse, then climbed up after her. The fireman stood back against an iron bulkhead, across from the closed firebox, looking wary and weary and holding his canvas-gloved hands chest high, fingers curled toward his palms. The engineer was flipping levers and crouching to inspect dials.

Glancing at Cuno, he said, "We can't go too damn far west, ya know. They're ain't track no farther than a mile beyond the camp."

"I want you to take us a hundred yards. No farther. See that corral up there?"

The engineer nodded.

"Stop behind it. No farther. Then get ready to put her in reverse and haul ass back east. Stop at the edge of town, no farther." Cuno rammed the Winchester against the man's right shoulder. "You got that, mister?"

"Hell, that'll put us right in the line of fire of . . ." The brakeman let his voice trail off as Cuno gave him a deadpan look. He dropped his eyes, crestfallen, to the locomotive's copper-riveted floor.

Camilla stood with her back to the locomotive's rear bulkhead, the split wood of the tender car mounded behind her. She held her Winchester in both hands, keeping the engineer and the fireman covered, but her incredulous eyes were on Cuno. He moved past her, climbed the rear bulkhead, and slid his rifle up onto the locomotive's flat roof.

"You stay here and make sure they follow orders," Cuno told her.

She grabbed the left cuff of his new denims and looked up at him worriedly. "You be careful, crazy gringo, huh?"

As the locomotive jerked forward, roaring

184

and panting and spewing thick, black, cinder-laced smoke from its stack, Cuno hoisted himself easily onto the roof. He grabbed his rifle and lay down flat just behind the base of the smokestack. The hot iron roof quivered beneath him as the train's wheels lifted a caterwauling.

Tent shacks and stock pens slid back behind him on both sides of the rails. Penned pigs, geese, and chickens raised a ruckus at the roaring, squealing locomotive. He kept one eye on the brothel from which more smoke was issuing and female screams emanated, and one eye on the timber and canvas structures across the broad street from it, very near the tracks.

Bodies lay around the hotel and slumped half out of windows. More lay on the other side of the street, twisted and bloody. Both factions had suffered what appeared to be heavy losses.

Still, the gunfire continued, albeit a little more sporadically than before. Smoke puffed, showing the shooters' positions. Only a few puffs appeared in the windows of the brothel. Mateo's men were probably scrambling around, trying to find their way out of the burning building. Already Cuno glimpsed half-clad girls streaming out behind the place and disappearing behind the thickening veil of smoke.

Maybe Mateo and most of his men had fled with the women. Still, it couldn't hurt to further thin the ranks of Ed Joseph's band of bounty hunters, give Mateo's group time to gather their horses . . .

Cuno clicked the Winchester's hammer back and drew a bead on a man crouched behind a water barrel outside a broad saloon building. He and several others, hunkered here and there along the street, had turned to stare incredulously at the train. Even from his distance of fifty yards, Cuno could see the sudden hope in their eyes as they began to figure the engineer had pulled the train up so they could reboard and get the hell out of the bailiwick they'd found themselves in.

Cuno offered a grim smile and settled his rifle sights.

The Winchester bucked and roared. A man running toward him down a break between two buildings flew forward and turned a somersault, dropping his rifle, raging, and clutching his left knee. Cuno blew another man off a shake-shingled roof, and drilled another through the shoulder while a man in a black hat with a pinned up front brim stopped suddenly and shouted, "Wrong train, boys! Fall back!"

A couple triggered bullets toward Cuno. The slugs hammered and rang against the side of the locomotive, but then virtually all disappeared as they ran westward from the main part of town, threading their way amongst the tent shacks and the wood-frame structures of the slowly growing camp.

Meanwhile, flames licked up from the far side of the brothel's roof. Movement in the street below caught Cuno's eye, and he quickly ejected the last spent cartridge from his Winchester, rammed a fresh one into the breech, and planted his sights on the man's broad chest. The black-bearded man wore a black, silver-stitched Sonora hat. He had a shell belt slung over one shoulder and a rifle in his other hand. He was waving the rifle high above his head.

"Mateo!" Camilla screamed from the engine's pilothouse beneath Cuno. "Head east, Mateo. *Del este!*"

The locomotive had shuddered to a halt, and now Cuno dropped his head over the edge of the hot steel roof to shout, "Reverse!"

"*Si!*" Camilla replied.

Then she shouted something to the engineer but Cuno couldn't hear above the din of squawking wheels and thundering couplings. Townsmen were shouting beyond the rails, running around and gathering wooden buckets to form a bucket brigade with which they'd try to put out the fire that would very likely consume the entire encampment if left unchecked.

As the train began jerking back the way it had come, Cuno stared out over the town, though he could see little now because of the smoke from the fire as well as the powder smoke from all the capped cartridges.

To the west, Ed Joseph's men were running into the brush along a creek that snaked around the town's outskirts and where apparently one or two of the gang had cached their horses. Only a few were actually running. Most of the nine or ten were limping or being helped into the trees by others steadier on their feet.

While the townsmen continued forming a bucket brigade obscured by the wafting smoke, Cuno settled himself against the locomotive's quivering roof. He lowered his rifle, doffed his hat, and ran a hand through his hair. His heart was hammering a persistent rhythm against his breastbone, and his mouth tasted like copper. His bones had turned to marrow. He laughed, giddy from all that had happened, electricity sparking through his veins and nerve ends.

Christ, he'd never seen such a thing, much less been part of such a dustup. He laughed again and held his hand in front of his face. It was quivering only slightly.

"Shit," he said and ran it through his hair once more.

15

Spurr's chest was tight, but he didn't think his pumper was acting up any more than it always did, lurching and chugging like a locomotive on a tough incline. No, it wasn't heart trouble that pestered him now. It was something far more worrisome.

The old marshal had for the past year or so, even before his first bad heart spell, been thinking he was losing his mind. Going loonier than a tree full of owls or a den full of coyotes during a full, blue moon.

The horrible things he'd witnessed throughout his life on the frontier, first as a soldier fighting Indians and then as a deputy U.S. marshal running down the worst hard cases imaginable, had started to trouble him to the point where he often found himself dropping to his knees, as though felled by a strong, unseen hand, and bawling.

Yes, bawling. Like a toddler in rubber pants who'd just had his sucker confiscated by a frisky pup. His chest would constrict and tears roll out of him like a dam had busted deep inside him.

It was happening again now as he rode eastward, trying to pick up the trail of McQueen, Mason, and McQueen's two deputies. He kept his head facing forward but he could not remove the image of those poor young children being carted away by the slaver traders.

And there wasn't a damn thing he could do about it.

Oh, he could summon Mason, and they could go after the cutthroats, but the lawmen would die long before they even got close to the children. They kept pickets, like the man Spurr had just beefed, far out from the main caravan.

Slavers were an especially tough breed, and it just didn't make sense for Spurr to try to run them down until he had a good-sized crew of seasoned lawmen or at least a modest-sized army contingent backing his play. He could go after them later, after he'd formed such a posse, but the men who traded slaves for a living all across the frontier would likely be lost in the Indian Nations in a week or two.

Gone forever.

Those poor damn kids . . .

Spurr sobbed into his gloved hand, shook his head, his swollen heart recoiling at the thought of the grief the children as well as the families of the children were going through. God, he wished there was something he could do. But first and foremost he had to go after Mateo de Cava and the young firebrand the desperado had busted out of prison — Cuno Massey. Those two and their gang were far more dangerous to more people than the slavers currently were. True, the Mateo bunch was too big for Spurr, Mason, McQueen, and McQueen's deputies to bring down alone, but they could follow the gang and stick to their trail until the soldiers from Camp Collins or another posse, possibly summoned via telegraph, could catch up to Spurr's party.

Then they could all run them to ground before more innocent men like the guards at the Arkansas pen and the posse from Limon were so savagely cut down. De Cava was probably headed back to Mexico, but he'd likely rob a bank or two or even a train or two, possibly stagecoaches, to fund his long, circuitous ride.

Spurr blew a long, snorting sob once more, thinking of the children and feeling as helpless as the children themselves. But there were only a handful of the little ones.

Spurr had to stay focused on his current problem, for de Cava and Massey were capable of a whole lot larger loss of life.

Spurr would remember the slavers, though. He'd remember their faces. And he'd run them down just as soon as he was free of his current mission and had help from the government. They'd sweep the Nations, find those children or as many as possible, and get them back to their families.

Spurr sighed and blew his nose into his bandanna. There. He felt better now. Deep down, he didn't really believe he'd be able to manage all that, or that he'd ever find those kids, but sometimes you had to manufacture your balms or roll down off your horse and sob the rest of your years away in the goddamn dust of the trail.

Crazy. He was going goddamned, old-woman crazy . . .

He rode another fifteen minutes, following the fresh tracks and droppings of four shod horses before he saw the horses standing near a copse of willows and cottonwoods. The horses had their tail-switching rears facing Spurr.

Left of the horses, Mason sat on a rock. Right of them, McQueen sat on a log, elbows on his knees. He had his hat off. One of his deputies was digging a hole with a small folding shovel. A long, blanketed lump lay near the fresh hole, two boots sticking up, pointed toes aimed at the sky.

Spurr rode over to where Morgan sat smoking.

"He didn't make it?"

The sheriff shook his head and let smoke dribble out his nostrils. "Blew a lung out his back. He was dead before they got here." He glanced in the direction from which Spurr had come. "What about that dust?"

"Slavers." Spurr choked back another con-sarned sob and swung his gaze away from the dead deputy. He had to get himself on a leash. "Too many for us to tangle with alone."

"Women or girls?"

"Boys and girls. Headin' for the Nations, most like. To be sold to the settlers there."

Mason stared eastward. "Been a problem out here. They raid the little settlements off the beaten path without telegraph lines. And small ranches and farms."

"I figure I'll track 'em later, after we finish up with the de Cava gang."

Spurr swung down from his saddle and loosened the latigo, then slipped the roan's bit from its teeth. He blew his nose, put some steel back into his nerves. He turned to Mason, found the man staring at the ground between his boots, pensively taking another drag off his loosely rolled quirley. Something was bothering him. Spurr glanced toward McQueen sitting near his sole remaining deputy still digging the grave with his shirt off, bandanna wrapped around his forehead. "McQueen taking it hard?"

"I don't know. I reckon."

"What's the matter with you, Sheriff?"

Mason looked up at Spurr, then lowered his eyes again as he drew on the cigarette. "Ah, hell, I don't know. I keep thinkin' about that kid, Massey. Somethin' don't seem quite right."

"I'll say it don't." Spurr filled his hat with water and set it down in front of the roan, which dropped its head to drink.

"No, I mean . . ." Mason let his voice trail off. "There was somethin' about him that didn't set right with me. I mean, there was somethin' about him that made me think I shouldn't have turned him over to the soldiers at Camp Collins."

Mason flushed a little, embarrassed at his own frankness, and shook his head as he gained his feet and field-stripped his quirley, letting it blow away on the breeze. "Ah, hell, I don't know what I'm tryin' to say. I gotta take a piss."

He walked off into the trees, fumbling

with his fly buttons.

Spurr stared after him. His eyes skeptical, speculative. First had come Mason's apology for the blond girl whom Spurr had had to shoot. Now, another expression of self-doubt.

Damn, Spurr thought. Was Mason turning human?

Spurr hauled a whiskey flask out of his saddlebags, sat down on Mason's rock, and sipped from the bottle as he rolled a fat cigarette and smoked it. He was feeling himself growing impatient with McQueen, wanting to get mounted and ride for another hour or so before the sun set, when McQueen and the deputy finally walked over from the mounded grave.

McQueen looked paler, grayer than before, his eyes deep sunk. There was a jaundiced look about the man.

"We're going home, Marshal," the sheriff said.

"Home?"

McQueen reached under his horse's belly to buckle the latigo. His deputy, a kid of about nineteen or twenty, pulled his shirt on after first using it to scrub the sweat from his bony, flour-white chest.

"Look, Sheriff," Spurr said, "we've all lost men before. Sure, it's a hard knock, but . . ."

"Jason was my son."

McQueen looked over his shoulder at Spurr. There was little emotion in his eyes, but the haggard look said it all.

"My oldest. We ranched before I ran for sheriff, and I wish to hell now I'd stayed on the ranch." He sighed and turned back to his horse. "Now, I'm going to take my one remaining son back home with me to face the unenviable task of letting the boys' mother know . . ."

He clucked and shook his head, still facing his horse. He set his fists atop his saddle and stared westward. When his other son had mounted up, McQueen mounted, too, and the reluctant sheriff of Holyoke pinched his hat brim to Spurr and Mason and booted his steeldust eastward.

He and his stone-faced son galloped off over the hogbacks, the thud of their horses' hooves fading gradually, until the darkening sky swallowed them both.

Spurr looked at the grave they'd left behind. The pile of rocks was fronted by a cross fashioned from two dead willow branches and wrapped rawhide.

Spurr cursed loudly. His chest felt raw as a rusty tin tub. He hoped he wouldn't cry again, but suddenly he felt all cried out and empty.

Mason said nothing. Spurr felt his chest tighten again, and he took a long pull from his bottle to loosen it.

He corked the bottle and returned it to his saddlebags.

"No point in dillydallyin' here," rasped the old marshal, climbing heavily into his saddle. He looked to the west. " 'Nother hour of good light left."

Mateo had lost a half-dozen men at the brothel.

It was a beat-up bunch he led out of the unnamed railroad camp on the horses they'd quickly saddled at the livery barn and drew to a halt beside the train that Cuno had ordered stopped at the camp's eastern outskirts.

A dozen or so riders including Frank Skinner swung down from their saddles, and while the locomotive wheezed and chugged, pressure valves releasing jets of stream around the iron wheels and gouts of cinder-laced smoke from its stack, the men led their horses up the stock car's ramp. Camilla stood near the base of the ramp while Cuno stood in the car, holding his rifle and peering back toward town.

None of the bounty hunters appeared to be following the gang. They'd had enough.

Mateo swung down from his saddle. He was nearly black from the fire smoke and bloody from several minor wounds. He hugged his sister and grinned up at Cuno.

"You think good for a gringo!" He stretched his beard in a grin as he glanced back at the town over which smoke rose blackly. "In that whorehouse, it was getting a little warm . . ."

Cuno was watching the others, who were still obviously sporting hangovers, leading their mounts up the ramp. Skinner looked bleary-eyed. He'd taken a graze across his right temple, and he, too, was basted in soot.

Hooves thundered on the plankboards. Horses blew. Cuno saw three or four wounded riders, though in light of their leader's policy regarding stragglers who might hamper the group, they kept their heads up, their upper lips stiff.

"He is good at many things," Camilla told her brother, beaming up at Cuno.

"I bet he is!" Mateo laughed lewdly as he led his big black up the ramp behind the others, blinking against a down swoop of coal smoke.

When all the riders had led their horses into the stock car, most of the men climbed an outside ladder to the roof where they could keep an eye on the town. Mateo stood beside Cuno and fired a stove match on his shell belt.

"How far can this thing go back east?" he said, touching the flame to a long black cheroot.

Cuno glanced at the engineer and the fireman, who stood along the freshly graded railroad bed, keeping their hands in the air as Cuno had instructed. "They said all the way to Amarillo."

"*Si*. But we don't go to Amarillo." Mateo looked speculatively eastward across the rolling prairie. "Tell them to take us east for an hour. Then we stop and take off on our horses. You tell them that."

He slapped Cuno lightly on the chest and frowned, nodding, obviously trying to formulate a new escape plan in light of the bounty hunters having caught the gang literally with its pants down.

Like Camilla had told Cuno earlier, the gang leader was getting careless. Cuno hoped he'd learned his lesson. When he and Mateo had the ramp back in place beneath the floor of the stock car, Mateo climbed to the roof while Cuno hazed the engineer and the brakeman back to the locomotive. Camilla followed, and soon Cuno had the train headed eastward as fast as it would go, thundering in reverse across the prairie, the new seams clicking under the wheels.

The fireman shoved a chunk of wood into the firebox and closed and latched the heavy door. He looked at Cuno, his brown eyes dark with worry. "You gonna let us go when this is done?" He licked his lips. "Or you gonna kill us?"

"You do as you're told," Cuno said, "and you'll be back at the camp by nightfall."

The brakeman nodded, a cautious relief in his eyes as he shared a glance with the engineer.

Cuno and Camilla sat together against the locomotive's rear bulkhead, taking turns napping while the other kept an eye on the trainmen. Cuno had fallen into a deep, exhausted sleep when a hand nudged him awake, and Camilla said above the train's roar, "It's been an hour."

Cuno grabbed his rifle resting across his thighs and heaved himself to his feet. He ordered the engineer to stop the train, and then he scrambled down the side of the locomotive and lowered the stock car's ramp. When all the outlaws had led their horses down the ramp and were resetting saddles and buckling latigos, Cuno and Camilla led their own horses down to the railbed.

Cuno slid Renegade's bit into the horse's

mouth and turned to Mateo. "We can let the trainmen go, now, huh?"

Mateo was looking away from Cuno at the locomotive, where his big gringo lieutenant, Wayne Brouschard, was holding a rifle on the fireman and the engineer. Raising their arms high, the trainmen had their backs to the locomotive's massive right rear wheel. Brouschard's head was turned toward Mateo, but now, receiving some unspoken command from the gang leader, the big man turned toward the trainmen.

He raised his Winchester.

"No!" Cuno cried, lurching forward but taking only one leaping stride before Brouschard's rifle cracked twice quickly, and both train men bounced against the side of the locomotive and fell in heaps to the railbed.

16

Cuno stared in shock at the two dead trainmen, both slumped on their sides, the
engineer with his head on his arm, blood
pumping from the hole in his chest.

"Mateo!" Camilla cried.

As the girl began to harangue her brother
in Spanish loudly and shrilly, Cuno walked
stiffly along the railbed, heading for the
panting locomotive. Brouschard walked
toward him, a devilish leer twisting the
man's bearded lips.

The gravel-paved railbed was narrow, and
Brouschard gave no ground to Cuno. As
they met, the man brusquely nudged Cuno
with the rear stock of his rifle, snorted, and
kept walking straight ahead toward Mateo
and the rest of the gang. Cuno only vaguely
felt the nudge. His body was numb with
shock. A weird, low shriek rose in his ears.

He stopped to stare down at the dead
men.

He dropped to his heels, absently picked up a handful of gravel, ground it around in the palm of his hand and let it dribble out through his fingers. Slowly, the shock of the killings receded. A strange sort of quiet calm oozed into his brain.

Why should he have felt such shock? True, he'd promised the men they'd live. But he'd known who Mateo de Cava was. He knew the brand of men he'd thrown in with. He himself had already killed a town marshal and several bounty hunters. If he hadn't killed them, he'd either be dead himself or back in prison. Riding with Mateo de Cava, he was as responsible for the sacking of the brothel as Mateo himself was.

How could it have been any other way?

That was the price you paid for running with a pack of wild wolves. And Cuno would likely go on paying it until he decided he'd had enough. The trouble was, he was just as much a fugitive as Mateo was. And leaving the gang would almost certainly mean he'd be run down and killed.

Not jailed. Never again would he allow anyone to jail him.

Killed.

Was he ready to die?

Cuno straightened, turned away from the dead men, and strode back toward the group. He straightened his hat on his head and grabbed up Renegade's reins. The others had mounted their horses and were galloping east along the tracks, dust sifting behind them.

Only Camilla remained. So did Frank Skinner, his horse facing east, the old bank robber's lean face turned to regard Cuno fatefully.

"Get used to it, kid," Skinner said. "It's a long way to Mexico."

He flipped his reins against his sorrel's withers and bounded after the others.

Camilla leaned back against her chestnut's saddle fender. Her face was drawn and pale, and her eyes were rolled up to stare at Cuno. She was furious with her brother.

She opened her mouth to speak, but Cuno cut her off as he swung up onto Renegade's back.

"Mount up," he said.

"He had no reason to kill those men."

"Yes, he did."

She frowned. "What?"

"They would have gone back to the camp and blabbed about the direction we rode off in." Cuno gave her a hard look, deep lines cutting across his broad, tanned forehead above the faded bluing of his broken nose. "What the hell's your problem, anyway? You killed plenty of prison guards."

"To save you!"

"Well, you saved me." Cuno hiked a shoulder. "Now, mount your horse and get the hump out of your neck. Like Frank said, it's a long ride to Mexico."

That they were headed for Mexico now, there was little doubt. Mateo led the gang straight south without wavering. Before they were more than two hours away from the stalled train and the two dead men they'd left there, two of the wounded were killed, their bodies left unburied upon the prairie.

Cuno rode up near Mateo and Brouschard. He felt the need to ride close to the leader, to prove to himself that he'd thrown in with the man and would follow through with whatever needed to be done to save himself as well as the rest of the pack. This wasn't a fully formed decision, but a decision it was.

Camilla rode back and to the outside. Cuno rarely looked at her, because he didn't want to see the reproof in her eyes. But when he did cast his gaze in her direction, the castigation was there, and it made him confused and uncomfortable — one, because she was why he was here in the first place, and two, because he knew that for whatever reason she loved him. He thought that, given time, he could love her as well and that they could maybe find happiness together somewhere down the trail.

But they had a long way to ride before he could start thinking about such things as happiness.

Late in the afternoon, they stopped at a creek to water the horses and refill their own canteens. It was here that Brouschard, apparently feeling as though his position as Mateo's first lieutenant was being threatened, made a fateful play.

When Mateo had ordered everyone to mount back up, Cuno walked over to Renegade. Brouschard had just slipped Cuno's saddle off the paint's back and tossed it into the brush.

"What the hell are you doing?" Cuno asked him.

"I've decided I like this horse." With a grunt, Brouschard leaned down to pick up his own saddle and tossed it onto Renegade's back. The horse jerked sideways with a start and nickered skeptically. "I'm going to take him. You can have mine, kid."

Cuno chuckled. "I don't want your horse. I want my horse."

"My horse is a perfectly fine horse. Good enough for you, anyway. This horse here"

— Brouschard gave Cuno a hard, challenging look over Renegade's back — "is my horse now."

Bitter fury flashed behind Cuno's retinas. Balling his cheeks but keeping his face implacable, he walked around behind Renegade and turned to face the big, bearded Yankee. A big bowie flashed in the man's hand. The jagged edges of coffee-stained teeth shone, set deep inside his shaggy blond beard flecked with steeldust gray.

He moved forward, crouching, shuffling to and fro, showing big yellow teeth through that menacing smile. Sweat dribbled down his dusty, red cheeks from his hat brim.

A murmur rose amongst the other men. A few of the horses nickered as the men moved around them to get closer to the two challengers. Cuno caught a brief glimpse of Mateo. The outlaw leader's attention had been directed toward Cuno and Brouschard, and his dark eyes lit with amusement.

Brouschard leapt forward, slashing the big bowie from left to right. Cuno stepped back, leaning forward as he sucked in his belly, avoiding a crossing slice from the wide, razor-edged blade by a hairsbreadth. Brouschard slashed again from the opposite direction. As the knife passed close once more, Cuno lunged quickly forward, bringing his big right fist up fast and hard. It smacked resolutely against the big man's heavy jaw.

Brouschard's eyes snapped wide. He shook his head as if to clear it. Cuno had opened a three-inch gash in the man's face, just above his jaw. Blood flowed to the corner of his mouth from a cut on the inside.

Cuno grinned. "You'll want to remove your saddle from my horse."

The men around them chuckled and sidestepped, pivoting to follow the action. Cuno glimpsed Camilla striding off toward the creek.

Brouschard's face turned crimson. He gave a furious yell and slashed at Cuno once more. A few years ago, Brouschard would have been a formidable foe. But he had a good seven or eight years on Cuno, and he'd packed on extra weight that slowed him down.

Cuno was quicker on his feet. He had more strength in his fists. The left he jabbed at the bigger, older man split Brouschard's upper and lower lips in the very front of his mouth.

Brouschard stumbled back, spitting blood and bits of his broken front teeth. Not letting up, Cuno followed him, dodging another blow from the knife to hammer the man twice more, savagely, widening the cut on his left jaw. Brouschard screamed and bulled toward Cuno, keeping the knife low but swinging it up, threatening the young freighter with a painful disemboweling.

Cuno stepped back, kicked his right foot high, connecting solidly with Brouschard's wrist.

There was a cracking sound. Brouschard screamed again and dropped the knife. His wrist hung crookedly. Cuno bulled toward him, head butted him twice, until the big man was staggering straight back, brows bloody, and shaking his head again to clear it.

"Best get your senses back, Brouschard." Cuno's voice was deep and tight. "Maybe I can help."

He slapped the man's fleshy face twice, then grabbed him by his collar and began pulling him toward the creek. Brouschard cursed shrilly, spitting blood and teeth, and then Cuno had the man's hickory shirt halfway up over his head as he led him, staggering and screaming and pinwheeling his arms, through the brush along the creek and then on into the water. The big man hit the creek with a splash.

Cuno followed him in, grabbed the back of his shirt collar with one hand, and shoved his head under with the other.

He held the man down, biting his lower lip with the effort.

Brouschard fought to raise his head but could not find purchase at the bottom of the creek. Frantic air bubbles rose around his head. He flung his arms up, trying to grab Cuno. Finally, Cuno released the man. Brouschard's head came up, his lower jaw dropping as he sucked a deep, loud breath, water streaming off his head and down his face and beard.

Cuno slid his pistol from his holster, rocked the hammer back. His eyes were like agates. "You wanna haul your saddle off my horse now?"

The others had followed Cuno and Brouschard into the brush. They stood along the shore of the creek, watching bemusedly. Mateo hung back, leaning a shoulder against a tree. Camilla was sitting on a log, separate from the others, elbows on her knees, staring grimly toward Cuno. The breeze brushed the yellow weeds around his boot tops.

Brouschard continued sucking air, rubbing water from his eyes.

Mateo said in a menacing singsong, "Better kill him . . ."

Cuno spread his boots on the creek's

gravel bottom and shoved his cocked Colt up to Brouschard's face. "Get over there, or I'll kill you here."

On his knees in the creek, looking like some overgrown, waterlogged muskrat, Brouschard slid his hand down his bearded face and looked grimly up at Cuno. He slid his eyes to the others standing in a shaggy line along the shore. He looked once more at the cocked Colt in his face, then rose heavily.

Lumbering past Cuno, he stepped onto the bank, stopped, glanced once more over his shoulder at Cuno. His right brow was cocked, the eye hard as granite in a mountain wall. The others stepped back, making way, sneering but saying nothing as the big man strode slowly in wet-squeaky boots over to Renegade and slipped his saddle off the paint's back. Swinging around, he hauled the saddle over to his blaze-faced coyote dun and tightened the belly straps.

He did not look up from his work but kept his head lowered, face hard and expressionless. The others shared mocking glances then, shrugging and muttering, and began moving back to their own waiting horses.

Cuno walked out of the stream and holstered his pistol.

Mateo said in the same menacing singsong

212

as before, "Should have killed him, Yankee."
Then he rolled off the tree and headed back
to his horse.

"Cuno."

He turned to Camilla sitting on the blown
down cottonwood. She was toying with a
long weedstock. She looked at him with
desperate pleading.

"Let them go to Mexico." Rising, she
dropped the weed and strode toward him,
the breeze bending her sombrero's broad
brim that cast a shadow over the top half of
her face. "We'll ride west. Nevada, Califor-
nia. It doesn't matter. But west." She
grabbed his suspenders and looked up at
him desperately. "Please."

Cuno wrapped his hands around hers,
leaned down, and kissed her.

"Damn cold in that Nevada high country
of a winter," he said softly. "Too hot in the
summer. Me — I never been to Mexico."

Fear made her voice thin as she shook her
head and said, "It is no good for us there.
Not with Mateo . . . Brouschard. You should
have taken Mateo's advice and killed him.
He will not rest until he kills you now."

"With them's as safe as anywhere. Come
on."

He snaked an arm around her slender
waist and guided her back to the horses.

She stiffened her body and pulled away.

They mounted up and followed the others south.

17

Spurr smelled the railroad camp before he saw it.

Usually, you smelled privies and stock pens before you reached a town. A half mile outside of the railroad camp, which he and Mason had spotted from a high bluff in the west, still on the relatively fresh trail of the de Cava gang, Spurr smelled charred lumber. The smell was almost as bad as filth.

Mason smelled it, too. The sheriff shook his head as he and Spurr booted their mounts into lopes. "Got a bad feelin' about that smell."

Spurr grunted his agreement. Gangs like that of Mateo de Cava had a habit of laying waste to anything and anyone along their trail.

It was dusk when the two followed the trail of twenty or so shod hooves into the encampment lying along the freshly laid spur-line rails. Off to the right of the trail, on the other side of the railroad tracks, a half-dozen men in rolled up shirtsleeves and battered hats were digging a large hole in the ground.

A few of the men smoked as they worked. Blanket-covered lumps that Spurr knew were bodies lay at an angle near the hole. A black-and-white collie dog lay near the bodies as if in attendance, one white paw curled beneath itself.

"Yeah, there was trouble, all right."

A few minutes later, they stopped in front of a large, black mound of burned timbers and gray ashes — the remains of what had once been a rather large building and likely one of the most permanent structures in the camp. Smoke still curled from the ash piles, and here and there small, intermittent flames leapt and chewed at what remained of ceiling beams.

There was the heavy musk of coal oil all around.

Blood smeared the dirt in front of what had once been the front gallery, which Spurr could identify only by part of a door and some frosted glass, a couple of posts, and a few lengths of scorched floorboards. Tent shacks surrounding the place had also been burned, a few patches of gray canvas remaining amongst the ashes.

Spurr glanced at Mason, both men scowling, then booted their horses forward. On the left side of the broad main thoroughfare, with a train depot and tracks on the right, was a large tent with a board shingle stretching out from it announcing BURT HOMETREE'S BEER PARLOR. A smaller sign beneath the first read: NICKEL BEER, TEN-CENT BATHS, FREE LUNCH COUNTER. Another sign had a pointing hand painted on it and the words: GIRLS ACROSS THE STREET AT MAY'S — CLEAN AND CHEAP!

Out front of the saloon tent stood a man supported on crutches. He was dressed in a clean but worn brown suit and a brown bowler hat, steel-framed spectacles perched on his nose. His right foot and ankle were wrapped in a thick gauze bandage spotted with blood. In one hand, he held a beer schooner, and he was staring through the saloon tent's broad open doors, wobbling on his crutches.

The man was so intent on the doings inside the saloon that he didn't see Spurr until Spurr's roan gave a snort and shook its head and bridle. The man snapped his head toward the newcomers, his round spectacles reflecting the yellow and reds of the sunset.

"Well, hell!" the man intoned, slurring his

words a little. "It's about time lawmen get here!"

"What happened?" Spurr growled.

"The de Cava gang is what happened. They set fire to a brothel and killed half of Ed Joseph's bounty hunters. The other half is in there."

The little man, who had a hawkish face and two-days' growth of stubble on his cheeks, nodded to indicate the inside of the tent. Through the open flap, Spurr could hear sporadic groaning. The old marshal swung down from the roan's back, looped the reins over the hitch rail fronting the beer tent, then peered inside.

Rusty railroad lanterns hanging from posts offered the only light. They showed five men laid out on cots along the wall to Spurr's left. A plankboard bar flanked by several beer barrels ran along the rear wall. A stocky, aproned Chinese man stood behind it, washing dishes in two porcelain tubs against the canvas wall.

There were a half-dozen hammered-together timber tables, and three of these were occupied by burly, bearded men in suspenders and oily denims — track layers, no doubt. They paid little attention to the groaning men on the cots. The wounded were being attended to by a tall, severe-looking man in his early thirties wearing a black vest over a white shirt and a stethoscope. His heavy, brown brows mantled as he drew a wool blanket up over the inert face of one of the wounded men. He turned toward the doorway and nodded fatefully.

Behind Spurr, the little, hawk-faced man turned his head west and shouted, "Another one for the boneyard, Dempsy!" His voice was shrill and raspy, and it made Spurr's ears ache.

"Christ!" complained the aging marshal, turning toward the little man while rubbing his right ear. "You gotta yell like that?"

"How in the hell else is them gravediggers supposed to hear me?" The little man took a swig of his beer and looked down at his ankle. "Thanks to Mateo de Cava, I can't exactly run hoppin' and skippin' on out there with the news in person."

Spurr looked the little man up and down, his salt-and-pepper brows furled critically. The little man smelled of sweat and beer and smoke from the recent fire. His eyes were dark and fidgety. Some men you didn't like from appearances and instinctively knew you would like even less the better you got to know them.

"Who're you, little feller?" Spurr asked him.

"T. Benson Grimley," said the little man, glaring up at Spurr defensively, as though he knew the bad impression he made. "Folks call me T-Bone. I'm the constable here in Mayville."

"Constable, huh?" Spurr said with a chuff.

Dusty Mason said, "Mayville?"

"That's the name we come up with and are now calling the camp though it ain't official yet. Mayville . . . after May over yonder. She was the first businessman here, even before the rails got here."

T-Bone glanced at the narrow, two-story building near the depot and railroad tracks whose front oil pots were now being lit by a man in a black, floppy-brimmed hat and a torn blue blanket coat. Blue curtains hung over the lantern-lit windows. A shingle on two posts reached out from the place as though to physically waylay prospective customers passing on the street; it read simply MAY'S.

"Thank god they didn't burn that, too," said the little man before taking another quick sip of his beer. "We'd have only one brothel in town, though there's still plenty of whores. Homeless whores, thanks to de Cava's bunch. They're in tents down by the creek. Rail layers're givin' 'em plenty of business, though."

The little man snorted and drained his beer glass.

"How long since de Cava pulled through here?" Spurr asked the man.

"Yesterday around noon. Helluva dustup. I got caught right in the damn middle of it, too. Took a ricochet." T-Bone looked down at his ankle. "Doc says the bone's shattered. I might never put full weight on it again . . ."

Mason was looking into the tent saloon, thumbs hooked behind his cartridge belt. "Who're the bounty hunters?"

A voice behind the two lawmen and the constable said, "Ed Joseph's bunch."

Spurr swung around to see a man in a long tan duster and tan hat walking toward him from May's. He adjusted his hat on his head. Long black hair dropped to his shoulders. He wore a deerskin vest adorned with large silver buttons beneath the duster.

"Where's Joseph?" Spurr asked the man approaching the beer tent.

"You're lookin' at him." Joseph stared out from beneath the brim of his tan slouch hat at Spurr. "You're Spurr Morgan, ain't ya?"

"Well, I'll be damned," Spurr said. "You're Joseph?"

"I told ya you was lookin' at him." Joseph stood beside Spurr, peering into the beer tent at his wounded men. "Shit, I lose another one, Doc?" he called.

"You might haul your friend out of here, Mr. Joseph," the harried sawbones said crisply as he washed his hands in a stone bowl on a table near his patients.

"That's what T-Bone's boys get paid for, Doc."

To Joseph, Spurr said, "Where the hell'd you come from, Joseph?"

"Bonner. Just east of here. Just got done running a bunch of claim jumpers out of Reynold's Park, and we was holin' up and waitin' for some new horseflesh from Amarillo. T-Bone there's my brother-in-law, and he knew where I was from my sister, and he cabled me just after de Cava rode in. We hired our own special train, don't ya know."

"How many men you start out with?"

"Seventeen."

"And these are all you're left with?"

"Them five . . . er . . . four, I reckon, since ole Jimmy-John seems to have kicked off, now, too." Ed Joseph shook his head and fingered his long black hair hanging down over his left shoulder — an oddly girlish gesture. He had a thick black beard and amber eyes, a knife scar reaching an inch down from the right side of his mouth. His face was like a roughly carved hunk of mahogany.

Spurr had heard he'd been raised in Tennessee, and the old marshal detected the faintest of Scottish accents mixed with the petal-soft drawl of the Appalachians. Joseph's gang, made of mostly ex-Confederate bounty hunters, was — or had been — notorious across the frontier.

Joseph looked at Spurr, then slid his eyes to Mason. "Where'd you come from?"

"The prison," Mason said.

"What prison?"

"The one de Cava broke Cuno Massey out of." Mason looked incredulous. "The one where he lifted the hair of Warden Castle, blew the man's nose off, and left him a howlin' cripple."

Joseph and T-Bone shared a glance. Then the ferret-faced, bespectacled little constable said, "We didn't hear about a prison break. We figured they heard about the whores in Mayville and was just here to raise hell. They done already had plenty of bounty on their heads for Ed here to be interested."

"Reckon they raised that hell, didn't they?" Mason said, rolling a quirley as he looked back down the street toward the charred brothel ruins.

"Look — all I want to know," Spurr said, "is how many rode out of here and in which direction."

T-Bone opened his mouth to speak, but his unlikely brother-in-law, Ed Joseph, shoved him brusquely back with an arm across his chest and stepped between the smaller man and Spurr. "Hold on. You don't get that information until we come to an agreement."

Spurr tipped his head to one side and scowled. He didn't like bounty hunters. And there was something particularly foul and morbid about the long-haired one before him.

"I'll be ridin' with you two lawbringers. And I get the reward on them I bring down. Or, like the deal I had with my bunch, we split it up even between the three of us."

Mason turned to Joseph, frowning and removing his quirley from between his lips. "We don't ride with bounty hunters, Joseph."

"Speak for yourself, Mason." Spurr's voice was toneless.

He was still staring at Joseph distastefully, taking in the two gutta-percha-gripped Smith & Wessons on the man's belt, a LeMat in a shoulder holster, and the two knives jutting from his high-topped black boots. Oddly, the man had a silver crucifix dangling down his chest. Few stranger men had Spurr ever seen, but he knew Joseph's reputation.

Mason switched his incredulous scowl to Spurr. "What're you talkin' about?"

"I mean, Joseph has a deal. We ride out tomorrow at first light, and we split the reward three ways. If we manage to run down de Cava's bunch, that is. And that's one hell of a 'that is.' "

Mason started to speak, but Spurr cut him off with: "Ah, shit, their trail'll be plain enough come sunup. But we can use all the help we can get, Mason. I don't like this man any better than you do, but if he wants to help us run down them killers, we'd be fools to refuse him, short-handed as we are."

He gave Joseph a pointed look. "But you play by our rules — understand? This is law business. You break the law, do anything whatsoever to set fire to my britches and burn my dick, we'll throw the cuffs on you and drop you off in the nearest hotbox to wait for a judge."

"Hell, Spurr," Joseph said, dropping his chin and bringing a shrewd look to his dark, devilishly slanted eyes. "You've got a reputation yourself. Tough as an old Texas boot with a sidewinder tucked inside. I won't cross you."

He held up a long, slender finger. "But you don't cross me, either, when it comes

time to split the reward money. You see" —
he stretched an even more cunning grin —
"I don't trust lawmen anymore than you
trust bounty killers." He returned the finger
he'd been pointing with to his hair, absently
smoothing it down against his shoulder.
"And I'm a bad enemy to make."

Mason balled his fists as he stepped
toward the bounty hunter. "Why, you — !"

Spurr threw a hand up, palm out, bringing the sheriff up short. "All right, then," he
barked, impatience in his raspy, gravelly
voice. "We're all partnered up. Friends for
fuckin' life!"

He hitched his pants and cartridge belts
up on his lean hips and sauntered into the
beer parlor. "Now that that's settled, I
believe I'll have a drink, then find me a
whore to pound a pillow with."

18

"Whoo-eee, doggies, boys! Grab your gals and lead 'em on out there, cause we're gonna have us a roarin' good time this evenin' in Mayville!"

The half holler, half howl had risen from a half-finished frame saloon not far from May's. It was followed by a washtub base and concertina backing up a feisty fiddle. Spurr, lounging in the suds of his steaming bathtub while awaiting a girl, heard the hoof stomps and hand claps of a raucous barn dance.

Even the burning of a brothel and the turning out of a dozen whores could not keep the proverbial lid on the fledgling little railroad camp. The track layers and gandy dancers, not to mention the homeless whores themselves, were going to have a hoof-stompin', tail-raisin' good time no matter what.

Spurr felt a smile touch his mouth as he

grabbed his whiskey bottle off the chair beside the tub. He had the bottle only half raised to his mouth when he heard the squawk of a loose floorboard in the hall beyond his closed door. He set the bottle back down on the chair and rose in the tub, pricking his ears.

Above the din of the barn dance and the moans and groans of lovemaking in Miss May's rooms all around him, Spurr heard nothing now. The old whore, Miss May herself, weighed a good three hundred velvet-and-crinoline-ensconced pounds and had been lounging, half drunk, on a red plush settee in the first-floor parlor, with a wooden cash box and a pistol beside her, when Spurr had entered her domain, introduced himself, and announced his desire for a bath and a woman.

She was likely passed out by now, leaving the watchdogging and bulldogging to a bent-up old ex-railroad inspector named Steaves and his double-bore shotgun, while the girls went about their business.

The board squawk in the hall was probably just a customer taking his leave from his few minutes of frolic and, having heard the jubilation in the half-built saloon, was heading that way. From somewhere below, a girl laughed loudly and phonily.

Spurr sank back down in the tub and reached once more for his bottle. He'd no sooner gotten a gnarled hand wrapped around the whiskey, however, than a shadow moved in the hall beneath his door. The shadow stopped moving and remained beneath the door. There was no sound from the hall. At least, none that Spurr could hear above all the other noises.

The fractious crab in his chest twisted, belched, and flicked its leathery tail. The withered organ was like a creaky old man itself, trying to heave himself up out of a chair and groaning and panting with the near-fatal effort.

Slowly hoisting himself up out of the water, trying to make as little noise as possible, Spurr kept his gaze directed at the unmoving shadow. The person out there might be the whore he'd been waiting for, as he'd ordered one sent up to him after enough time for him to have had his badly needed bath.

On the other hand, the shadow wasn't moving . . .

Spurr's recalcitrant old ticker squawked almost audibly as he drew a breath and slid his big Remington from his holster on the chair beside the bottle. Quietly clicking the hammer back, he lifted one old veiny leg over the side of the tub, then the other. Dripping wet and blowing water from his lips, he felt like a fool as he knelt down on the other side of the room's single bed, which lay perpendicular to the tub.

Spurr drew another breath then hollered, "Come on in, little darlin'! Ole Spurr's been awaitin' on ye!"

Spurr's yell hadn't finished echoing around the room before the door blew open as though from a dynamite blast.

It slammed against the wall, causing the room to shake and for Spurr's bottle to tumble off the chair and hit the floor with a thud. A man burst into the room, stopping the door's bounce with his left boot — a red-haired gent with blue eyes and a cherry-red, clean-shaven face. Eyes spitting sky-colored fire and gritting his teeth, the man extended a walnut-gripped pistol and drilled three shots at the tub that stood six feet in front of him.

Plink! Plink! Plink! went the slugs hitting the water before clanking against the tub's copper bottom.

The shooter held fire and stared wide-eyed at the tub he seemed to just now notice was empty. No more than a half second had passed, however, before he saw Spurr kneeling behind the bed, and he swung his gun in the old lawman's direction.

Spurr had him dead to rights.

Bam! Bam! Bam-Bam!

The redheaded bushwhacker was picked up off his feet and thrown straight back out the door and against the wall on the opposite side of the hall, cracking it. He seemed to hang there for several seconds against the long jagged crack, moving his arms and legs as though trying to climb the wall backward to some perceived escape hatch in the ceiling.

Then his chin dropped to his left shoulder. His knees hit the floor with a loud thud. He slumped forward, rolled onto his side, sighed heavily, and died.

As the usual shouts and screams rose around him, and doors opened, and jakes flanked by whores rushed out to see what had spawned the fireworks, Spurr shambled barefoot and naked into the hall himself and looked at the stiff. He didn't recognize him. Or maybe there was a dim recollection. He couldn't remember.

He swung his cocked Remington around at three men filing toward him — two naked, one in balbriggans, all wielding pistols. "Drop them hoglegs or join your friend in hell!"

The three lowered their guns. Spurr

turned to face the other direction, where a portly man nearly his own age and with long snowy hair hanging down from a bald pink pate was also shuffling toward him. He was clad in only moccasins and a shell belt, squeezing an old Patterson revolver in his pudgy, brown hand.

"Drop that horse pistol, Samuel!" Spurr was surprised to remember that Samuel Loggins was the man's name. An army packer and whiskey drummer, he was sometimes a fort sutler when he was in the government's good graces. Spurr had also known him when the man had professionally skinned buffalo hides.

"Spurr?" Loggins scowled in disbelief. "I thought for sure you'd be stakin' a claim on St. Pete's back forty long before now!"

"Drop that pistol, Samuel."

"Ah, shit — I don't have no beef with you, Spurr." Loggins depressed the big pistol's hammer, lowered the gun to his naked white thigh mottled with blue cornflower veins.

"Memory's getting' so bad," Spurr growled, "that I'd have forgotten if you did have a reason. Can't believe I remembered your name."

"What's his name?" Loggins gestured his pistol at the dead redhead who seemed to be staring at a black spider crawling across the floor near his nose.

"I don't remember . . . if I ever knew it." Spurr looked at the other men, a couple of whom had already slipped with their whores back into their rooms, the entertainment being over. "Anyone know this kid?"

"Rusty Hammond." This from down the hall. Spurr stared past two men and a blond girl who'd just come up the stairs carrying a bottle of whiskey, to a door on the hall's left side. Two eyes and a nose peered out from behind a cracked door. "Waddie out at the Crosshatch. He seen you ride in last night, Marshal. Said you took his brother, Omar, to be hung by Judge Parker in Fort Smith last year."

"Ah, shit," Spurr said, mostly in response to having his memory nudged.

He remembered Omar Hammond's bright red hair, apple-red cheeks, and eyes so frosty that just a glance would freeze a man's pecker. Hammond had killed three Indian girls along a freight road near Sutter Creek, Nebraska Territory, after he'd led them all by pistol point into the breaks of the Niobrara River, raped each one before he'd locked them all in a farmer's spring-house, then shot them through the walls. Him and a friend of his, Wheeler Whitfield, whom Spurr had not been saddened to have gut-shot and caused to take a long, loud time dying . . .

Spurr looked at the eyes and the nose in the foot-wide gap between the door and the frame. "You might have talked him out of dyin' for a no-account brother."

"We figured it was a family matter." The door closed. The latch clicked.

Spurr snorted, cursed again.

Downstairs, a woman started to yell profanities. May, no doubt. Presently, old Steaves appeared, wheezing at the top of the stairs at the far end of the hall, holding his shotgun as though it weighed as much as a steel-shod wagon wheel. "Sorry for the commotion, sir," Spurr said. "I reckon you can have this one buried with the others out yonder."

Spurr lowered his pistol and grabbed the arm of the blond girl, who was staring down at the dead redhead and cradling a whiskey bottle, baby-like, in the crook of her right arm. "Think I'll return to my room and flush out the old boiler. Come on, missy. You're mine, ain't ya?"

"I reckon, mister," the girl said tonelessly, still staring down at the dead redhead. "If you're the one they call Spurr, that is . . ."

Stiffly, she followed Spurr into the room. He closed the door and looked down at her, pleased to see that she was a full-bodied gal, with large, creamy breasts jutting from her pink corset, full hips swelling from a waist that was pleasantly plump. Not fat, mind you. Plump. The way a girl oughta look. Too many of them were so thin that you could snap them between your fingers, like a stove match.

Curly blond hair fell to her shoulders. It was sort of layered and adorned with a black ribbon. The locks on the right side of her head were pulled taut against her right ear and caught under the black silk choker she wore around her neck and which was trimmed with a small, fake diamond pin. Her face was small and china-doll pretty. One might even call the girl beautiful. At least, to Spurr she was comely enough to give his leaky heart a painful tickle.

He wished she wasn't blond, because it reminded him of the blond Murphy girl. But you couldn't have everything.

The girl turned reluctantly from the door and looked up at him. "You do that a lot, do you? Shoot . . . men . . . ?"

"Only when they try to shoot me first, especially while I'm bathing. I don't take baths all that often, and when I do I consider it a private affair."

Spurr took the bottle from the girl, who

still appeared shocked by the dead man in the hall though girls in her profession should be accustomed to such experiences. Brothels were colorful places.

"I do apologize for my appearance, but I'm clean enough."

He set the bottle on the dresser that was missing its mirror, a brick propping up one short leg. "I'd dress if we was goin' to an opry or somesuch, but, since . . ."

He grabbed a mineral-stained water glass, splashed whiskey into it, and threw it back. He shook his head against the delightful burn and raised a hand. It shook. He frowned at it, troubled. Killing men who'd tried to kill him first usually didn't trouble him. So why was he shaking?

Why, too, did he suddenly feel as hollowed out as an old corncob pipe?

He backed up to the bed, sat on the edge of it, and gave a phlegmy sigh. "Shit."

The girl was unlacing her corset and watching him curiously. She had amber eyes. Her hair was nearly as gold-yellow as sunflower blossoms. "You all right, Mr. Spurr?"

Spurr watched the corset fall away from her breasts. Her tender, pale, pink-buttoned bosom spilled forth, but the wonderfully shaped orbs could have been a blank wall for all the feeling they evoked in Spurr's nether regions. He admired the girl's breasts as one might admire a beautiful oil painting or a sunset, but his dong did not stir.

"You look sorta pale," the girl said, the faintest concern in her voice as she stepped out of her stockings while keeping her sheer, powder-blue wrap draped across her shoulders. Her full breasts swayed behind it.

"Must be the hot bath." Spurr threw back the whiskey. "I'll be all right in a minute."

The girl, naked now except for the wrap, walked toward him, rolling her hips slightly, staring at him with a coquettish little smile on her ruby lips, cupping her breasts in her soft hands. "Sure you will. Most fellas feel all right when they get under the sheets with Miss Lilly." She stopped before him, slanting a sparkly-eyed look at him while continuing to cup her breasts.

She was a professional, this girl, and she'd overcome her distaste for what she'd seen in the hall to earn her keep here at May's. She was a right beautiful girl, but Spurr had liked her better before she'd put the phony lust behind her eyes.

He was old and ragged, big-boned but stringy as jerked beef, and everywhere the sun seared him he was the color of old saddle leather. Where it couldn't find him, he was white as talcum. His face was un-shaven and the texture of a falling-down chicken coop, with brown moles and droopy eyelids.

Of course, he repulsed her. Age was beauty's nemesis. It was natural to shy away from it.

But you couldn't tell by her slightly parted lips, the tip of her pink tongue poking out between them, nor by the way she entic-ingly kneaded her breasts, shoulders rising and falling as she breathed. He usually liked older women, but this girl, at twenty, was as old as they came here at May's. She'd have to do.

Spurr held his glass out to her. "Pour me another drink. Then lets you an' me pound the pillow, darlin'." He cracked his own phony grin, trying to drum up some of his old, rakish charm, and reached behind her to squeeze one of her plump butt cheeks.

"I bet you can really pound it, eh, Mr. Spurr?"

"It's just Spurr. And no, I can't really pound it. But I can give it a tap or two." Spurr chuckled as the girl filled his glass. When she'd swung around from the bed, enough of her hair had slipped out from beneath the choker to reveal her right ear.

Or what had been her right ear before

most of it had been hacked away, leaving little more than a ragged pink stub.

"Good lord," Spurr said softly, rising up from the bed in shock, "what happened to your ear?"

The impulsive exclamation had escaped his lips before he'd realized it. He'd always been one for sticking his boot clean up to its mule ears in his mouth. The girl jerked her head toward him, flushing and covering her ear with her hand.

"Don't look!" she squealed, slamming the bottle back down on the dresser, then dropping her chin to her chest in horror. "You're not . . . no one's supposed to see! Miss May warned me — word gets out, she'll fire me!"

Spurr rose and walked over to her. "What happened, honey?"

The girl shook her head.

"Come on — you can tell ole Spurr. What happened to your ear, dear girl?"

She kept her head down, hand over the stub of her ear. "Market hunter. Crazy drunk. Decided to take a trophy, I reckon."

"Ah . . . hell. I am sorry."

"It ain't your fault." She looked up at him skeptically, searchingly, wonderingly. Then she dropped her chin again to speak to the floor near her plump, bare feet. "If you'll turn away, I'll cover it back up. If you want me to stay, that is . . ."

Spurr's heart swelled again. He choked back a sob. Christ, what a world . . . The blond girl he'd killed flashed through his mind once more, and so did the children the slavers had been hauling across the prairie. The dead killer in the hall had been a shaver once, lumbering around in swaddling clothes . . .

He said thickly to Lilly, blinking back a wet sheen from his eyes, "A little thing like a torn ear don't take nothin' from your brand of beauty, sweet girl. If anything, it makes you purtier."

Spurr took his whiskey glass, turned away from her, and went back over to the bed. His throat was dry; it had a throbbing knot in it.

He climbed onto the bed, leaned his back against the headboard. The girl had tucked her hair back down over her ear and secured it beneath the choker. She stood resting her hands on the edge of the dresser behind her.

Spurr patted the bed beside him. "Come on over here, my beauty. Let Spurr have another shot of this who-hit-john, and then you can see if you can get my third old wooden leg up far enough to give you a ride on it. If you don't mind climbin' into the saddle, that is. Truth be told, my old ticker ain't what it used to be, and . . ."

The girl had walked over to him, shedding the silk wrap. She tossed it over a ladder-back chair and climbed up onto the bed, full breasts jostling to and fro. Her nipples were pebbling. Her smile had returned, as well as that lusty sparkle in her eyes. Only this time it looked a tad more authentic. Her amber gaze and ruby lips stroked the old lawbringer gently, warmly.

"I can do that for you, Spurr." She crouched over him and began using her hands to manipulate him, giving him a playfully admonishing sidelong glance. "Promise you won't tell?"

Spurr finished the whiskey, smacked his lips. "Your secret's safe with me. As long as you keep mine."

"What secret's that?"

"I'm old and slow," Spurr said with a sigh, setting the glass onto the bed beside him. "Though sometimes I'm old and way too fast." He chuckled. "Tell no one."

He clipped the chuckle with a choking groan. Lilly's hands were caressing him magically, unexpectedly sending little tendrils of desire through his belly.

Lilly smiled. "Secret's safe with me." She lowered her head over his crotch.

Spurr spread his hand out across the top

of her head. "One more thing."

The girl lifted her head, wrinkling the skin above the bridge of her pretty nose.

"I only paid for an hour, but I done changed my mind. I'd like you to stay the night. An old man gets lonely, don't ya know." He gave her chin a playful nudge with his thumb and tried once more to swallow down that consarned knot in his throat. "I'll settle up with Miss May in the mornin'."

"You don't need to do that."

"Yeah, I do. For me, not you. An old man gets spooky at night."

Lilly's red lips spread wide, showing her small, white teeth in a genuine smile. Her eyes sparkled. She lowered her chin and closed her mouth over him, making soft sucking sounds. Spurr sank his hand into her hair again, soft as the first grass of spring.

She moved her head around.

Spurr sucked a breath and groaned louder as he discovered that, in the right company, he wasn't so old and slow, after all.

19

In the single sphere of magnified vision, curtains of sand and gravel blew this way and that on the savage wind. Cuno adjusted his spyglass's focus slightly until a ridge about three hundred yards away clarified slightly on the other side of a miniature badlands of broken rock and dry river courses carved through a spine of sandstone and limestone.

Three riders appeared atop the ridge — so vague from this distance and through the fluttering curtain of sand that Cuno would not have recognized them had he not been looking for them. He would have thought them inanimate objects blowing on the wind — large tumbleweeds, a trick of the light, or cloud shadows.

Cuno blinked, and when he looked again the riders had dropped out of sight in the badlands. There was only the howling wind and the blowing sand now, and the bits of

weeds and whole tumbleweeds and other
debris that the fierce northwestern wind had
been kicking up for several hours.

Cuno lowered the spyglass and rubbed his
cheek thoughtfully as he continued staring
out across the badlands. Three riders. Could
be part of Ed Joseph's bunch — those that
had survived the dustup in the fledgling
railroad town.

Or they could be lawmen.

Cuno and the other members of de Cava's gang had learned they were being followed nearly a week ago, when Mateo had
sent an outrider to peruse their back trail
and the man had come upon the still warm
ashes from a recent cook fire and a recent
set of shod horse hooves.

Three days ago, Mateo had sent four riders back to wipe the shadowers from his
trail, but the four riders had returned looking sheepish. They'd found no tracks where
they were certain they'd spied the riders
through field glasses, and found no more
ashes from cook fires. It was as though the
men had decided against their dangerous
mission and simply gone back to where
they'd come from.

Or maybe they hadn't been following the
gang but were coincidentally crossing the
same country. Other desperadoes, most

likely, hightailing it toward Mexico.

The wily Mateo had not been satisfied with that explanation, however. He'd kept a rotating string of men out flanking the main gang, scouting a broad area around the gang's back trail. Cuno was one of those outriders today, and a half hour ago, around noon, peering through his spyglass from the ridge of a near bluff, he'd seen one of the riders cross a ridge — or what he'd thought had been a rider. Now, having seen all three from this ridge he now hunkered upon, between two cracked boulders, closer to the badlands, he was sure.

The gang was being shadowed.

He looked around at the vast country around him — distant mountains looming cool and blue in the west and south and northwest, dry washes scoring the nearer land bulging with bluffs, rocky spurs, and tabletop mesas on pedestals of red sandstone. Clay-colored boulders had been strewn around the rolling, sage- and greasewood-carpeted bluffs by ancient glaciers or sent to the earth's surface by violent quakes or gradual upthrusts.

They were somewhere in southern New Mexico, possibly skirting the Arizona line, not far from Old Mexico. It was impossible to know for sure, as they were following no beaten path, though they occasionally crossed a seldom-used stage road and even fainter Indian trail. Small, isolated mountain ranges cropped up everywhere.

Cuno had never been through this country — maybe a northeastern corner of it when he and his father had hauled freight for the frontier cavalry several years ago. There were no near towns. One knew such country only by its landmarks.

Cuno crabbed on his knees and elbows back down the hill. He heard something behind him, and twisted around, reaching for his low-slung .45.

He froze, his hand over the gun's carved ivory grips, and looked down the hill where Wayne Brouschard sat with three other gang members — Chisos McGee, "Dirty" Leo McGivern, and the squat man with the shabby bowler hat, little pig eyes, and silver eyeteeth — Eldon Wald.

Brouschard leaned negligently forward, gloved hands on his saddle horn, his yellow eyes slitted devilishly. He'd mostly healed from the pummeling Cuno had given him, but the cut high on his jaw was a long, thick scab outlined in red.

All four men were holding rifles. Wald held his out from his stout right hip, aimed at Cuno. It didn't appear to be cocked. The apprehension that Cuno felt nip the back of his neck when he saw his enemy here, out here away from Mateo's supervising eye, where anything could happen, settled to a mere prickling of the flesh.

Brouschard had something else in mind, all right. That was plain by his cunning, shit-eating stare, as well as that of Wald and the others. Apparently, he wasn't planning on back-shooting Cuno and throwing him into a deep ravine. The young freighter was a little surprised.

"You seen 'em." Brouschard made it a statement, not a question, lifting his eyes to indicate the northern distance beyond Cuno.

"Yeah, I seen 'em."

Cuno closed his spyglass against his knee and heaved himself to his feet, brushing off his denims. Already they were soft and sun-bleached, the dust ground into the tight weave despite the cowhide leggings he'd bought — or Camilla had bought for him, to his nettling chagrin — in Mayville. "There's three of 'em, all right. We'd best —"

"Uh-uh." Brouschard grinned and shook his head. He raised his voice above the howling wind. "Not we'd best. You'd best ride on over there and get shed of them three . . . whoever they may be. You go on. You showed you can fight with your fists all right. But out here cold steel's the language spoken."

The big devil gritted his teeth and jerked his head in the direction of the badlands. "Go ahead. Show us what you got, freighter boy!"

Eldon Wald, Dirty Leo Givern, and Chiso McGee all smiled, Wald keeping his Winchester aimed casually at Cuno. He had his thumb on the hammer.

Cuno hooked his thumbs behind his cartridge belt. "Mateo order this?"

"Mateo ain't here. I'm here. I'm ordering you to ride on over there and wipe them dung beetles off our trail. You do that, and then maybe you got the right to strut some. Then maybe you've earned the right to be pokin' Mateo's sister every night."

Chisos McGee sneered and let his cold eyes rake Cuno up and down. "Thinks he's some young bull in the studdin' corral."

Wald laughed, spittle showing at his mouth corners.

"All right." Cuno walked over to where he'd tied Renegade to a sage shrub. "You're the second in command, I reckon. I follow your orders, Brouschard."

He looked at the big man and grinned.

Then he swung into the saddle. He was tired of Brouschard. He wished he'd killed the man when Mateo had sanctioned it. Now he was just tired enough of him to want to do what the big man obviously thought was a tall order, a damn near impossible challenge, and shove it back in the man's face. It would be the best payback Cuno could think of.

His voice was hard, toneless, his sunburned cheeks flushed with fury. "If they have badges, I'll bring 'em back in about an hour or so. Sound good to you?"

Brouschard narrowed a skeptical eye and said out of one side of his mouth. "You do that. Three tin stars."

"And what'll you do for me?"

Brouschard pressed his lips together.

"You get off my back," Cuno said, holding Renegade's reins taut. "And stay off my back. And Camilla's back. One more cross-eyed look at me, one more ogling look at her . . ." He shook his head darkly. "And I'm gonna drill you for keeps without one word of warning. One forty-five pill through your fat gut, and I'm gonna watch you crawl while your miserable life drains out."

Cuno turned the horse around and galloped off down a crease between the bluffs, heading for the badlands.

Behind him, the four devils stared after him. Brouschard's nostrils flared.

Foolhardy machismo had compelled Cuno to follow Brouschard's order, to accept the challenge. He knew that, and he didn't care. He had no reason not to kill the lawmen — if lawmen they were. Out here, if he didn't kill them, they'd likely kill him. Besides, he'd already killed another lawman.

They can only hang you once.

Besides, lawmen or those who professed to ride on the side of the law were little better than Mateo de Cava's pack of unabashed gun wolves. Lawmen had tried to take Cuno's life away for no good reason. He owed them nothing.

They'd made him a wolf, so he'd live like one. From now on it was kill or be killed. He'd live for himself and only himself and whatever girl was warming his blankets at night.

He intended to kill the three men on his back trail, and it didn't matter who they were — bounty hunters, lawmen, or three nuns who'd decided to take up bounty tracking to make a little money for the orphanage.

They'd die however Cuno had to do it.

And he'd ride back to Mateo's camp,

laughing like a banshee, and he'd toss those silver stars at Brouschard and relish the expression on the fat man's scarred face.

He found a game and cattle trail into the badlands that appeared to have once been an ancient riverbed, the water having wildly eroded the gray rock into bizarre and twisted shapes, with meandering corridors carved between sheer stone walls. From the cracks in the stone walls, brown, bristly tufts of brush grew raggedly.

As Cuno put Renegade toward the broadest corridor he could find and which appeared to lead in the direction of the other side of the bed, he saw part of a stark, white cow skeleton. The skull had bits of hide remaining around the ears. Otherwise the carcass was completely nude, most of the smaller bones having been carried off by carrion eaters.

Clucking to his horse, Cuno rode on into the corridor that was so narrow in places that both walls often scraped his knees. Mud swallows flitted and shrieked above his head. The wind here was cool and fresh against his face, drying the sweat on his chest and back, but there was also the tangy stench of mineral springs.

Not far from the corridor's mouth, a man's skeleton in ragged cowboy garb sat back in a dim alcove, the skull dipped toward the sun-bleached chest, the white ribs bulging through a tattered and frayed denim shirt.

An arrow protruded from between two of the ribs. A Schofield revolver lay near one of the man's bony hands. Cuno glanced at the boots that were stylishly red though the color had been faded by the weather. Stars had been tooled into the toes.

Cuno wondered how long it had taken the poor drover, who may have ridden down here after stray cattle, to die after his tussel with the Indian who'd killed him. He must have been alone, and he'd likely crawled in here to escape his attackers, never to see the light of day again.

The young freighter shivered involuntarily and rode on down the corridor, the moaning of the wind sounding even eerier now in light of his grisly discovery.

After he'd ridden fifty or so yards, the corridor branched sharply left and dwindled to a foot-wide crack. The gap was wider above, so Cuno stepped off Renegade's back and onto the right side wall, planting his boots on a narrow, gravelly ledge. The walls were deeply and broadly pitted, and he saw a funnel of sorts leading at an upward slant toward daylight and tan, windblown grit.

Cuno reached down and slid his Winchester from his saddle boot. He racked a round into the breech, set the hammer to half cock, and glanced at Renegade, who gave his head a wary shake, nearly slipping his bit from his teeth.

"Cool your heels, boy," Cuno said. He swallowed as he looked up, tracing the funnel with his gaze. "I'll be back in a minute."

Using the small ledges and fissures and nubs of protruding stone, Cuno climbed the funnel to a broad gap filled with sky and sunshine. Just below the ridge, he doffed his hat and, holding it in his hand, poked his head up above the ridge's lip, looking northward.

All he could see were humps and thumbs of gray rock spotted with white bird shit, here and there a bristly weed clump. About seventy yards beyond the knobs of eroded rock, the other bank rose gently to rolling prairie sprouting massive bluffs and mesas with slopes stippled with cedar shrubs.

Cuno doffed his hat and climbed up and out onto the ridge, staying low as he looked around, planning a route over the precarious terrain here atop the dinosaur spine of a stone ridge crest. He strode northward, leaping several narrow precipices, then climbing a higher ridge pocked with what must have been volcanic air vents.

He was almost to the top of this ridge when he stopped suddenly.

He stared at the rock facing him, the fingers of his left hand curled into one of the vents, his right hand gripping his Winchester's receiver.

Voices. Men's voices.

They carried almost inaudibly on the howling wind. If he could trust the sounds that the wind tossed this way and that, the voices originated just beyond the scarp he was on. Hard to tell how far away. He could hear only intermittent bits and pieces of the conversation between wind gusts.

Slowly, he continued climbing until he reached the top of the ridge. Again, he doffed his hat and rose slowly, looking around. There were several boulders up here and a stout cedar twisting up from a wide crack in the mottled gray and black rock. He hunkered down behind a boulder and lifted a look over the top.

Sucking a sharp breath, he quickly lowered his head. He crawled on one hand and both knees to the boulder's far left side, where there was a gap between this rock and a large stone knob farther to his left. Cautiously, gritting his teeth, feeling his blood surging in his veins, Cuno edged a look through the gap and held there, eyes wide in spite of the wind-tossed grit.

On the other side of the ridge, in a rocky hollow and with their backs to another ridge behind them, sat three men.

They had to be the same three who'd been dogging the gang. Before them was a low fire. The flames were sheltered enough by the surrounding ridges that the wind only harassed them slightly. Two of the men were a few years older than Cuno, maybe in their late twenties or early thirties. One had long black hair, a black beard, and dark eyes. He was dressed in a black vest over a dark blue shirt down which hung a silver crucifix. He had high-topped black boots bristling with knife handles and black denims. He was pouring coffee from a black pot into a speckled blue cup.

The other younger man hunkered back in a slight hollow between the black-haired man and the third man. He wore a tin star on his wool vest. A sweeping dragoon mustache mantled his upper lip.

His eyes were . . .

Cuno's heart quickened. He drew his head sharply back behind the boulder, lower jaw hanging. The second younger man was Sheriff Dusty Mason — the man responsible for throwing Cuno to the wolves at the

Arkansas River Federal Penitentiary.

Cuno caught his breath, squeezing his rifle in his big, gloved hands.

How in the hell had Mason gotten on his trail? Why? Had the sheriff made it his own personal and professional responsibility to make sure that Cuno sweated out the remainder of his life at Arkansas? It appeared so. But why? Mason had honestly thought that Cuno had killed those other lawmen in cold blood, but the young freighter had certainly done nothing to justify a personal vendetta.

Cuno gritted his teeth, felt the indignant rage surge behind his breastbone, making his head light, his fingers and toes tingle. Rarely had he wanted to kill a man more than he wanted to kill Dusty Mason if for no other reason than the sheriff was responsible for Cuno's being right here, his heart red as molten iron, swollen with hate.

A wolf dogged by those he'd once considered his own kind . . .

When he'd gotten his emotions under control, he edged another look through the gap between the rocks. The third man sat back against the base of the opposite ridge, legs stretched out before him, ankles crossed, arms crossed on his chest, broad-brimmed hat tipped over his eyes. What

Cuno could see of his face was deeply lined and furred with a thin salt-and-pepper beard. His hair was longish, mostly brown but streaked with gray.

He'd been a large, rawboned man at one time, but age had chiseled him down to rawhide and sinew. A walnut-gripped Remington was thonged low on his right thigh. A bowie was sheathed on his opposite hip. To his right, an older model Winchester rifle, its stock worn smooth with use, leaned against the stone wall.

On his vest was pinned the moon-and-star copper badge of a deputy United States marshal.

The wind's moans and weird yowling were echoed in Cuno's ears. Despite the wind and the fact that at least two of these men were lawmen, Cuno felt a strange calm sweep easily over and through him. A killing calm . . . He raised the Winchester, drew the hammer back to full cock.

He felt the most animosity toward the sheriff, but because the older, federal man was asleep and farthest left, making him an easier target, Cuno would drill him first.

20

Cuno rested his Winchester's sights on the old lawman's chest, left of his badge. Just over the man's heart. He drew half a breath, held it, and took up the slack in his trigger finger.

A shrill rattling rose, instantly drowning out the wind's keening.

Cuno jerked the trigger back. The Winchester roared. The slug puffed dust from the ridge just above and left of the old lawman's head. At the same time, the snake struck — a stone-colored blur flying toward Cuno from the shade beneath a rock to his left. The rattler sunk its fangs into his left forearm, a sharp searing pain, instantly hot and throbbing.

Cuno gave an involuntary cry and threw his arm up and out, flinging the snake whip-like away from him. The viper hit the ground and coiled instantly again about six feet away, the tiny beadlike eyes fixing its victim with a threatening stare.

Cuno lowered the Winchester. He glanced toward the fire. The three stalkers were reaching for rifles, shouting and running for cover while loudly levering cartridges.

Cuno backed away from the boulders, gritting his teeth against the pain in his forearm. Rifles roared from below, slugs hammering the rocks around him. He donned his hat and spun, feeling like a fool for having to retreat like a damn tinhorn, but the snake had sunk its teeth resolutely into his forearm, and already he could feel the arm burning and aching and starting to swell.

Snakebit, he could not take on the three stalkers, all of whom were bearing down on him furiously, their slugs spanging off rocks with enraged, echoing whines.

Holding his burning arm close to his side, Cuno hopscotched the knobby surface of the rocky ridge. He leapt the fissures over deep, blue-dark, stone-walled corridors, got disoriented for a moment, and looked around wildly before recognizing a landmark.

A minute later he was half falling down the funnel that he'd taken up from the box canyon in which he'd left Renegade.

The horse nickered as Cuno approached

and shied back a ways. "Hold on, boy," Cuno said, breathless, holding his rifle out away from him for balance. "Don't bolt on me now . . ."

He pushed himself away from the gravelly incline and dropped clumsily into the saddle. Trying to remain calm in spite of the black poison he imagined being pumped through his veins, coursing toward his heart, he backed the horse along the corridor. He reached a bulge in the stony gap, managed to turn the horse around, then batted his heels against the stallion's flanks.

"He-yaaah!"

Shod hooves clacked on the rocky, gravelly floor of the corridor, echoing. The wind whistled through the gap high above Cuno's head. Swallows shrieked and fluttered about their mud nests. Cuno's arm grew heavier and hotter by the second. His mouth was dry. He could feel cold perspiration popping out on his forehead.

He stormed out the mouth of the corridor and angled sharply right, heading back the way he'd come. As he rode, the wind pelting his face with grit, he pricked his ears to listen for the two lawmen and the black-haired man. If they were on his trail, he couldn't hear their hoof thuds above the devilish wind.

There were other craggy corridors in the maze of rock jutting around him, probably wide enough gaps for the stalkers to thread as they tried to cut him off. He kept his rifle up in his right hand, ready to fire if one of his pursuers dashed out of a gap. He hadn't seen their horses near their camp, though, so it would likely take some time to gather them.

He'd climbed the bank and was booting Renegade into a hard gallop when he heard a shout behind him. A rifle popped, the report quickly clipped by the wind.

He glanced over his shoulder to see two riders galloping out of the riverbed about fifty yards left of where Cuno had left it. A third man, Sheriff Mason, was galloping up out of the bed now, too, lowering his head over his horse's neck and batting his steel-shod heels against his horse's flanks.

The black-haired gent was in the lead, though the old marshal was riding up fast behind him and slanting off to his right as he lifted his rifle to his shoulder, reins in his teeth. The black-haired gent had his own rifle raised.

Smoke puffed from it. There was a crack like that of a branch snapping.

Cuno heard the bullet spang off a rock to his right. Another crack. Another bullet curled the air near Cuno's head. He flinched, ducked lower in the saddle, then cursed and slid his rifle from his boot, taking his reins in his left hand, which felt as though a tender, red heart were throbbing in it.

He doubted he'd outrun those three on their three fresh horses. He'd have to make a stand right here. The thought had no sooner passed through his brain than near rifles thundered around him.

He flinched again and looked around, disoriented. Brouschard, Eldon Wald, Dirty Leo McGivern, and Chisos McGee were firing their rifles toward Cuno's pursuers from behind a boulder and a spur of rock humping up from the ground and sheathed in bear grass.

Cuno leapt out of his saddle, dropped his reins, and whacked Renegade's left hip to send the mount galloping southwest out of the line of rifle fire. He hunkered down beside Brouschard whom he was incredulous to see had suddenly become his unlikely ally.

"Good work, kid," the yellow-bearded devil cackled, triggering another shot over the spur. "Was figurin' you'd either give up the ghost in them badlands . . . or lead them trail wolves right into our rifle sights!"

Cuno triggered his Winchester twice, but his three pursuers were holding back now, and all three were obscured by the blowing curtains of dirt and sand. "You should have waited another minute," Cuno growled. "They'd have been another fifty yards closer!"

Brouschard turned to him, away from the rear stock of his cocked rifle, and flashed his broken teeth in anger. "Shut up, shaver. You was supposed to bring me their stars!"

Brouschard narrowed an eye as he aimed down his rifle, then tripped the trigger. Cuno couldn't tell if he hit anything. He could no longer see his pursuers. They'd likely taken cover themselves or hightailed it back to the badlands.

Pain bit his arm like a whipsaw blade, and he groaned as he fell back against the earthen shelf. His vision dimmed, his stomach bucked and pitched like a bronco mustang, and suddenly he stumbled to one side as the conflagration in his guts surged bitter-hot to his throat.

He dropped to his knees and threw up all the contents of his stomach, which wasn't much, as the gang was low on food and Cuno had eaten a spartan breakfast of jerky and coffee boiled with yesterday's grounds.

Brouschard laughed. "What the hell's the

matter with you?" When he saw Cuno's knob-knuckled hand, both the hand and the wrist swollen half again their normal size, and red as as raw beef, the big man scowled. "Christ!"

"Get after 'em," Cuno said, panting and running his sleeve across his mouth. He tossed his head in the direction of the badlands. "Get after those sons o' bitches, Brouschard. Talk's cheap. You got three other men — a fairer fight than mine was!"

Deep lines cut savagely across the big man's forehead. "I was about to!" he roared, leaping to his feet and cupping one hand to his mouth to shout toward where McGee and Wald were hunkered behind a boulder. "Let's go, boys. Grab your horses. We got 'em on the run!"

When all three had run off to an escarpment to the east and behind which they'd tethered their horses, Cuno sank back once more against the knoll.

His heart thudded. Sweat dribbled through the dust coating his face. His arm felt as though it had been dipped in burning tar. His heavy lids drooped over his eyes. He opened them when a sound drifted to his ears beneath the wind.

Through the blowing dust a horse and rider galloped toward him. Camilla's sombrero flopped from its thong behind her shoulders; her hair blew about her head like a wild, brown tumbleweed. Cuno tried to keep his eyes open, but the lids closed like heavy iron doors, and everything went black.

Only vaguely and briefly, he heard the girl calling his name . . .

Spurr put Cochise into the riverbed and reined the big roan to a stumbling halt, curveting him. Mason and Ed Joseph galloped down the slope behind him. "Split up!" Spurr shouted above the wind. "We'll take the bastards from cover!"

He leapt off Cochise's back, twisted an ankle against a rock, and dropped to one knee, cursing. He held the roan's reins, used them to pull himself back to his feet.

Beside him, Mason yelled, "You all right?"

Spurr ignored the question. Getting old and having to display your decrepitude at every turn in the trail was a pisser.

He managed to get his rifle out of his saddle boot, slapped the roan's rump with the Winchester's barrel, then hopped on one moccasined foot behind a slanting shelf of rock at the very edge of the riverbed. Cochise gave a shrill whinny and galloped off down the bed, soon disappearing behind a veil of blowing sand, down a corridor of jutting rock. The other two horses followed him.

Mason scrambled into the rocks a dozen yards to Spurr's right. Joseph dropped behind a boulder nearly straight out from where their trail dropped into the riverbed, another twenty yards beyond Spurr.

Spurr brushed a sleeve across the blood streaking the right side of his face, wincing at the pain of the dozen small cuts inflicted by the flying rock slivers when the bushwhacker's bullet had slammed into the stone wall behind him.

The side of his head, his ear, and neck were peppered with the shards, as well. They burned like buckshot. He could have lost that eye. Damn foolish to get caught like sitting ducks out here, but he, Mason, and Joseph had figured Mateo's bunch to be several miles ahead. They hadn't expected de Cava to send bushwhackers back in the windstorm.

Stupid mistake. The truth was, Spurr grudgingly acknowledged to himself, he and Mason had been tired and had used the storm as an excuse to rest their weary bones. A hard lesson learned. Spurr would never again underestimate the cunning of de Cava's desperadoes. They were capable of anything a tracker could imagine and then some.

He couldn't afford to be tired. He couldn't afford to be old.

He hunkered low, right index finger taut on the Winchester's trigger, and waited. He kept his ears pricked, his eyes sharply focused on the slanting embankment about forty yards straight out away from him and the boulder he was crouched behind. The wind continued to blow the sand in curtain-like waves, obscuring the top of the bank and making visibility beyond nearly impossible.

But that's where the four killers would come from. Had to be. Unless they'd turned back . . .

Gooseflesh began to rise on Spurr's back as one minute became two and then three.

He could feel the tension rising in his two cohorts. He could see Mason down on one knee behind his own boulder, the man's Henry repeater extended out across the top of the rock's flat surface. He couldn't see Joseph because of the blowing sand and the mortar-like slab of stone protruding from the larger mess of fossilized minerals between him and Mason.

He kept staring down his Winchester's barrel, right eye narrowed. In the periphery of his vision, he saw Mason glance at him.

He wanted to tell the sheriff to keep still, stay his ground, but he'd have to shout madly to be heard above the wind.

He had a feeling that the de Cava riders, as canny as the rest of the bunch, were stealing up slowly, probably afoot, to the bank of the dry, rocky riverbed. That's what Spurr would have done, expecting a bushwhack. Again, he'd wrongly assumed they'd storm into the bed like wildmen, flinging lead every such way to try to bring their quarries to ground before they forted up in the rocks.

Spurr had sent a telegram to the little New Mexico town, Cicorro, that lay somewhere south of here — he wasn't sure how far. There was a cavalry outpost nearby that had been set up to handle the Mescalero Apache problem.

Spurr had sent the telegram to the post commander, alerting the man of de Cava's breakneck ride south on a course that would take him and his band to or within close proximity of the village, which was a little supply settlement for the mining camps in the mountains owning the same name and looming tall in the northwest. He wanted like hell to reach the town and the dozen riders Captain Wilson had promised to have waiting there. As it was, out here, Spurr's trio was badly — one might even say *hilari-*

ously, terminally — outnumbered.

A gust of windblown sand slithered along the riverbed from Spurr's left to his right. When the tan-colored curtain had passed, Spurr spied movement on the opposite bank — just the quick jerking movement of a hatted head and a rifle slanting down from a low boulder and a snag of juniper the wind was wildly beating, smashing almost level with the top of the bank itself.

There they were.

21

Spurr looked at Mason.

The man was aiming his Henry just right of where Spurr had seen the rifleman. Mason didn't see the shooter.

Spurr picked up a small rock, side-armed it, bouncing it off Mason's back. The sheriff turned with a start. His face was an angular brown smudge beneath his low-tipped hat brim, his mustache a slightly darker line beneath his nose.

Spurr canted his head toward the opposite bank. Mason turned to look across the wash and hunkered lower, tensing. When he glanced at Spurr again, the old marshal gestured with his head once more, this time indicating up the wash on his left. He couldn't tell if Mason had understood, because just then the wind threw more sand and grit between them. Just the same, Spurr stepped back from his boulder cautiously. He turned and made his way through the rocks, finding a circuitous route that roughly paralleled the wash for about thirty yards. Limping slightly on his gimpy ankle that wasn't so gimpy now that he'd gotten some blood to it, he crossed the wash and pressed his left shoulder against the steep-cut bank.

He blinked against the sand and tightened his grip on the Winchester. Damn hard to get your bearings out here in this dry prairie blowup. He was liable to waltz right up to one of the de Cava men before he knew it, get himself gut-shot.

Swallowing back his apprehension — he hoped to hell he wasn't losing his gravel along with his health and his youth — he climbed the slick, eroded clay bank, grabbing roots and then a shrub at the top to help hoist him up. Slowly, he made his way back along the wash.

He hoped Mason had gotten his message and wouldn't spy his movement and drill him. The de Cava men were enough to worry about.

Setting each moccasined foot down carefully and holding his rifle straight out from his right hip, Spurr walked twenty yards, then thirty. He meandered around buck-brush clumps, prickly pear, and rocks.

A rifle barked in the distance, the report swallowed almost instantly by the wind.

Spurr stopped. There were two more quick shots, then another and another. Was that a man's shout? The sounds were swirled and tormented by the hot, demonic wind, but they seemed to be coming from the wash's opposite side, possibly farther back in the rocks than where he'd left Mason and Joseph. Spurr's mouth dried, tasted like stale tobacco. He moved forward, quickening his pace.

A rifle bellowed from nearly straight in front of him. The sound, so loud and close on the heels of the more distant though no less menacing reports, caused him to nearly leap out of his moccasins.

The rifle exploded twice more, and Spurr saw the blue-red flames stab in the direction of the wash on his right. They were flashes in the blowing grit. Just then there was a lull between gusts, and Spurr saw a big man hunkered in the brush at the edge of the bank. About six feet in front of Spurr. He wore a duster. A felt hat hung down his back by a leather thong. He had thin, sandy, sweat-matted hair, a bright pink, bulging forehead and a yellow-blond beard.

Spurr racked a fresh shell into his Winchester's breech. The ejected cartridge arched toward Spurr and dropped in the gravel in front of him.

The man must have sensed or glimpsed Spurr a half second after Spurr had nearly stumbled over him. He rolled onto his left shoulder, bringing his rifle to bear, yellow teeth flashing, yellow eyes widening and brightening.

He screamed with shock and savage fury. But Spurr had him.

The old marshal's aged Winchester barked three times, the spent cartridges flying back behind Spurr's right shoulder. The big man fired his own Winchester one handed, kiting the slug over Spurr's head. He fell back hard, then slid headfirst down the bank to the wash, his spurs grinding against the clay.

Rifles continued thundering in the windy distance across the wash. Spur could see no movement, only ragged, obscure glimpses of the rock wall and ledges through the blowing grit.

He moved ahead quickly, but when he figured the other three de Cava men were no longer on this side of the wash but had attempted the same maneuver that Spurr had tried in reverse, he dropped down the bank and lit out running toward where he'd left Mason and Joseph.

He lost his bearings, and it took some time to find where his cohorts had been. They weren't there. Only the body of a short, stalky gent, his silver eyeteeth showing in a death grimace. Spurr's heart thudded. The gunfire had fizzled to only sporadic bursts originating from somewhere deep in the stone corridors. It echoed eerily. Spurr tried to hone in on it and stole down a gravel-floored hallway with slanting walls and a slanting ceiling.

From ahead emanated the rotten-egg odor of burned powder. Something lay on the ground against the right side wall.

He slowed his pace as he approached, then crouched over Ed Joseph. The bounty hunter's rifle lay beside him, one hand on his belly, the other over the rifle barrel. Blood bibbed the black-haired man's shirt and his silver crucifix. His dark eyes stared sightlessly at the stone ceiling, blood trickling from a corner of his mouth.

Spurr heard another shot from somewhere ahead. He continued forward and followed a right-angled dogleg. Ahead, another corridor intersected Spurr's. Wind blew sand through it, pelting the gray stone wall beyond. A shadow slid across the wall. Spurr stopped, dropping to one knee and extending his Winchester out from his shoulder.

A dark, man-shaped figure appeared — short and wiry and wearing a calico shirt and a bleached-yellow Stetson with a torn brim. The man turned toward Spurr. His eyes widened, and just as he started to swing his carbine around, Spurr shot him through the brisket.

The thunder of Spurr's rifle in the close confines set the old marshal's ears ringing.

The slug plowed through his target's chest and spanged off the stone wall behind him, painting the wall with blood. The man fired his carbine into the ground at his boots, stumbled back against the wall, then dropped straight down to his rump. His head sagged to one side, eyes squeezed shut. Holding the rifle across his knees, the man let his head drop to the gravelly ground and shook violently as he died.

Spurr ejected the spent cartridge, heard it cling to the gravel at his boots. He rammed the lever home, seating a fresh shell, then freezing there and pricking his ears to listen. There was only the moaning of the devil wind in the sky above the gray stone walls, the occasional sift of sand down the walls around him. The walls themselves were absolutely still and dumbly silent.

No more shots sounded. No more cries.

Spurr continued forward, hearing now the soft crunch of gravel beneath his moccasins. In here, the wind's cries were farther away, muffled, but just as eerie. They seemed to be taunting him. Jeering. He heard something just as he approached the dead man at the intersecting corridor. It came from his right. He held his Winchester steady, then stepped around the corner, spreading his feet and tightening his trigger finger.

He held fire.

Another man lay facedown on some stone rubble littering another gap on the corridor's left side. Thick blood was gushing out around the rocks beneath his body and head. His right hand was draped over one of the rocks, squeezing it desperately. Otherwise, he was still.

Beyond him, Dusty Mason sat against the corridor's right wall. Mason's hat lay beside him. One of his legs was stretched out wide, the heel of the other one curled under the knee. His chest rose and fell sharply as he clamped his left hand over a bloody hole low on his right side. He had a cocked pistol in his right hand, but when he recognized Spurr in the rocky shadows, he depressed the hammer and cursed raspily.

Spurr moved forward. "How bad?"

"How the hell should I know?"

"You ain't never been shot before?"

"Nope."

Spurr looked at the man wagging his head

against the wall behind him. "Really?"

"First time." The sheriff winced then pounded the ground with his pistol. "Hurts good, too. Hot."

"Let me see."

"What the hell can you do?"

"I can look at it," Spurr growled in irritation.

"I think it musta cracked a rib or two. It hurts like holy hell to breathe. Feels like my ribs on that side are gonna splinter apart."

Spurr set his rifle aside then leaned forward, pried Mason's hand away from the bloody hole above his right hip, and examined the wound. He couldn't see much but blood. The sheriff was losing it fast. Spurr tipped him forward.

"Ouch! Goddamnit, Spurr — what're you . . . ?"

Spurr pushed Mason back against the stone wall. "Can't tell if it went all the way through or not. If it's still in there, it'll need to be dug out."

"Not by you!"

"No, hell, I wouldn't dig around in your yaller guts!" Spurr brushed a pensive fist across his nose and looked around.

"Joseph?" Mason asked him.

Spurr shook his head. "We're gonna have to get you to Diamondback. Probably a sawbones there of some kind. At least a butcher."

"Ah, fuck." Mason lifted his chin and glared at the fine line of washed-out sky above the cavern. "Don't take me to no butcher, goddamnit. My old man was a butcher." He laughed bizarrely — a high-pitched chortle through clenched teeth. "Shit, I think I'd rather you did it."

"You're gonna have to get up. Can't sit here all day. I think Diamondback is just south of here — a couple miles is all. I'm gonna go out and fetch our horses, and then I'll come back and help you out to 'em. All right?"

Mason sniffed and nodded, his jaw hinges dimply.

"Stuff your neckerchief in the hole there so you don't bleed out before I get back."

Mason reached up with his right hand to untie his dirty red neckerchief. He wadded the cloth in his fist and pressed it gingerly against the wound.

"Harder."

Mason pressed harder, making a face.

"Harder than that." Spurr reached over and pressed the cloth down hard.

Mason stiffened his legs, arched his back, and screamed.

"Like that!"

Spurr turned to fetch their horses.

"Spurr," Mason shouted in a weird, pain-wracked voice that echoed around the corridor. "I hate your cussed old guts!"

Spurr snorted.

He had the devil's own time running down Cochise and Mason's strawberry whose name he didn't know. If it even had a name; Mason didn't seem the type of man who named his horse. Most men weren't. Horses died too damn easily, so it was best to not get too attached.

After wandering half blind in the storm for twenty minutes, Spurr found one of the four bushwhackers' mounts not far from the riverbed. It stood with its tail to the wind, and seemed so frightened by the storm that it didn't lurch away when Spurr approached nor when he grabbed its ground-tied reins and mounted it.

He used the horse to run down his roan, which he found nearly a mile up the riverbed, having doubtless been hazed there by the harassing wind. Cochise was sheltering himself in a little alcove in the high, stony ridges. He nickered with seeming relief when he saw his rider materialize from the dust storm, the old lawman wearing his bandanna over his nose.

Spurr released the killer's claybank, and astride Cochise he found Mason's horse nearby, on the other side of the riverbed. The horse was so unnerved by the storm that he ran as Spurr approached, and the marshal had to throw a rope on him and dally him in.

He'd marked the spot where he'd left Mason, with a handkerchief tied to a stick, but the stick had blown down, so Spurr overrode the spot and wasted another half hour finally locating the place once more. When he got back to the sheriff, he thought the man was dead; he was slumped forward, chin drooping to his chest.

Spurr called his name.

Mason lifted his head, blinking. "What?"

"Damn — you're alive. I thought my life was gonna get a whole lot easier."

"Sorry to disappoint you."

Mason doffed his hat and tried pushing off his left knee. He groaned and nearly fell sideways, but Spurr grabbed the sheriff's arm and, wrapping his other arm around his waist, hauled him to his feet. They staggered like two sentimental drunks down the craggy corridor and back out to the riverbed, where Spurr had tied both mounts to sage shrubs.

Spurr had the devil's own time again getting Mason mounted. He wasn't as strong as he used to be, and Mason was too weak and in too much pain to lift his leg into the stirrup. Finally, Mason stumbled over to a rock, which he managed to step onto, and then onto his saddle. Spurr turned away from the wind and heaved a sigh of relief.

"Now to find Diamondback," he said as he swung up onto Cochise's back.

"Shit," Mason grunted, pressing his spurs to his own mount's ribs. "What about the rest of de Cava's crew? They could be anywhere out here."

"Yeah, and the way our luck's holdin'," Spurr said, following the sheriff up the riverbank, "we're liable to ride right into 'em."

22

Cuno rode hunched in his saddle, his arm hanging down by his side, feeling like a twenty-pound slab of meat that was slow-roasting over a low fire.

Camilla rode ahead. He felt too much the fool for having gotten himself bunged up again to let her lead him, so he held Renegade's reins in his right fist and kept the horse just behind Camilla's horse's tail, which was blowing wildly in the incessant wind.

He felt both hot and cold. Cold sweat dribbled down his cheeks in short streams that were dried or blown away by the wind. He straightened himself in his saddle and tried to stay conscious, but when he felt Renegade slowing, he opened his eyes to find himself slumped nearly to the paint's buffeting mane that whipped his face like whang strings.

Ahead, Camilla reined her mount to a

stop. Beyond her, several riders materialized from the blowing sand, dusters or serapes whipping around them. Several of Mateo's riders' hats flopped down their backs by their chin thongs. Hatless, they were hard to recognize but Cuno could make out the lean, hard-chiseled, angular face of Frank Skinner riding beside Mateo. The gang leader put his horse up to his sister. They were in a crease between two sandstone scarps that tempered the wind but caused the dust to swirl like mini tornadoes.

Mateo said something in Spanish that Cuno could hardly hear above the wind, let alone understand. Camilla glanced at Cuno. The young freighter heard the word *serpiente.* Mateo rode back to Cuno, who tried to straighten his back again but felt as though his spine had turned to jelly. He winced, tried to keep his eyes open, but the effort caused him to vomit more bile.

Mateo's horse started at the violent upheaval. The gang leader shook his head and slid one of his big Colts from its holster.

"He's finished," the man said in English, for Cuno's benefit. He rocked the pistol's hammer back.

"No!" Camilla swung her horse around until its was angled toward the tail of Mateo's Arab. "Put it away, Brother!"

"You know the rules, *mi hermana.*"

"He isn't that bad. We're forting up soon, right? He'll be better tomorrow."

Mateo shook his head stubbornly. Cuno was too sick to care much if he lived or died, but he felt his own hand sliding toward the ivory-gripped Colt on his right thigh. It was on the opposite side of his horse from Mateo. He knew the gang's rules and accepted them, but the instinct for self-preservation was too strong for him to go down without a fight.

"He'll slow us down," Mateo said, swinging the long, silver-chased barrel toward Cuno's head. "He dies."

"I said no, *mi hermano!*" Camilla whipped her serape above the handle of her own .44, and slipped the pistol from its brown leather holster with surprising speed for a girl Cuno had once known as meek and deferring.

Aiming his revolver at Cuno's head, Mateo glared fiercely at his sister and cut loose with a string of Spanish Cuno couldn't keep up with. The only word he recognized was whore. Camilla parried the verbal onslaught with a fiercer one of her own that caused her brother to fall suddenly silent and just stare at her, eyes turning as hard as obsidian ore.

She'd insulted his manhood. It was obvious from the deep cherry color rising in Mateo's tan cheeks above his beard.

"Hold on," Frank Skinner said, putting his horse up to Camilla's. "Why not give him a chance? We're gonna need all the help we can get for pulling the next job, Mateo."

"Shut up, Skinner. This is between *mi hermana* and myself."

"No, it's not." Skinner smiled to offset his defiance. "If we're gonna make it to the border, we're gonna need guns and money. We're already short-handed after the dustup at the whorehouse, and we ain't seen Brouschard's group of late, neither. I say give the kid till tomorrow. If he's still pukin' his guts up at first light, I'll drill the hole in his head myself, save you from havin' to do it and gettin' any more on your sis's bad side than you already are."

"She is on *my* bad side!"

Cuno had his hand on his pistol's ivory grips. He'd unsnapped the keeper thong from over the hammer and was very slowly and inconspicuously sliding the revolver from its holster.

Camilla spat a retort at her brother, but Skinner cut her off with, "Come on, amigo. Why make your sister angry? We don't have much farther to ride today. Let's head on over to Diamondback, set up camp, and

285

wait for morning." He paused before adding with a slow blink: *"Por favor, el capitan."*

Cuno was bringing his gun up slowly, keeping it hidden behind his right hip. He had his thumb on the hammer and was slowly starting to rock it back.

Mateo glanced around at the other men. There were only a handful left besides himself and Skinner. From their scowls and the tense sets to their eyes, they weren't in any hurry to lose any more firepower, either.

Mateo looked at Cuno. Cuno met the man's gaze before flicking his eyes to the black maw of the man's silver-chased revolver. Chicken flesh rose on the back of Cuno's neck. He edged his own pistol a little higher and had the hammer half cocked when Mateo suddenly raised his own gun's barrel and depressed the hammer.

He cursed wickedly in Spanish, turning another frigid glare on his sister, then reined his black around and galloped southward through the gap between the escarpments and out of sight. The other men, all looking relieved, booted their own mounts after their fractious leader.

Camilla looked at Skinner. She didn't say anything. Cuno guessed she didn't need to.

Skinner pinched his hat brim to the senorita, then reined his horse around and headed after the others. Camilla turned her horse close to Cuno and reached over and grabbed his shirt collar.

She gritted her teeth angrily. "Are you going to make it? You make it, all right?"

"I'll make it," Cuno said, straightening his back and dropping his Colt back down in its holster.

She saw his right hand release the gun, then raised her dark eyes to his and smiled. Reining her horse around, she booted it on up the trail. Cuno nicked Renegade's flanks with his dull spurs, and the horse broke into a trot after the girl.

After another long, painful half hour ride, Cuno heard the windblown sand ticking against something nearby. He opened his eyes. To the right of the trail that he and Camilla were following was a sign that read DIAMONDBACK, NEW MEXICO TERR., POPULATION 156.

There was another, smaller sign below the main sign, both worn to a pewter-gray from weather and time, the few chips of remaining paint quickly being worn away by the current blast.

In faint letters, the bottom sign warned: HELL-RAISERS WILL NOT BE TOLERATED!

Ahead of Cuno, unseen in the storm, one of the gang members laughed.

Nearly an hour after he got the wounded Sheriff Mason on his horse, Spurr found the old stage trail that he, having traveled through this southern New Mexico country on several occasions over his years hunting tough nuts and hard cases, knew would eventually take him to the little town of Diamondback, just east of the Organ Range.

Surely there he'd find a doctor for Mason. Once he got the sheriff taken care of, he'd rendezvous with Captain Wilson from the cavalry outpost on Hackberry Creek, about ten miles south of town. Together, they'd ride down the de Cava devils before they gained the Mexican border, less than twenty miles away.

But only after the storm died, Spurr thought, wincing as another wind gust peppered his face with sand, weed bits, juniper berries, goat heads, packrat shit, and whatever else it picked up along the desert floor.

His saddle-brown cheeks were raw, and his horse balked at every blast. He glanced behind at Mason, hunkered low in his saddle, tipping his face downwind, his features taut with agony.

"You still with me, Sheriff?" Spurr yelled

as he put Cochise westward along the trail.

Mason yelled something in a pinched voice that the wind tore, rendering the words incoherent.

Spurr snorted and urged more speed out of Cochise. He glanced up but could see little except the red-brown waves of blowing grit set against a sky that appeared cloudless. A clear sky meant the wind could continue for a long time. He hoped it would eventually blow in a rainstorm, settle the dust, and clean the air.

He held Cochise at a spanking trot for only a short time, pulling Mason's own horse along behind him by its bridle reins. He didn't want to beat the sheriff half to death, cause him to lose more blood than he already had. Despite his sour feelings for the man, which for some reason had grown a little less sour over the many long days they'd ridden together, he didn't want to see him die.

He was a little too precious about himself, Mason was, but given enough experience, enough seasoning, enough humility, he'd make a good lawman one day.

Maybe even one as good as old Spurr himself . . .

Spurr snorted again at his own conceit. A hazard of the job, maybe. Or maybe the attitude you had to have to keep wearing a badge in the face of often insurmountable odds not unlike the ones, regarding the de Cava bunch, that he was facing now.

A sign took shape along the trail's right side, growing in size as Spurr approached. Mesquites and alders flanked it, hammered by the wind so that two branches fell as Spurr watched. He returned his slitted gaze to the sign and snorted at the lower one's warning against "hell-raisers," and rode on, glad to finally be reaching the town.

Corrals and stock pens pushed up along both sides of the trail. Buildings materialized out of the blowing dust. Spurr could hear the shrill squawks of shingle chains up and down the broad main street.

Keeping Cochise moving, he saw a large building on the right — three stories tall with a broad front porch. He made out the words ORGAN HOTEL painted across the second story, and his pulse quickened as he angled the big roan in that direction.

He pulled up suddenly as bulky shapes half clarified in the dust. They were horses milling in front of the hotel. Not just horses. Horses and men. The men were filing up the hotel's front porch steps, saddlebags slung over shoulders, rifles in their hands.

One was being helped up the steps by a

shorter figure in a serape. Spurr squinted his weary, sand-blasted eyes. The shorter figure owned female curves. Long hair blew in the wind.

Spurr stared at the hotel until the newcomers had all filed up the steps and gone into the saloon, leaving three men gathering up the reins of the horses and beginning to lead them on up the street. The whinnies of the storm-frightened beasts mingled with the bizarre howling of the wind and the raucous rattling of the shingle chains.

Spurr glanced back at Mason. The sheriff's eyes were closed, chin dipped to his chest, the wind smashing the crown of his Stetson nearly flat against his skull.

Spurr reached down and shucked his brass-framed Winchester from his saddle boot. He racked a round into the breech, lowered the hammer to half cock, then set the rifle across his saddlebows. He looked around, then neck-reined Cochise off to the left and into a broad gap between a corral and a barrack-like mercantile with a broad front loading dock. Mason's horse balked at the sudden pull, then trotted along behind the roan, Mason half asleep but automatically clinging to his saddle horn.

Spurr swung the horses around behind the buildings lining the main street, wanting to stay out of view from the hotel, and reined up when he saw a beefy man in an apron splitting wood between a small building on the right and a privy on the left.

He asked the man where he could find a sawbones, and the man said, his black hair around his bald pate blowing wildly, "Little white house at the other end of town. White picket fence. You can't miss it." He shuttled his gaze from Spurr to Mason and then sunk his maul into a pine log, cleaving it cleanly in two. "Nicest place you'll find in this hellhole."

"Hellhole?" Spurr said. "Last time I was in Diamondback, it was growin' from all the gold camps in the Organs."

"Not no more it ain't," the man said, hefting the ash-handled splitting maul in his hands. "The gold's gone, and the pilgrims done pulled their picket pins for the San Juans and the Sawatch Range. We're holdin' on by a thread here, amigo. When the stage switches its run, that'll be all she wrote."

He glanced again at Mason. Spurr knew the man was curious about what had happened to the sheriff, but he'd lived out here too long to ask fool questions of strangers. Especially a couple of raggedy-heeled, unshaven lawdogs — one of whom had likely been shot — fresh from the high and rocky. He merely shook his head and sunk the head of his maul into another pine log.

Spurr rode on along behind the buildings of the main street until he came to the end of town and rode up to the little white house sitting neatly under cottonwoods and alders, a little buggy shed behind it, beside a privy with a half-moon carved in the door. The door was loosely latched and the wind was slamming it back and forth in its frame.

Spurr dismounted, ground-reined both horses, and went over to tug on Mason's shoulder. "Come on, Sheriff," he yelled above the wind.

Mason pulled away and groaned.

Spurr tugged on the man's shirt once more. Mason jerked his head up, blinking and looking around. "Where . . . ?"

"We're in Diamondback. The sawbones is in yonder. Looks like he's done right well for himself, too, so maybe he's worth his salt."

"Probably some cranky old drunk who only knows how to use a bone saw." Mason let Spurr help him down from his saddle.

Spurr supported the man with one of the sheriff's arms around his neck as they pushed through the well-tended gate in the picket fence. They were halfway up the narrow cobblestoned walk when the front door opened, and a woman in a plain blue and white muslin dress walked out onto the gallery, pulling a white shawl around her shoulders. Spurr could see right away that the woman was about as well set up as the old marshal had ever seen — full-busted, with nice hips, long legs, and red-blond hair piled richly.

"The doctor in?" Spurr called.

"I guess you could say that," the woman responded, stepping out and holding the screen door wide with both hands. The wind threatened to tear it from her grip.

Spurr led the heavy-footed, knock-kneed Mason up the three porch steps and on into the house that smelled of a meal cooking — a smell so rich and inviting that it almost drove Spurr to his knees. It made him feel lonesome, too, as most such smells tended to do to a man who so seldom enjoyed such domestic delights.

"What happened?" the woman said as she stepped into the foyer behind the two lawmen.

"Got a bullet in his side."

The woman latched the screen door, closed the inside door, and gestured down the hall beyond the short foyer, extending into the heavy shadows beneath a stairs that presumably rose toward a second story.

"Straight ahead. That door there's the office."

She hurried around both men, and again Spurr caught a glimpse of her comely features — clearly defined jaws above a patrician neck, skin tanned a little darker than ripe peaches, complimenting her honey hair and indicating she didn't hide from the sun.

Her eyes were brown and alight with a warm intelligence. Fine lines at their corners bespoke a woman in her thirties, maybe even late thirties — relatively easy years, at least physically, for she appeared straight and strong. The brown eyes also showed concern as she took a quick glimpse at Mason, then pushed through a varnished oak door beneath the stairs.

Spurr helped the sheriff into the office. It was a lavishly appointed room, though lit by only two tall, curtained windows, with a rolltop desk, leather divan, and several shelves and glass and metal cabinets. It smelled of camphor, carbolic acid, and leather. Maybe a tinge or two of aromatic pipe tobacco though a pipe hadn't been smoked here lately. The walls were papered light green with yellow corn patterns.

Two doors opened off the main office, and Spurr and Mason followed the woman into the room beyond the desk. There was a leather-upholstered examination table in the middle of the room, and Spurr helped Mason onto the table and then to lie back on it. Blood oozed out from the wound against which Mason was still pressing the bloody bandanna.

The woman glanced at the wound, shook her head, and clucked. "Why do you men do such things to each other?" She turned those large, soulful brown eyes on Spurr, and they sparked with urgency. "Out!" she commanded. "Fetch my neighbor, Alvina Winters. The little blue house to the east."

Spurr stared at her, clumsily doffed his hat, and held it over his chest. "No offense, ma'am . . . but shouldn't we get the doctor in here?"

"I am the doctor, Mister . . ."

"Call me Spurr."

She looked him over with vague appraising. "Spurr," she said, her eyes flicking to his badge, which didn't seem to impress her.

Spurr looked her over in kind. "You're . . . the sawbones here in Diamondback?"

"That's right . . ." She hesitated, as though the single syllable word were too much for her delicate lips. "Spurr. Dickinson is my name. June Dickinson."

She planted a fist on her hip and gave the

dusty, sweaty, unshaven frontiersman a slightly challenging look. "I took over the doctoring duties in Diamondback after my husband was killed by Apaches. Now, will you fetch Mrs. Winters for me, please, Spurr? Before your friend here bleeds dry on my table?"

Spurr clamped his hat on his head and hurried out.

23

Spurr fetched the crow-like little woman, Mrs. Winters, from her little blue house next door to June Dickinson's, split an armload of wood with which to stoke the Dickinson stove, and hauled water from the well. When he figured he was no longer needed, the women having retreated to the room in which Mason was parked and closed the door, Spurr went out and gathered up the reins of his and the sheriff's horses.

He led the mounts up to the main street, which a wooden sign proclaimed as First Street, and looked it up and down. Through the blowing dust, there didn't appear much here anymore. Many of the wooden or adobe-brick buildings had been boarded up. There was a church, a post office, a stone jailhouse, a blacksmith shop, and a few stores, including a furniture store and a drugstore, even a haberdashery. There was also a stage relay station — a large, low box of a place with a large corral and stable and a roof of red scoria. The establishments doing the best business, judging by the horses standing hang-headed at hitchracks, were the town's three or four saloons. Spurr passed all but one of the saloons as he headed east, toward the hotel, looking for a livery barn.

He found the Saguaro Livery and Feed Barn beside the Ace of Hearts Saloon, and went in to make arrangements with the middle-aged black hostler for his and Mason's horses to be curried, stabled in separate stalls, and fed. He looked around at the other horses munching oats from wooden buckets.

There were half a dozen or so. They all looked a little wild-eyed and sweaty. Recently ridden hard. The black man, who'd said his name was Earl Hedges, was rubbing down a tall skewbald paint as Spurr shouldered his rifle and looked around the barn's dusty shadows rife with the smell of oats, straw, and hot horses.

"These mounts come over from the hotel?" he asked the hostler.

"I believe that's where they come from, yes, suh," Hedges said with a bored air as he rubbed down the paint, not looking at Spurr.

"You know who their riders are?"

"No, suh, I do not." From his tone, Hedges didn't care to know. If he had known, he wouldn't have said. Spurr decided he didn't need to ask the man to not mention that he'd inquired.

Spurr went back out into the wind, slid the heavy door closed behind him, and turned to look east along the street in which dust danced and tumbleweeds bounded out from breaks between the northern buildings to pile up with hundreds of others against the forlorn-looking establishments on the street's south side.

Were the men he'd seen through the dust the de Cava gang? If so, Spurr might have run into a bit of good luck . . . if Captain Wilson's soldiers arrived to lend him a hand, that was. And if the gang didn't learn that the lawman dogging their trail was here in town before he wanted them to know . . .

Having to face them alone would be suicide.

Curiosity buzzing like blackflies around his ears, Spurr tramped eastward up the street, staying to the boardwalks beneath the awnings, swerving now and then to avoid the wooden shingles dancing wildly on their squawky chains. He passed a barbershop and a boarded-up saloon, a couple of rickety parlor houses, and stopped suddenly when a figure moved toward him on his right, descending the steps of the mercantile's broad loading dock.

The figure was slender and dark and holding a rifle under his right arm. Her right arm. Dark hair blew about her shoulders. She had her straw sombrero tipped low against the wind while cradling a small burlap bag in her left arm, against her side. She didn't see Spurr until she'd placed a boot on the street and begun to turn.

Spurr had stopped near the base of the steps. The girl stopped now with a start. The sombrero's broad brim tipped back, and two coffee-brown eyes stared out at him from a fine, Indian-dark face with pursed but pleasant lips and smooth, tapering cheekbones coated in tan dust.

She had a pistol on her hip — not a dainty thing, either. Her right gloved hand closed over the receiver of the Winchester, ready to bring it up.

Spurr locked curious gazes with the girl. His vest blew out away from the badge pinned to his shirt. Her eyes flicked to it before sliding back to his face, the skin above the bridge of her nose crinkling slightly and the eyes narrowing a bit.

Spurr kept his own rifle down as he said

cautiously, "Afternoon."

The girl stared at him.

Spurr glanced at the hotel on the street's left side, then looked at the girl once more, canting his head to one side. "From around here?"

The girl studied him for a time, then said, "No." A pregnant pause, a slight arch of her right brow. "You?"

Spurr shook his head. He looked at the burlap pouch cradled against her side. She looked at it then, too, then again at the badge on Spurr's chest.

Her gaze lingered there for a time, and then she swung her attention to the hotel. A thin strand of dark hair fluttered against her cheek, beneath her right eye.

She swung her body away from Spurr while keeping her cautious, thoughtful eyes on him for two more beats. Hefting the pouch slightly, she dropped down off the boardwalk and strode across the street toward the hotel. She glanced back at him once, turned completely around once as well, as she continued to the hotel.

Tumbleweeds bounded around her. The faint trills of her spurs faded beneath the wind.

Spurr watched her climb the hotel's porch steps, then disappear inside, the door closing soundlessly behind her.

Spurr gave a dry snort, brushed a gloved fist across his nose, then turned away and headed back toward the Dickinson place.

Camilla pushed through the hotel's heavy outside door and into the saloon hall, where Mateo and his men had gathered. The gang was now only half as large as that which had overtaken the Arkansas prison, and they all looked wild-eyed and haggard from the long, harrowing ride.

The only customers in the place, they sat at several tables left of the bar, not talking or playing cards but only smoking while hunched over their beer glasses and whiskey or tequila shots.

There were three Yankees and four Mexicans aside from Mateo. The Yankees, including Frank Skinner, sat at a table separate from the Mexicans.

A Yankee bartender stood with his back to the room, stirring soup in a big pot behind the long oak bar. He'd glanced around when Camilla had entered, but now he kept his eye on the steaming pot.

The wind howled. It sounded like wolves circling. Dust rattled the cracked panes of the windows that lent the saloon's shadows a wan, gray light.

Mateo looked at his sister as he blew out a long plume of cigarillo smoke and grunted, "Any sign of Brouschard?"

The others looked at her expectantly, hopefully awaiting her answer.

Camilla shook her head. She remembered the old lawman she'd seen outside, with a face like the eroded desert floor itself.

A Mexican named Calderon turned to the gang leader and said in Spanish, "We should have waited for him, maybe, huh?"

"What?" Mateo threw back a half a shot of tequila and refilled his glass from the clear bottle with a white label on the table. "You think he's lost?"

Mariano Azuelo squashed a spider on the table with the heel of his hand and said, "They could be. It's blowing worse now, I think."

"Brouschard wouldn't get lost. He never got lost in Mexico, and we had worse storms in the desert." Mateo shook his head and stared at the big window flanking Camilla. "He's dead. All four are dead. Forget them."

Frank Skinner was leaning back in his chair, ankles crossed casually in front of him, one hand holding his whiskey glass. He was staring inquiringly at Camilla, and now he jerked his head toward the ceiling. "The kid say what happened? He must have

304

been the last one to see Brouschard and the others."

These men were nervous about being so short-handed, Camilla knew. Nervous because of the job they had planned here in Diamondback. Good. Maybe they would forget the job, and they could all head back to Mexico when the wind lifted.

There'd been too much trouble here in the States. She didn't like it here anymore. Once, it had seemed her sanctuary from the revolution-torn provinces south of the border. Here, she would find wealth and happiness. Now, she felt as though her heart lay back in Sonora. A little mountain village far south, perhaps.

She'd wanted for her and Cuno to leave Mateo, because she was frightened of Mateo's influence on the young freighter she'd once known as a good, strong young man. A young man of integrity. But now she and Cuno must get back to Mexico. The lawman was after them, and there were probably others. Many others.

She wished she'd never gone back to summon her brother northward to help her free Cuno from the prison. She wished that she'd stayed in Mexico but remained far, far away from Mateo. He was her *hermano* in name only. Now, she wanted only to be rid of him, and she would be once they were back in Mexico.

Camilla shook her head as she walked forward, heading for the staircase at the back of the hall.

"Hey." Mateo glared at her. "Skinner's right — the kid would have seen Brouschard last. He must have said something to his senorita?"

He smiled insultingly and let his gaze flick to his sister's bosom.

Camilla felt anger flame in her chest. "He said nothing. What does it matter, anyway? Even with Brouschard, you've lost half your men, Mateo. It is time to go home!"

"Oh, so you have your gringo stallion!" Mateo said. "Now it is time to go home! Why so hasty, *mi hermana?* I told you — I've got some business up here. I didn't ride this far only to save your gringo boyfriend, you know."

"You took revenge on Warden Castle," Camilla said. "Let that be enough. When the wind dies, let's go back to Mejico!"

"I told you!" Mateo pounded the table and stared fiercely at his sister. "One more job! I will not go back to Mejico empty-handed."

"*Si, si,*" said a desperado named Nervo. He sat alone at a nearby table. The only

306

whore in the place was on his right knee —
a chubby, Indian-dark girl in fake pearls and
a thin black dress. "We are low on money,
and American money will take us far in
Mexico."

Camilla saw a couple of the men look
toward the bartender. The man must have
heard what Nervo had said, but he did not
react. He only kept his back to the room as
he slowly, tensely stirred the steaming pot.
Neither Mateo nor his men seemed to care
whether the apron heard or not.

"If we ever get back to Mexico!" Camilla
hefted the burlap bag of liniments and other
concoctions, crossed the room, and
mounted the stairs.

She, Cuno, and the others in the gang had
all rented rooms on the hotel's second story.
The room she shared with Cuno was the
second one on the right. The door was
unlocked.

Inside, she was surprised to find Cuno sitting on the edge of the bed, looking out the
window. He was naked. She'd swabbed his
feverish body with cold water before she'd
left to see what she could find to doctor a
snake bite.

The room was dusky, so she could see
only the silhouette of his thick, sunburned
neck, his broad back, and heavy, sloping

shoulders. His hair was rumpled. From this angle he looked at once boyish and brawny — quite enticing, in fact.

"You're sitting up," she said, moving into the room.

He glanced over his shoulder at her then lifted the forearm that the snake had bit. It was swollen almost twice the size of the other one. "I think I'm better."

"Really?" She leaned her rifle against the room's sole dresser, and, carrying the burlap pouch, walked around to his side of the bed. "So soon?"

Cuno nodded as he stared out the window. "I don't think I got a full dose of poison. If I did, I don't think I could have even gotten into town." He lifted his hand and looked at the swollen forearm again; a large, purple lump sporting the two puncture wounds had risen like a large stone pushing up from beneath the skin. "Oh, I still feel like shit. But I think the worst has passed. That cold water got my fever broke, I think."

He looked at the bag, which she'd set on the bed as she dropped to her knees beside him. "I hope you didn't spend too much on that. I owe you enough the way it is."

"Don't be foolish. You are my gringo stallion" — she slid her hand over his thigh —

"and a good senorita takes care of her stallion."

She smiled at him, but he'd turned his head to scowl out the window. "Gotta get some dinero. A man who can't take care of himself . . . who has to be taken care of by his girl . . . ain't much of a man." He shook his head and pursed his lips.

"Don't speak about that." Camilla removed a tin from the bag. All that the mercantile had had on hand for snakebites was paregoric, some powders from crushed roots for tea, and potatoes. The proprietor's wife was part Pawnee, and she'd said that potato peels would draw the poison from the wound. Red elm worked especially well, but Camilla would find no red elm anywhere around Diamondback. The potato peels and the paregoric would have to suffice. And time for the poison to work its way out of Cuno's body.

Camilla set the tin on the bed, opened it, then reached up to clamp her hand across Cuno's forehead. It was still clammy but not as hot as before. Maybe he was right, and he had indeed gotten only a small dose of the poison. Now that the initial shock was passing, maybe he would be well again soon.

"You are better." She dipped two fingers

309

into the liniment and smeared the greasy concoction gently on his forearm. The sweet smell of the opium in the salve filled the room. "I am glad. We will be able to head to Mexico all the sooner."

Cuno glanced at her. "When?"

"Whenever . . ." She looked down as she worked the liniment into his arm. "Whenever Mateo pulls this next job he insists on pulling before he'll leave."

Cuno sounded excited. "Really? He has a job planned here?" He got up, pulling his arm away from Camilla, and looked westward along the dust and sand-blasted street. "I haven't seen a bank . . ."

"Oh," Camilla said, trying to put some levity into her voice though she didn't feel at all cheerful, "you want to be a bank robber now . . ."

Cuno hiked a shoulder. "Why not?"

She stared at his profile as he stared out the window, sort of cradling his arm against his side. A rock fell in her stomach as she took in the hard lines of his face, the cold light in his eyes.

Somewhere between here and the prison, he'd changed. The change had likely started inside the prison, but now it seemed nearly complete.

The young man she'd fallen in love with

— the young boy-man whose inner warmth and easy kindness had been so evident in his eyes, in the subtle, boyish charm that put a jaunty swagger in his thick, hard, muscular body — was gone.

Now his handsome face and brawny physique seemed carved from stone. The Cuno Massey who had saved her and Michelle Trent and the Lassiter children from the Utes, who had exchanged his own life for theirs, had vanished. He'd been replaced by one of Mateo's desperadoes — one who would no sooner give his own life to save others than Mateo or Frank Skinner themselves would.

Loneliness howled inside Camilla. Her life had been a violent one, raised by peasants embroiled in *revolucion.* She'd grown up fast; she'd learned how to ride and shoot by the time she was twelve and killed a man — a vaquero who'd tried to rape her and her mother — by the time she was thirteen. All the boys and men around her were, understandably, fierce warriors. Camilla herself was a warrior. But a warrior with a soft heart and a desperate yearning for peace and happiness.

For so long she'd looked for a good, kind man to marry and to raise children with. To work side by side with in a field of watermelons or corn, or herding cattle or horses with. She'd looked for such qualities in nearly every man she'd met. A man she could grow old peacefully with. How ironic that her very act of saving the one man she'd finally found — or thought she'd found — had changed him.

Camilla jerked slightly with a start. Cuno's eyes, his strange, dark eyes, were on hers. She was vaguely shocked to see how much a person's physical features could change in so short a time, but she doubted that she'd recognize him now if she saw him on a crowded street.

"You all right?"

"*Si.*"

"Don't worry." He set a hand against her face, and she could feel the pressure of his fingers against the underside of her jaw. "I haven't robbed a bank before, but I'll hold my own in there. I'll pay you back for the duds and the gear, and we'll make a fresh start in Mexico."

"Fresh start?"

"Why not?"

Hope rose in her. "I thought perhaps we'd buy a horse ranch. I know an old man who traps wild horses. He said he would teach me . . ."

Cuno dropped his hand from her cheek

and returned his distracted gaze to the window. "I don't know — I reckon we'll see. Hard for a wanted man to settle in one place." He glanced at her again, trying to encourage her with his stranger's gaze. "But we'll see, Camilla. All right?"

Again, the stone dropped in her belly. She nodded dully.

He sat back on the bed, lifting his bare legs and tugging on her arm. "Come on. Lay here with me a bit."

She lay down beside him, ran a hand across his thick chest and his heavy, sloping shoulder. She closed her eyes and kissed his arm, pressed her hand against his flat belly, feeling desire rise in her, needing him to hold her close to him in his big gentle arms and take her fears away.

"Cuno . . ." she whispered.

He said nothing. His chest rose and fell heavily. She looked up at his face. His eyes were closed. A soft snore drifted up from his chest. Feeling a cold tear trickle down her cheek, she pushed up slightly and gently touched her lips to his.

She rolled away from him and, curled on her side, wondered for a time why she had not told Mateo or even Cuno about the old lawman she'd seen on the windy street.

Finally, she closed her eyes, emptied her mind, and willed herself asleep.

24

His mind heavy, his old heart quarrelsome, Spurr walked westward along First Street. There was no one about except for a few dogs braving the wind to sniff around the trash heaps between the buildings. He angled across the street, bent forward against the grit-laced gale, and stepped onto the weather-silvered boardwalk fronting the stone jailhouse.

He'd thought he might be able to find a lawman here, but the place looked abandoned, weeds growing up between the gray boards at his moccasin-clad feet and between those of the three steps fronting the stout, timbered door. There was a padlock on the door latch. The windows were not shuttered, but they betrayed a cave-like darkness inside.

To satisfy his curiosity, he pounded on the heavy door twice with his rifle butt, then looked in the window left of the door.

Abandoned all right. There were three cells comprised of banded steel cages at the back of the place. There were cots in only two of the cells. Aside from a few curled, yellowed wanted posters on one wall, where a desk had apparently once sat, the place was empty of all furnishings.

Spurr wasn't surprised. He hadn't figured on finding a lawman here in Diamondback. Most towns this far off the beaten track couldn't afford lawmen. They usually relied on the irregular services of a county sheriff or a sheriff's deputy from the county seat. If the county in which Diamondback lay even had a seat. The courthouse might only be a saloon somewhere, the law enforcement being handled by remote cavalry outposts or by passing deputy U.S. marshals like Spurr himself.

No, Spurr hadn't figured on finding any help here, but now that it indeed appeared that Diamondback was without a marshal or even a constable, he felt a twinge of apprehension.

He stepped down off the boardwalk and into the street, casting his squint-eyed gaze eastward toward the Diamondback Hotel. He'd be alone against the gang — if the de Cava bunch was indeed who the newcomers were. He could no longer rely on the backing of Sheriff Mason. The only help he was likely to get was from Captain Wilson and his troopers at the outpost, but he'd seen no sign as yet of the captain, who might have gotten held up in any number of ways. Spurr knew from past experience that army outposts were not only often small and remote but unreliable. He'd known many that had been wiped out by the desertions of their garrisons.

Wilson might be waiting for a summons from Spurr. The old marshal knew that Diamondback was equipped with a telegraph, though he'd not yet seen any lines. He'd find the office soon, after he'd checked on Mason, and see about sending a telegram to Wilson. He'd have the man make his way to Diamondback pronto with as many troopers as he had in his arsenal.

Back in his prime, he might have taken on seven or eight men alone. He wasn't that stupid anymore. Nor capable, he mused dryly, nibbling his mustache as he swung away from the hotel and tramped eastward up First Street, resting his old Winchester on his sagging shoulder and keeping his gloved index finger curled through the triggerguard.

The Dickinson house came into view behind wavering curtains of tan dust above which he could see the washed-out blue of the sky.

Hard to tell what time it was, but it was likely getting on in the afternoon. Night soon. Even if the wind lightened, the de Cava bunch would stay here in Diamondback until tomorrow morning. No point riding after dark, though that they were making hard for the border was obvious. If they headed out before help arrived for Spurr, the old lawman would continue to dog their trail and wait for help. Maybe he'd even figure a way to take them down one by one or two by two, until he had the entire gang six feet under.

Noting a chill adding to the wind's bite, Spurr walked up to the house's front door and knocked twice. Since Mrs. Dickinson and the birdlike Mrs. Winters were likely still with Mason, he went ahead and stepped inside.

"Ah, there you are, Mr. Spurr." Mrs. Dickinson stood in the open doorway just beyond the foyer, on the left side of the short hall. There was a range and an eating table behind her, and a teakettle was starting to whistle.

Spurr moved inside and closed the door. "Howdy, ma'am." Quickly, awkwardly — the neat, little house made him feel big and

318

unwieldy, for some reason — he doffed his hat and looked at the woman regarding him expectantly, long-fingered hands intertwined in front of her slender waist, beneath the high, proud bosom. "I figured you'd be with Mason."

"He's fine. Resting now due to the chloroform."

"You work fast."

"I have a lot of experience as of a couple years ago. When there were more miners and cowpunchers around, we had a booming business, my husband and me." She hiked a shoulder. "Besides, the bullet wasn't deep. It must have been a ricochet, and when it struck the sheriff, it bounced off the side of a rib. Came right out."

"What's the prognosis?"

"Oh, I imagine he'll be up and around by tomorrow. I don't recommend that he stray too far from bed, though, for several days. A week would be best." She hooked a thumb to indicate behind her, where the steam kettle was whistling in earnest. "Would you care for some tea, Mr. Spurr?"

She did not wait for his response but swung around and strode into the kitchen, her muslin skirt swishing about her long legs. Spurr couldn't help taking a quick appraisal of her full, round ass, then found himself blushing when she glanced at him sidelong as she removed the teapot from the stove lid. She kept one eye on him and arched her brow with apparent, albeit subtle, reproof.

Shit, she'd caught him. You'd think he'd learn . . .

"No, ma'am. No, thank you," he said, feeling the warmth in his sand-blasted cheeks as he let his gaze crawl like a truckling dog across the polished hardwood floor. "I'd best look into a hotel room somewheres . . ."

"No need for that, Mr. Spurr."

He looked up at her as she poured steaming water into a delicate china teapot adorned with painted daffodils. "Say again, ma'am?"

"You can bed down here, with your friend. At least, I assume you're friends though under the chloroform Sheriff Mason cursed your name several times." Mrs. Dickinson gave him that penetrating sidelong glance once more, and her lips spread a bemused half smile as she sprinkled dried tea leaves from a tin canister into the teapot.

Spurr brushed a gloved hand across his nose. "He did, did he?"

"Come on in and sit down. There's only one hotel in Diamondback, and it's way on the other side of town."

Spurr felt like a bull in a china shop, but he couldn't very well head across town and try to secure a room in the same hotel as the de Cava gang — if they were the de Cava gang, which they likely were. But he could bed down in a livery barn, which was what he'd do when he'd had a rest. His feet were sore from all the walking he'd just done, and the wind was hard on a man with a weak pumper.

"I reckon I'd have a sip of tea," he allowed, lowering his rifle and looking around for a place to put it. The house was so neat and orderly and crisply papered and painted, he was worried about damaging something, even of scuffing the floor with his hide-bottomed moccasins.

"If you'd prefer coffee, it wouldn't take long . . ."

He hesitated, finally leaning his rifle in a corner near the front door, holding both hands out in case it slid down the wall, scratching the mauve wallpaper with gold vases of cattails imprinted on it. "No, no — tea's fine."

He strode into the kitchen, making sure not to brush his clothes on the walls or door casing.

She'd set the teapot on the table covered by a white tablecloth embroidered with red roses and green leaves. Now she went to an open, white cupboard above a dry sink, and pulled down two china cups and saucers that matched the teapot.

"What brings you to Diamondback, Mr. Spurr?" She looked at him as she carried the cups and saucers to the table and dropped her eyes to the badge on his chest, partly concealed by his vest. "Or is it . . . Marshal Spurr?"

"Just Spurr's fine. Thank you, ma'am." He closed his hand over a chair back but his moccasins seemed glued to the floor. He was staring at the delicate china, hoping against hope he wouldn't break it. Maybe he should skip the tea, head on over to the livery barn.

"I reckon law business brought me and the sheriff to your fair town."

"Sit down, sit down." She was pouring tea into one of the cups, holding the lid on with the third finger of her other hand. "Can I ask you what kind of business?"

"I'd rather not say at the moment."

He'd known the woman only a few minutes. He thought he could trust her not to spread the word that he was here, after the de Cava gang, but he hadn't nearly outlived his ticker by throwing caution to the wind. He slid the chair at one end of the table out carefully and sagged into it even more carefully.

"I would ask you where you telegraph office is, though, ma'am. I'd like to send a telegram to the soldiers out to Hackberry Creek."

"Just south of town, on the other side of the creek. Homer Constiner has a little shack out there that was supposed to be a train depot, when a spur line was considering running a track through Diamondback. Those plans, of course, went the way of the gold, the rain, and everything else out here."

Spurr removed his deerskin gloves, set them down beside his cup and saucer, hoping he wasn't littering the table with too much sand and dust, and wrapped his hand, or as much of it as possible, around the teacup. He lifted it slowly to his lips.

He couldn't remember if he'd ever drunk from any vessel as small and delicate as this. When in hell would he have had the opportunity? He didn't care for it. In fact, as he lifted the steaming brew to his lips, he felt himself growing irritated that anyone would fashion a cup so small and obviously fragile.

Wasn't life, for chrissakes, difficult enough?

He tried to close his upper lip over the

rim of the cup but his mustache got in the way. He hadn't trimmed it in a month of Sundays so it had become a soup-strainer without his knowing.

"Christ," he grumbled, glancing over the cup at the woman sitting across from him.

She was watching him, a bemused twinkle in her large, brown eyes.

"Uh . . . sorry."

"I do apologize for the cup, Spurr."

"It's no problem." He applied a little more pressure to push the rim between his lips, and drew about a half-teaspoon of the tea into his mouth, let the sour-tasting brew roll back over his tongue, and swallowed. "Ooh," he said, smacking his lips. "That's right good."

"I'd be happy to make you a cup of coffee."

"No, it's good."

Spurr took another sip and set the cup back down in the saucer, wincing at the too-loud clink of china on china.

The woman was gazing at him obliquely over the rim of her own cup, which she held in both her fine hands, and he couldn't tell what she was thinking. To break the pause, he looked around the kitchen that appeared bright, clean, and happy despite the dull gray-tan light angling through the room's two windows that the wind rattled in their frames. "You live all alone here, eh? Do all the doctorin' by your lonesome?"

Mrs. Dickinson nodded as she swallowed a sip of her tea and set the cup down in its saucer. "The house isn't worth much here, I'm afraid. I'll hold on to it as long as I can. As long as there is some doctoring to do. I've had to cut my expenses since my husband died, of course, but I'm comfortable here. I do have some family in Ohio, but all those I was close to are now passed."

She'd said it very matter-of-factly, without a trace of self-pity. Spurr was cheered by the warmth in the woman's pretty eyes. She smoothed out a small wrinkle in the tablecloth with her right hand and gave him something close to a shy smile. "Do you have a woman, Spurr?"

"Me?" Spurr said. "Nah. No woman." He thought of Abilene, but he didn't consider her his. She belonged to no man, and that's how he liked it. That's probably how he would like it even after they both went to Mexico together, if they ever got that far. "Oh, I been married. Three times, in fact. It wasn't right for me, ma'am."

"How long have you been marshaling?"

"Longer than I care to remember. Soon done, though. After this here . . . well, after

I head back to Denver, I'm gonna turn this hunk of copper in to my boss, Chief Marshal Henry Brackett, collect my time, and head south with a gal I know. If'n she'll ride with me. I think she will, but . . ." He chuckled wryly. "Women are notional."

"Yes, we are."

"Well, maybe you aren't," he said, backing water.

"Oh, no — I am, too." She sipped her tea once more and favored him with a penetrating stare that fairly seared his own, windburned eyes. "And this is my current notion, marshal. Why don't you let me heat water so you can take a bath and get some of that trail dust and grime off of you. And then I'll make you supper, and you can spend the night right here, in my spare bedroom. It's all very neat and clean, and the mattress is stuffed with goose down. It's been slept in maybe a total of three times."

She let her voice trail off when she saw the curious cast to Spurr's own, lilac-blue gaze. Lowering her own eyes demurely, she ran her hand over the wrinkle in the tablecloth again, and said, "I don't mean to be forward, Marshal. I'll admit it gets lonely here. I do miss the ministrations of a strong man. The touch and the warmth of a strong man. But I am not a charlatan."

She lifted her eyes to his once more, and there was a boldness and sincerity there, as well as a haunting sort of mad lonesomeness, that was like a razor-edged knife poking the backside of Spurr's heart. He was buoyed, however, by her seeing him as strong.

"Well, I'll be damned," Spurr said in genuine disbelief, a boyish embarrassment touching his cheeks again with warm irons. "Ma'am, I ain't all that strong. Not anymore I ain't. But I sure never been so charmed, and I sure ain't up to refusin' a beautiful woman's offer of lodging." He arched a brow. "That said, I am a stranger to you, Mrs. Dickinson. Are you sure . . . ?"

"If a woman can't trust a man with a badge, who can she trust?"

Spurr stared at her fine-boned hands. On her right hand, she still wore a gold wedding band. He lifted his gaze to her full bosom, which heaved against her dress, pulling the material so taut that it puckered along the sides of her breasts, beneath her arms.

Spurr leaned back to reach into his pants pocket.

She stretched a waylaying hand on the table between them. "I certainly want no money from you . . . aside from what you owe me for doctoring your friend in there. I suspect from the coin I found in his pockets, he'll be paying for that himself."

She sat back in her chair, drawing a deep breath that lifted her bosom again. "Shall I get started on that bath?"

"No, ma'am." Spurr had taken another sip of his tea, which was beginning to taste better, and set the cup back down in its saucer with both hands. "I gotta go find the telegraph office, send a telegram to Hackberry Creek."

She was looking at him, faintly incredulous, skeptical.

Spurr smiled warmly and winked. "Then I'll be back for that bath and them vittles." He slid his chair back and rose, grabbing his hat off the table. "Don't look like the storm's gonna let up any time soon, an' I figure I can keep an eye on the town from here as well as anywhere."

"You don't think me brazen, inviting a strange man into my house?"

"Brazen? I find you nothing less than a saint, Mrs. Dickinson."

"I reckon you might as well call me June, Spurr."

"June," Spurr said with a smile. "I like that. See you in an hour or so, June."

He turned reluctantly away from the
woman, grabbed his rifle, and left.

25

As June had said it would be, the telegraph office sat on the far side of the creek from Diamondback, just east of a sprawling, dead cottonwood.

It was an unpainted shack of rough lumber and a shake roof, several of the shakes appearing to have been blown away by the wind. Several others fluttered like paper as Spurr approached, tramping across the crude pine bridge traversing the creekbed.

Spurr had figured the creek would be dry, but several inches of adobe-colored water swirled down it. He looked upstream, to the west, and beyond the flying grit he saw that a bank of charcoal clouds edged with cottony gray had settled over the Organ Range. Thunder rumbled and lightning flashed wanly.

Spurr stopped to consider the storm, which, judging by the direction of the wind, was moving toward Diamondback. The chill air was spiced with the smell of sage and brimstone. That deluge would likely be upon the town in an hour or so.

That would keep the de Cava bunch sitting tight. The problem was it would probably also keep Captain Wilson hunkered down at his Hackberry Creek outpost.

There was a cracking sound. Like a gunshot, ripped and torn and nearly drowned by the gale. Spurr jerked his head toward the telegraph office.

Realizing the shot had come from the little shack off both ends of which telegraph wires trailed away on tall pine poles, he dropped to one knee on the plankboard bridge. An especially heavy gust of wind blew up dust and sand in front of him, momentarily blotting the unpainted shack from his view.

He closed his eyes against the grit, and lowered his head, wincing and muttering curses.

When the gust relented, he looked at the shack again. There was only the shack and the blowing dust and tumbleweeds and the whipping telegraph wire. He saw no one around. Pushing up off his knee with a grunt, he broke into a shamble-footed stride, crouching and holding his Winchester up high across his chest. Weaving around boulders and rabbitbrush and sage clumps, he gained the building's west wall, pressed his shoulder against it. He looked ahead and behind him, making sure no one had gotten around him, then strode cautiously up to the shack's west front corner.

He took a second to listen for any unnatural sounds emanating from inside the shack or in front of it, then stepped out away from the corner, bringing his Winchester's barrel to bear on the unroofed stoop running along the south wall.

Nothing.

Only, now the telegraph wire was sagging from a post that stood about twenty feet off the shack's far side.

"Well, I'll be a shit-house rat."

Spurr stood gaping at the sagging cable that was buffeted by the chill wind. He looked around wildly, swinging his rifle's barrel around, as well. It was as though a ghost riding the teeth of the wind had cut the wire. For a moment, he wondered if indeed the cable had been cut by the wind. Then he walked over to it, pinned the end down with a moccasin, and inspected it.

A clean slice that had undoubtedly been made by a large wire cutter.

Spurr looked toward town, then jerked his rifle up once more. Three vague figures were striding away from him — dark shadows wavering amidst the veils of blowing sand and growing gradually smaller as they crossed another bridge, heading toward Diamondback. One was wearing a duster, which flapped wildly about his legs.

Flickering in and out of the sand curtains, the three figures were finally swallowed by the storm. Spurr lowered his rifle and looked down once more at the cut cable.

"You bastards," he said, running a gloved hand across his bearded cheek. "Now, why in the hell did you have to go and do that?"

That was all right, Spurr thought, hope rising in him. He'd spliced cut telegraph wire before. Indians were forever cutting telegraph wire. If he could climb that pine post, which might not be so easy now in his later years, he could repair the wire and get the telegraph operational again.

If he could climb that damn post . . .

He remembered the gun crack. Raising the Winchester once more, he strode on back to the door of the telegraph shack.

The door was open, swinging back and forth in the wind. Sand and bits of tumbleweeds lay strewn across the crude wood puncheons just beyond the doorjam. A man lay there, as well. An older gent in a wash-yellowed dress shirt, the sleeves rolled up his freckled arms, and brown wool broadcloth trousers. He wore armbands and a green eyeshade. He had a pale, craggy face with a pencil-thin mustache and a chin like the mouth of a whiskey bottle.

He also wore a bloody hole in the middle of his chest. Blood was pooling on the floor around him. His sightless, wide-open eyes stared at the low ceiling. His teeth were gritted, his jaws clenched as though against the death that was consuming him.

Had comsumed him. He lay perfectly still.

A cat meowed from somewhere back in the room's shadows. It sounded loud in the quiet building despite the wind's howling outside, and Spurr jerked his head and rifle up, his heart thudding irregularly.

"Shit, pussy. Don't do that to ole Spurr."

He moved forward and stepped away from the door, habitually wary, so that the outside light wouldn't silhouette him. He couldn't see the cat until he'd moved a ways into the shed, toward a cage and wicket that stood on the shack's opposite side.

The liver-colored cat sat atop the narrow counter running along the front of the cage, hunkered down and curling its tail anxiously, its yellow eyes glowing. It was a fat cat, well fed. It had probably belonged to poor, dead Constiner, who'd been killed most likely only because he'd been Diamondback's telegrapher and he'd been in the wrong place at the wrong time. The killers had wanted to cut the telegraph wires, and they hadn't wanted anyone in town knowing about it.

Why?

Speculation careened haplessly across Spurr's brain as he looked around the small shack outfitted with a charcoal brazier and a rocking chair in a corner, a knitted afghan draped over the back of the chair. There was a half-eaten sandwich, glass of milk, and small whiskey flask on a table beside the chair, with a saucer of milk on the floor beneath the table.

The telegrapher's cage was outfitted with a small desk and a small filing cabinet. The telegraph key sat on a small, tin table against a dirty sashed window in the outside wall.

A yellow-covered codebook sat beside the key, which had been smashed all to hell by the outlaws so that it was hardly recognizable. Springs and weights from the badly smashed instrument were spread out across the codebook and on the floor all around the cage.

So much for sending a telegraph. He could possibly repair the cable, but the key was finished. And he doubted Diamondback had any spare ones lying around.

The cat meowed again. Spur turned to it. It jumped off the counter, hitting the floor with a soft thud, then hurried over to the dead man on the floor and, curling its tail, sniffed the man's forehead. It sniffed the blood, as well, then gave a baleful yowl and padded back over to the counter, pressing its side against it and curling its tail up high above its head.

"Poor puss," Spurr said. "You got anywhere else to go?"

Thunder rumbled in the distance, louder than before. The wind seemed to be lightening slightly, judging by the diminished creaking in the whipsawed timbers of the telegrapher's shack.

The cat sat, curled its tail to one side, looked at the dead Constiner, and gave its head a quick shake of revulsion and fear.

"You'll get by," Spurr said. "Someone from town's likely to take you in. If not, hell, I'm sure there's plenty of rats around here. Rats love a town."

He stepped around Constiner and moved to the door. He went out and then reached back inside for the door handle. Glancing at the cat again, he frowned. The cat was watching him. It looked desperate, frightened, worried.

All alone in the cold, cold world.

"Christ," Spurr grumbled. He had far more worse things to worry about than a damn orphaned cat. Just the same, he moved around the dead man again and dropped to a knee beside the liver-colored puss. "If I pick you up, you won't scratch me, will you?"

Spurr removed his right glove and stuck his hand out toward the cat's nose, giving the frightened little beast a whiff. Like most animals, cats could tell if they'd trust someone by smelling them. Spurr hoped the cat wouldn't hold his gamey trail sweat and horse lather fetor against him.

The cat was too preoccupied with the dead man on the floor to pay much attention to Spurr's proffered hand, however. So Spurr reached around the cat carefully, slowly, and when he had his arm crooked around the beast, he picked it up and nestled it against his side.

"There, there, now, pussy-puss," Spurr said. "How 'bout if I see about findin' you a home? I bet Mrs. Dickinson likes cats. Smart, purty women like cats, and she's about as purty an' smart as they come. If not, maybe Mrs. Winters, though she ain't half so purty . . ."

Sort of cradling the cat against his side

and gripping his rifle in his left hand, Spurr left the shack and the dead man inside, closing and latching the door, then retraced his steps back in the direction from which he'd come.

Rain started pelting him by the time he reached the bridge crossing the creek. Small, cold drops were hurled slantwise by the biting wind. The creek itself was far from a dry wash. The depth of the water had more than doubled since Spurr had first crossed, and small branches and bits of cactus were swirling down the tea-colored stream that caught and eddied around rocks and sage roots.

"Holy shit in the nun's privy, cat," Spurr said, quickening his pace, "we're in for a gully washer!"

By the time he reached the Dickinson house, the sky had turned murky and the rain was hammering in earnest, turning the roads of Diamondback into veritable creeks, with the silver raindrops drilling into clay-colored puddles like small-caliber rifle fire. The wind had indeed lightened some, but its former ferocity was matched by the thunder and lightning of the fast-approaching storm.

Thunderclaps sounded like near cannon fire, causing the earth to leap beneath

Spurr's soaked moccasins as he hurried up the nearly submerged cobbled walk to the Dickinson front gallery. Lightning lit the entire sky from horizon to horizon. During such flashes, Spurr could see low clouds being hurled every which way and not all that far above the Diamondback rooftops.

He opened the screen door with the same hand with which he was holding his rifle, and held it open with his left foot. He didn't have to open the inside door. It swung open, and June Dickinson was there, looking at him worriedly as she stepped back, drawing the door wide, her brown eyes sliding to the sodden cat in Spurr's arm.

"What on earth?"

Spurr walked inside, and June closed the door behind him. He said, "Is this the telegrapher's cat?"

"Homer Constiner's. Indeed. What're you doing with it?"

"Poor thing don't have a home no more. Leastways, not the telegraph office."

She narrowed her eyes at him.

Spurr set the cat down and, avoiding the woman's gaze, leaned his rifle in the corner near the door. "I was hoping you could take him. They say you never have rats if —"

"What's happening, Spurr?" June's voice was quietly insistent. "Who killed Homer?"

Spurr sighed and held his hat down so it could drip onto the rug at his feet and not on the woman's polished oak floor. "There's a bunch in town, June." He brushed rainwater from his brows with his wet shirtsleeve. "The de Cava bunch. Led by a border rat named Mateo de Cava. They sprung a prisoner from the Arkansas River Federal Pen up in Colorado, turned all the prisoners loose, and . . ."

"And they're why you and Sheriff Mason are here in Diamondback."

"That's right. We followed them here."

"And they killed Homer Constiner." June sounded as though she couldn't believe what she was saying as, frowning in befuddlement, she bent down and picked up the wet cat. "Oh, poor dear Josie," she cooed, holding the cat against her despite how wet it was. To Spurr, she said, "I'll find Josie some milk. The sheriff is awake and has asked for you. He's in my room, the door off the parlor." She tossed her head at the doorway opposite the kitchen.

Spurr held his arms out away from himself and grunted in frustration as he looked down at his wet, muddy moccasins. "I'll get you a robe. We can dry your clothes out in front of the stove. I've stoked it for supper. Your bath is waiting for you upstairs when you're ready."

She walked into the kitchen stroking the pathetic-looking cat. Spurr stared after her admiringly, not so concerned with her ass now but warmed by her generous heart. He'd figured she'd take in a homeless cat. After all, she'd sort of taken in his homeless, old ass hadn't she?

The world was a shitty place, he mused, as he stooped to unlace his moccasins. But here and there he ran into folks like June Dickinson; those were the people who kept his heart ticking — even a squawky old ticker like Spurr's.

Leaving his moccasins on the rug in front of the door, the old marshal tramped in his loose, wet socks through the parlor, pausing at the door flanking a potted palm on one side, a curio cabinet stuffed with trinkets of all shapes and sizes on the other.

He knocked softly on the door. No answer. He knocked once more, harder.

"Come in," Mason said, raspy-voiced.

Spurr went into the room that could only have been June's own bedroom, for, though it was small, it was filled with rich, well-kept furniture and a canopied, four-poster bed, with many oval-framed photographs on the walls. Opposite the bed stood a large oak wardrobe carved with a trim of apples and bananas.

Spurr closed the door behind him. Mason lay in the bed, covered in quilts and sheets, his head sunk deep in a crisp, white pillow that was likely stuffed with down. The sheriff was wearing a striped pajama top and, despite his shaggy beard and un-trimmed dragoon mustache, looked almost like he belonged there. He didn't look bad despite having taken a bullet. He had a little gray around the eyes, was all.

"Where you been, Spurr?"

"What do you mean, where I been?" Spurr asked as he stepped up to the bed, glancing around and finding June's wedding photo-graph showing her in a veiled bridal gown and standing beside a seated man in a three-piece suit and holding a bowler hat on his knee. A neat young man with a dragoon mustache much like Mason's. Neither, after the fashion of the times, showed much emo-tion in the daguerreotype. June had her hand on his forearm.

"I thought maybe you got the notion to take off after that bunch alone," Mason said. "Don't leave here without me, Spurr. I'll be up and around in no time, and I want to personally put that Massey firebrand behind bars again. Bastard fooled me . . . almost had me thinkin' he didn't belong there . . ."

Mason coughed and clutched his side.

"Rest easy, old son." Spurr set a hand on the sheriff's shoulder. He glanced at the window against which lightning flashed, silhouetting the hammering raindrops. "The gang's holed up right here in Diamondback, and from the look of this weather, they won't be goin' anywhere soon."

Mason glanced at Spurr sidelong, skeptical. "They're here?"

"Holed up in a hotel on the other side of town."

"Shit."

"That's what I said."

"They know we're here?"

Spurr remembered the girl he'd seen in the street. She'd likely told others in the gang about seeing an old lawman about, but he hoped they were all too involved in whores and whiskey to give a damn. Sooner or later, though, they'd come looking for the badge-toter. He had to be ready.

"Yeah, I reckon they do. One does, anyway. But I doubt they'll come lookin' till the weather clears."

"If they come here . . ."

"I know, I know." Neither had to say what would happen. June's life could be in danger. Mason would be trapped. "But you're not goin' anywhere for a while, so I reckon I'll stay here and make sure they don't come in and shoot your sorry ass." Spurr gave a dry chuckle. "I sure would hate to bury you in all this rocky mud."

"The doctor," Mason said, narrow an ironic eye at the old lawman standing over him, "is right purty. You don't make a fool of yourself, now, hear? But you might put in a good word for me."

"Too late." Spurr winked and glanced at the man's pajama top. "She already seen ya naked." He snorted and turned toward the door. "You sleep tight, heal your ass . . ."

"Spurr?"

The marshal turned. Mason gave him a penetrating look as he jerked his head toward a chair to Spurr's left. On the chair were Mason's clothes, his boots set neatly on the floor in front of it. His shell belt and pistol were draped over the chair back.

"Hand over my six-shooter, will you? Couldn't sleep knowin' de Cava and Massey are that close, unless I had my hogleg under my pillow."

Spurr gave the man his gun, and Mason tucked it under his pillow, then rested his head back against it, shaping a slow, satisfied smile. "There, that's better."

" 'Night, Mason."

" 'Night, Spurr."

Again, Spurr set his hand on the door-knob, poised to leave the room. Again, Mason stopped him.

"What the hell is it this time?" Spurr said.

The sheriff gave him another penetrating look. "Thanks for savin' my ass."

"Ah, shit." Spurr shambled on out of the room.

26

In the kitchen, June was checking a pot roast cooking in the iron range while the dead telegrapher's cat, Josie, lay on a thick blanket that June had folded atop a chair, making a thick bed for the orphaned beast.

The cat appeared considerably drier than when Spurr had brought it into the house; June must have run a blanket over it. The milk bowl was empty and the cat now sat crouching, yellow eyes staring at Spurr through the spools of the chair back, looking a little disoriented but also sated and relatively comfortable.

June slid the roasting pan into the range, closed the squawky door, and glanced at Spurr standing in his stocking-feet in the doorway. "Good lord — you're still dressed? Shuck out of those soggy clothes before you catch your death of cold! There's a robe there," she said, nodding toward the red-and-brown plaid robe, frayed around the cuffs, hanging from a wooden peg near the kitchen doorway, beside another peg from which a pink apron hung. "Leave your clothes here. You can wear that upstairs to your bath. Hurry, now. I don't need two sick men on the premises. I'll bring some hot water up shortly."

"You want me to undress in front of you?"

She crossed her arms impatiently. "Spurr, do you have any idea how many naked men I've seen?"

"Oh, now, milady," Spurr said with a wink and a lewd grin, "you ain't seen this one!"

June flushed but smiled in spite of herself, turning quickly away to busy herself at her cupboards. Chuckling, Spurr began shucking out of his wet clothes.

Hell, if she didn't mind, he sure didn't. She certainly wouldn't be the first woman to see him in his birthday suit. She kept her back to him, however, when, all but naked, he sat down to peel his wet balbriggans down his legs, then, dropping the garment over the chair he'd been sitting in, plucked the robe off its peg and pulled it on.

"Much obliged, Miss June," he said, donning his wet hat.

She turned from her dry sink, and laughed. "Spurr, why the hat and six-gun? I guarantee you that there are no bad men in

347

your room upstairs."

He looked down at the gun and shell belt he'd buckled around the outside of the robe, then lifted his eyes to the brim of his wet Stetson. He shrugged and grunted, "Old habits are hard to break, I reckon . . ."

He pinched the hat brim to her, then headed on up the stairs where he found the spare bedroom with the faintly steaming bath in it. After he'd doffed the robe, sunk down in the tepid water, and begun soaping himself, June came in with a bucket of near-boiling water, and added it to the bath, being very businesslike about it and not blushing but politely averting her eyes from the sudsy bathwater.

"Much obliged, Miss June."

"Don't soak too long," she said as she walked to the door, bouncing the empty wooden bucket against her leg. "Supper will be ready in an hour but I thought we'd have a drink first."

Spurr looked over his shoulder at her, incredulous. "You got whiskey?"

"I *have* whiskey, Spurr," she said, correcting his English and tucking a loose lock of her honey-blond hair behind her ear. "Of course, I do. What do I look like — a pious parson's wife?"

Spurr gave her the up and down, brashly

enjoying her figure, and the look must have been answer enough for her, because she let a coy little smile play across her eyes before she turned away and left the room, drawing the door closed behind her.

Spurr continued soaping himself, singing a bawdy song that was often nearly drowned by the thunder that hammered around the house like near cannon blasts. Lightning flickered in the room's otherwise dark window, and silver rainwater sluiced off the roof overhang just beyond it. He continued to sing the bawdy Irish ballad as he rinsed himself off, then stepped out of the tub and dried with the soft, thick towel that June had set out on the bed.

"Spurr, why did those men kill Homer Constiner?" she asked him after they'd each taken a seat across from each other in the parlor, near enough to Mason's room that they could hear if the sheriff called out for June's assistance.

She'd poured them each a double shot of whiskey, cutting the hooch with water, and they held their glasses now, June on one end of a horsehair sofa, Spurr in a brocade-upholstered armchair. The old marshal still wore the luxuriously soft robe while his clothes dried over kitchen chairs positioned near the range.

June had changed into a fresh dress — a cream one with brown checks and lace edges — though Spurr hadn't seen anything wrong with the other one. They both clung to her wonderfully womanly form right nicely.

Spurr turned his whiskey glass in his thick, callused brown hand, staring down at it. He was fairly salivating at the succulent aromas of the cooking roast that hung almost palpably in the air around him.

"You don't need to sugarcoat it for me," the woman said, stroking the orphaned cat asleep on the sofa beside her, snugged against her thigh. "I wasn't born on the frontier, but I've lived here nearly twenty years now. In fact, I came out here on the Oregon Trail, lost my parents during an Indian attack, and spent several frightening years on my own in rough-and-tumble gold camps in the northern Rockies. Before I met Richard, that is. I've been through a lot. So, tell me, what's happening here in Diamondback?"

"To be honest with you, I don't know. All I know is me and Mason followed that bunch of curly wolves led by Mateo de Cava here. I figured they was just holin' up till the weather passed, but now they went and killed Constiner and cut the telegraph wire.

Seems to me they must be plannin' to stay awhile, to do a thing like that, to make sure no one can use the telegraph to report their presence here. But, hell . . ." Spurr hiked a shoulder and took a sip of the whiskey, which was several notches above the grade of hooch he normally imbibed in. Smacking his lips and sucking his mustache, he said, "I just don't know. There ain't no bank in town here, is there?"

June shook her head. "There hasn't been a bank in Diamondback for well over a year. Lord knows there hasn't been any money to put in it for longer than that."

"Any other businesses that might be a lucrative mark for trail dogs?"

June shook her head and bunched her lips. "No. Oh, the mercantile used to do a nice business, but even that's on its last legs. Soon, I'm sure the hotel and the other stores will close and all Diamondback will be is a ghost town with a stage relay station."

Spurr frowned and waited for an especially loud blast of thunder to wane before he said, "The relay station. When's the stage pull through?"

"Once a week. It's due tomorrow, but I doubt it will make it in all this rain."

"What's it carry?"

"Passengers between Las Cruces and Snowflake, mostly. Drummers. Barbed-wire salesmen, speculators, cardsharps . . ."

"No strongbox?"

"Sometimes a strongbox for the Red Devil Mine up in . . ." June let her voice trail off as she widened her eyes at Spurr. "Yes, that's it — isn't it? Once a month the Gila Transport line hauls payroll money to Snowflake, to pay the men who work at the mine in greenbacks."

"Once a month?"

"Yes. Regular as clockwork. Word gets around when the payroll goes through, of course, because it means the miners will likely head to Diamondback to spend their money. It's even good news for me," she added with a guilty flush, lifting her drink to her lips. "Invariably, they get into a fights and injure themselves." She gave a dry chuckle. "And that means I have a little extra on Monday for buying coffee and fresh eggs at the mercantile."

"Why, Miss June, you are a caution," Spurr chastised her.

"Yes," she said, her brown eyes acquiring a buoyant whiskey sheen, "and an enterprising businesswoman."

"Is it time for that strongbox to be pullin' through town?"

Pensive lines cut through her forehead as she looked toward a corner of the room before returning her gaze to the lawman. "Yes. I think so, Spurr."

Spurr nodded and stared at a rain-streaked window. The storm continued to hammer the roof. When lightning pealed, Josie would lift her head from the couch and look around as though afraid the walls would cave in on her. June absently stroked the cat's fur that had curled a little, looking more shaggy, as it dried.

"Oh, Spurr," June said, frowning at him with concern. "If the gang is here to rob the stage, you can't go up against them alone!"

Spurr thought it over as he stared at the window. He wished to hell he'd gotten a telegraph off to Hackberry Creek before the de Cava gang had cut the wire. Being the veteran desperado he was, de Cava probably knew that stage's timetable. That had to be what he was waiting for.

Spurr took another sip of the delicious whiskey, and despite the perplexity of his situation, he enjoyed the burn in his throat and belly, the limbering warmth it spread through his flinty old arteries. "Times like these, I've learned to eat the apple one bite at a time," he said as much to himself as to June.

"Maybe it won't make it," she said, following the old lawman's gaze to the moisture-streaked window. "All the washes between here and Las Cruces are bound to be flooded. The stage will probably be holed up at a relay station for several days, until the water goes down." She sighed, gave the cat one last pat, and rose, smoothing her dress against the backs of her thighs. "Speaking of eating, I don't want my roast to dry out. Shall we?"

"Ma'am," Spurr said, rising to his feet and grinning, though the stage was riding heavy on his mind, "if it tastes as good as it smells, I'll race you into the kitchen!"

"It's not going anywhere. Let's just walk, Spurr." She extended her hand to him with a warm smile. He took it, pressed his lips to it tenderly, and hand in hand, the two strode off to the kitchen and the beckoning smell of the roast.

Spurr couldn't remember when he'd last enjoyed a meal as much as he enjoyed the one cooked by June Dickinson.

The pot roast, fresh garden beans, and mashed potatoes and rich, dark cream gravy were a joy to behold, so much better than café fare he'd become accustomed to; they padded out the old lawman's hollow belly deliciously. The follow-up peach pie and whipped cream were fresh and sweet, the coffee hot and black.

Best of all, however, was the companionship of this beautiful woman. They'd known each other only a few hours, but Spurr felt nearly as comfortable around her now as he did with his dear Abilene, and he felt no guilt in Abilene's regard.

He did not belong to Abilene, nor did she belong to him. They both knew that life was as mercurial as mountain weather, and there were no guarantees they would ever see each other again. Abilene was likely taking comfort where she could find it; she would expect Spurr to do the same.

He dropped his fork on his empty dessert plate and took his last sip of coffee, regarding June sitting across from him warmly. "That was truly a delight the size of the entire frontier, Miss June. I do thank you for it."

"It was my pleasure, Spurr. How 'bout another piece of pie?"

Spurr sat back in his chair. "Couldn't hold another forkful."

"How 'bout another cup of coffee with some added elixir?" June held up the whiskey bottle and looked at him alluringly. "Help you sleep . . ."

Spurr held up his stone mug. "Don't mind if I do!"

Later, after a long, leisurely conversation and when they'd politely and somewhat shyly bid each other good night, Spurr drifted off to his room while June disappeared into the one beside his room upstairs, leaving her own larger and more comfortable bed to her patient. Spurr closed his door and turned to the window in which lightning still flashed while thunder ravished the heavens. He ran his hands through his long, thinning hair, knowing a keen frustration.

The night seemed incomplete. And he didn't think it was only his own goatish hungers that made it seem so, either.

He lit a lamp and crawled into bed. He could hear June moving around in the room next door. He heard the faint chink of her lantern's chimney as she lowered the wick in the room next to his, and the gentle complaint of the bed's leather springs.

Finally, the sounds stopped, and then there was only the boisterous clamor of the storm.

Spurr sighed. He closed his eyes and tried to sleep.

"Spurr?" June's voice was like a tonic. He snapped his eyes open.

"Yes, June?"

"If you need anything over there," she said, pausing to clear her throat, "you know where I am."

Spurr wrinkled his brows as he stared up at the ceiling lit only by lightning flashes. Shadows of tree branches shunted this way and that across the wainscoting rising in peaks above the bed. He replayed the woman's message in his head, and a slow smile shaped itself on his craggy face.

Two minutes later, he tapped his knuckles lightly against her door and winced. What if her message had not been the invitation he'd taken it for?

On the other side of the door, June chuckled. "Get in here, you. But you better not be wearing your hat and six-gun!"

Spurr laughed and went in.

27

Camilla's left breast bulged tenderly out from beneath her arm as she lay in the deep, soft bed in their second-story room in the Diamondback Hotel.

Pale light touched it softly. Cuno lowered his head and kissed the vanilla orb.

Camilla groaned and moved a little but kept her head pressed against the inside of her other arm, which was curled atop her pillow. She breathed slowly, deeply, drifting back into the depths of sleep made more inviting by the all-night tempest that had put a chill in the air and left a broad, wet stain on the peaked ceiling above the bed. The wind must have blown some shingles off and let the water in.

Cuno lifted his head from Camilla's back, and dropped his feet to the floor. He groaned a little at the burn in his left arm. The limb felt tight and hard, and it throbbed as though a rat had eaten into it during the long, stormy night and was nibbling away at the bone.

The purple skin of his forearm bulged; a sickly yellow color outlined both puncture wounds in the middle of the swell. Despite the soreness, he was damned lucky. Apparently, only a little venom had been fired into his system, making him about half as sick as he would have been had the viper not spent its poison on a rabbit or gopher before sinking its teeth into Cuno. He was a little queasy and light-headed, but otherwise he felt all right.

He hoped he wouldn't have to ride today, but if he had to, he could.

Now he tramped barefoot over to the room's single window and swept the flour-sack curtain aside with his right hand. He looked out over the shake-shingled and darkly wet roof angling over the saloon's front gallery into the street. Puddles lay everywhere, and long wheel ruts were overflowing with water.

The mud was six inches deep. Roof shingles and newspapers and other bits of windblown trash and tumbleweeds littered the mud.

The sky was the color of greasy rags; it hung low over the false facades west of the hotel. The wind had died, and a moody silence had descended in its wake. A fine mist quietly beaded against the window that had a long jagged crack in it. There was no movement on the street except a single wet dog trotting along the street's opposite side with its head and tail down, splashing through the puddles.

Cuno picked up his battered timepiece and saw that it was nine thirty. He'd slept in after a fitful night with his stinging, burning arm.

He was a light sleeper, and he'd heard no sounds coming from the hall, so most of the gang must still be asleep. They'd had a long, wild night downstairs with two whores and much whiskey and cards. Cuno and Camilla had holed up here together, Camilla fetching food and beer and tending his arm before they'd made love, then fallen asleep together despite the booming voices from the saloon hall below.

Now he could hear several sets of snores pushing through the walls around him as he dressed quietly, letting the girl sleep. He grabbed his hat and Winchester, stepped out into the hall, and pulled the door closed quietly behind him.

Downstairs, he found Frank Skinner sitting alone at a table in the hall's deep shadows. The wiley, sinewy, old train robber sat hunched over an oblong plate of eggs, bacon, and fried potatoes. He was wearing a long, wool coat and had a Spencer carbine on the table in front of him.

The only other person in the saloon was the beefy bartender, who had a long, straggly mustache drooping down both sides of his thin-lipped mouth. He was chopping up a roast while eyeing Cuno cautiously, dropping the small chunks of meat into an iron stew pot on the bar beside him. His face looked haggard, the skin around his eyes sagging, the eyes themselves bloodshot. He hadn't had much sleep after a doubtless harried night.

As Cuno stepped off the staircase's last step, Skinner, chewing, glanced over his shoulder at him. The train robber stopped chewing to grin, then began chewing again as he said, "I was snakebit once, and I begged my brother Earl to blow my head off with his shotgun."

He shook his head and swallowed his mouthful of food. "I was sure we'd seen the last of you yesterday. Or figured I'd have to finish you off today so's you didn't hold us up any."

Cuno strode over to the bar. "Sorry to disappoint you, Frank."

"I ain't disappointed. We're gonna need

all the guns we got to pull this next job and then get down deep into Mexico. And, in case you ain't noticed, we're startin' to run a little short."

"Give me a beer," Cuno told the barman. "Break three eggs into it."

He turned and rested his elbows against the edge of the bar, facing Skinner who'd continued to hungrily scoop food into his mouth. Since busting out of the hellhole of the Arkansas River Federal Pen, Cuno had had the same inclination — to eat and keep eating until he burst like a blood-sucking deer tick. In the pen, if Castle hadn't wanted you to eat, you didn't eat. Only, this morning Cuno wasn't hungry. He'd get his appetite back when the last of the venon had made its way from his belly.

The barman sullenly set his beer with three eggs in it atop the bar. Cuno flipped a dime onto the counter, then took the beer over to Skinner's table.

He set his rifle on the table near Skinner's carbine, removed a chair from on top of the table, which was the position all the other chairs in the saloon were in, and straddled it. He sipped the foam off the top of the beer.

"What's the next job?" he asked.

Skinner was swabbing yolk from his plate

with three large chunks of potato. He rolled his eyes over to the bar, where the apron had resumed chopping the roast and tossing the chunks into the pot. He had a stack of washed and topped carrots beside his cutting board.

Keeping his voice low, Skinner said, "Stagecoach. Mateo said the Gila Transport Company hauls a strongbox through here and occasionally moneyed passengers — wealthy businessmen — from Las Cruces to the mines in the mountains. Sounds like Snowflake is boomin' sorta the way Diamondback was a few years ago, and speculators are movin' in to, you know" — the old train robber grinned — "speculate. No doubt with their pockets full."

"When's it due?"

"Noon. Keeps a rigid schedule in these parts."

"What about the rain?"

"Yeah, well, that's why Mateo and his fellers are sleepin' in. It likely won't make it till the washes empty out. I was restless, so I got up early and rode out, and there's a wide creek about three miles south of town, on the road from Las Cruces. That won't be passable for a day or two, and who knows how the washes look farther south."

Skinner shook his head and shoved a

wedge of yolk-soaked toast into his mouth. "Nah, it won't make it today. Maybe tomorrow, even the next day. Or . . ." He shrugged and clapped crumbs from his hands as he sat back in his chair. "Maybe the next day after that."

"You think it's safe — us holin' up here that long?"

"Mateo cut the telegraph wires, so if any of the fine citizens of Diamondback decided to shout for help against the owlhoots holed up in their fine hotel, they couldn't do it. But I'm gonna suggest to Mateo we ride out and meet the stage at the flooded wash. No use waitin' around here. Just settin' ourselves up for another ambush. Besides, the whores ain't much good."

Skinner looked edgy. He likely had enough warrants and bounties on his head that he'd have to spend the rest of his life in Mexico. Cuno knew how he felt.

The young freighter wasn't thirsty for the beer, but he figured it would take some of the burn out of his arm, so he guzzled a good third of it and felt one of the eggs slide down his throat and into his belly. The beer was, indeed, soothing. And the egg was instantly nourishing.

He felt better. But he didn't like the pensive cast to Skinner's gaze. The man was an experienced robber, and Cuno knew not to take the man's moods lightly.

"What's the matter, Frank? You don't like the setup?"

Skinner pursed his lips and slid his plate to one side, absently brushing crumbs from the table and onto the floor that still looked damp from a recent mopping. "I know we need this job, as it's likely our last chance at good money before we hit the border, but I sense our gates closin' on us fast."

"Brouschard ever show?"

"Nope."

Cuno couldn't work up much sympathy for Mateo's pugnacious first lieutenant. "That the reason you're worried?"

Skinner lounged back in his chair, shoulders tilted to one side, his hat tipped back off his forehead to show a wedge of gray-flecked hair combed back from a pronounced widow's peak. "We got men on our trail. Maybe not many, but in this age of the telegraph, we could have 'em ahead of us, too. And there's a goddamn cavalry outpost just south of here, on Hackberry Creek. It ain't much. I've been through there a time or two in the past; it's a rat-infested little cracker box outfitted with kids and old drunks. But they got a group, just the same."

Skinner leaned forward suddenly. "And in

case you haven't noticed, our ranks are thinned. That was a crack-brained move Mateo made, holin' up in that little railroad camp for that long. When you're on the run, you run. That's the definition of runnin', see?"

"Them bounty hunters whipsawed us."

"If not for you and the *chiquita,* kid, we'd all be dead." Skinner stared at Cuno across the table, and a bemused light shone in his frosty blue eyes. "You take to this kind o' livin', haven't ya? I never figured you for a career criminal, but maybe I had you figured wrong."

"Do yourself a favor and don't try to figure me. I've stopped tryin' to figure myself." Cuno polished off the beer and the last egg and sleeved the hoppy malt from his mouth. "But I agree with you — I'd like to get to Mexico. But I'm gonna need some cash soon, so I'm willin' to risk waitin' for the stage."

"Well, I reckon Mateo is, too. And it's his dance, so I reckon he calls it." Skinner sighed and snapped his fingers for the barman to bring him another beer and a shot of whiskey. "Join me?" he asked Cuno.

"Nah, I'm gonna go out and stretch my legs, get my strength back." Cuno slid his chair back, and rose, stretching, wincing at the tight knot in his left forearm.

"All right, kid. See ya later. I know I'll feel a whole lot better when we're down in Mexico."

"Yeah, me, too," Cuno said, grabbing his rifle off the table and heading for the front door. "With a few coins in my pocket."

"If Mateo's right about this stage," Skinner called, "it'll be more than a little, and you'll be knowin' you're in the right profession, after all."

Cuno glanced back at him. The bartender had just set a fresh beer and whiskey shot in front of Skinner. He was nervously rubbing his hands on his apron. Skinner arched a brow at the man and said, "But all that'll stay under this roof here — won't it, pard?"

He grinned malevolently. The barman swallowed and shambled on back to the bar.

Cuno opened the door and went out into the soggy morning, lifting the collar of his denim jacket against the damp chill, looking around the gray, sodden town. A fine mist was still falling from a cottony sky. There were a few people out now — mostly shopkeepers sweeping tumbleweeds from their stoops or setting planks out in the street in front of their businesses on which potential customers could scrape the mud from their boots.

Aside from those three or four proprietors, the town looked as though it had been abandoned during the windy deluge. All that told Cuno that citizens remained was the smoke curling over and around the rooftops, emanating from both the north and the south side of town, where private dwellings and whores' cribs were arranged amongst stock pens and corrals and hay barns.

He walked down off the porch and into the street, his boots sinking heel-deep in the mud. Shouldering his Winchester, he walked westward along the street, his boots making sucking sounds in the mud, splashing in the puddles too numerous to be avoided.

When he'd walked a block and a half, he stopped in front of the stage relay station identified by the Gila Transport Company sign running along the roofline of the gallery. It was a shabby log building with a red dirt roof. It was rectangular, and its logs were silver with age. Likely, it had been the first building here, when Diamondback was only a relay station, before color showed in the Organ Mountains to the west.

Blue smoke curled from the tin chimney pipe. The front door was open, and an old woman with gray hair drawn back from her forehead and wrapped in a taut bun was sweeping dirt out the open doorway onto the porch where there were several wicker chairs and a sandbox spotted with chewing tobacco and cigarette stubs.

Three crows sat on the pole rail running along the right end of the porch, preening and digging mites from under their wings, one cocking its head to see what the old woman swept out.

The woman didn't lift her head toward Cuno but kept her attention on her work. She was getting ready for the stage. Cuno kept moving westward along the street and stopped after another block.

He was nearly at the west edge of town, where the soggy street became a soggy trail angling off through the sage and greasewood. On the left side of the street was a boarded-up general store with a faded green sign announcing LOGAN'S DRY GOODS.

A broad boardwalk ran the length of the place's log front wall, and on the far west end of the boardwalk, facing a rain barrel, a man was hunkered on one knee, holding his head down while reaching across himself, toward his left shoulder, with his right hand — obviously in some sort of distress.

Cuno canted his head to one side, studying the man with furled brows.

A rifle lay on the boardwalk right of the

man's right, moccasin-clad foot. In the dense, morning quiet, Cuno could hear the man's raspy breathing, his desperate grunts and sighs. Cuno recognized the man's shabby, broad-brimmed slouch hat with a rawhide chin thong hanging down his hickory workshirt. He wore patched, smoke-stained buckskin trousers. His hair was brown and gray, and it hung several inches over the collar of his deerskin jacket. Cuno could see only the man's right profile, but he'd know the rest of his craggy, saddle-brown face when he saw it.

Cuno lowered his Winchester from his shoulder and, snugging the butt against his right hip, tramped across the street.

The man must have heard the wet sounds of Cuno's boots in the mud, but he did not turn his head toward the young man approaching him. He was fooling with something in his right hand. It was a small hide pouch, and he was trying to bite the drawstring open with his teeth. His left hand appeared uselessly curled at his side.

As Cuno stopped beside the man, aiming his Winchester at him one-handed, the man whom Cuno would have drilled through the chest if the riled rattler hadn't sunk its teeth into the young freighter's arm popped something into his mouth.

He tossed his head back, and the stone-sized Adam's apple in his leathery neck bobbed as he swallowed. It was like a rock being shaken in an ancient deerskin sack.

He turned toward Cuno. His lilac blue eyes narrowed at the maw of the Winchester aimed at his neck.

"Hold it right there," Cuno said.

The old gent who had a deputy U.S. marshal badge pinned to his shirt, just visible behind the flaps of his jacket and deerskin vest, lifted his implacable gaze toward Cuno's face.

"What can I help you with, sonny?"

"Don't call me sonny."

"What should I call you?"

"Cuno Massey."

The old man's shrewd, pain-sharp eyes held Cuno's stare. He was breathing hard but now after taking his pill he seemed to be in less distress than before.

"Who're you?"

"Call me Spurr."

The old man sagged down onto his left butt cheek and pressed his back up against the wall of the abandoned dry-goods store. The rain barrel was to his left. His rifle lay near his moccasins, and he gave it a faintly longing look.

"Deputy U.S. Marshal Spurr Morgan,

371

that is. Most folks just call me Spurr." He glanced at the maw of Cuno's rifle once more and scowled angrily. "If you're gonna shoot me, younker, go ahead and pull the trigger and get it done with."

"It'd be so damn easy," Cuno said softly. "A hell of a lot easier than back in them badlands."

Spurr raised his eyes to the young freighter's face once more, and he narrowed an eyelid shrewdly.

Cuno said, "That was me who peppered that rock dust into your cheek. A diamondback saved your hide."

Spurr nodded slowly, pursing his lips in fateful disgust. "Like I said, if you're gonna finish the job you started, go ahead and finish it."

"Where's Mason?"

"Who?"

Cuno smiled without humor. "I seen Mason with you and the other gent. I would have drilled him first but I had an easier shot at you."

"You won't get an easier shot than this one, kid." Spurr spread his arms and looked defiant, challenging. "Might as well kill me now. Mason ain't here; he rode out to the Hackberry Creek outpost to get some soldiers. Should be here anytime, though."

Cuno considered that for a moment, then remembered what Frank Skinner had said about the washes around Diamondback being filled with rainwater. He shook his head slowly and sucked a heavy breath. "After that rain? I doubt it." He hardened his jaws and raised the Winchester butt to his shoulder, aiming down at the old lawman's forehead. "You tell Mason he's a dead man. Cuno Massey's going to kill him."

"He was just doing his job, son."

"And my job is to kill the son of a bitch responsible for locking me up in that goddamn hellhole of a federal prison. I'm gonna kill both you sons o' bitches for tryin' to take me back."

"You killed marshals, boy. Where'd you expect 'em to put you?"

"I killed those men because they had it coming. Mason wouldn't listen to any of that. I was no cold-blooded killer."

Again, Cuno spoke slowly through gritted teeth, narrowing an eye as he stared down the Winchester's barrel. "But I am now. And Mason's next on my kill list. You tell him that. Tell him if he wants me so bad, sees it his mission in life to lock me up again, he's got another think comin'. He can either find me or I can find him. But sooner or later, we're going to meet. And I'm gonna kill him."

Cuno lowered his rifle, pressing the butt again to his right hip. He backed slowly away, keeping the gun on the old marshal.

Unbridled fury blazed in him. He knew he should kill this man called Spurr, but he needed Spurr to relay his message to Mason. He wanted Mason to know that he was now the one being hunted.

Besides, Cuno couldn't kill a man who had no chance at all. Especially an old one with a weak ticker. He didn't know why, but he couldn't. He'd likely regret it later, and he had to learn to kill when he had to, but he just couldn't kill the old man now.

When he was half a block away, he turned around and tramped back in the direction of the hotel.

28

Because of the flooded washes left in the wake of the storm, the stage was delayed by three days.

Luther Haines, a Yankee desperado from Abilene, Kansas, lowered his field glasses and turned to Mateo de Cava. "Here she comes, Boss."

"Alabar a Dios — es sobre tiempo!" Praise god — it's about time!

Mateo was hunkered down behind a rocky scarp with Cuno, Camilla, Luther Haines, and Frank Skinner, using a Green River knife to trim his fingernails. He looked like a man waiting for a train. Cuno could smell the hooch on him, and on Haines as well. Their eyes were bloodred. "How many men are guarding it?"

Haines lifted his field glasses again to gaze through a slight notch in the lip of the black-rocked scarp that humped just beyond a wash that was nearly dry again after the storm. Cuno lifted his head to follow the man's gaze.

He saw the stage moving up from the south across the distant desert, following the meandering stage road behind a brown blotch that was its six-horse hitch. With his naked eyes, he could see a couple of the outriders in front of the stage, but none behind it. They were still too far away, and the cedars and junipers were thick amongst the boulders that some glacier had dumped here eons ago.

Haines drew his lips back from his teeth as he stared through the glasses. "Holy shit — there must be six." He narrowed his eyes and moved the glasses slowly from left to right, tracking the stage through the chaparral. "No . . . seven." He lowered the glasses and turned to Mateo. "Seven outriders. One shotgun messenger." The gray-eyed man grinned. He wore a gold stud earring and a snakeskin armband. "She's comin' in heavy, Boss!"

"Seven outriders, nine men total," Frank Skinner said, sitting with his back against the scarp a little ways from Mateo. "How many we got now?" Quickly, he counted them off on his gloved fingers. "Mateo, Camilla, Cuno, Calderon, Azuelo, Nervo, Luther, and myself. Eight."

He pooched his lips and arched his brows as though he thought the odds weren't so bad that the job wasn't doable. Challenging but doable.

"Eight left of nearly twenty men," Camilla said awfully, shaking her head and eyeing her brother who continued to trim his nails with the obscenely large, razor-edged knife. "My god, Mateo — we should have headed straight for the border."

"We did head straight for the border," Mateo said with a bored air.

"I mean we should have headed straight for the border without stopping in that railroad town so you could fuck whores and get half your gang whittled away by bounty hunters!"

Mateo snapped his dark eyes to his sister, his chest heaving. Before the outlaw leader could respond to his fiery-tempered sibling's tirade, Cuno said, "No point in arguin' over that now. What's done is done." He took the field glasses from Haines but cast an admonishing look at Camilla who was still staring, flushed with fury, at her brother. "Now we'd best get into position to take that strongbox."

He raised the glasses to his eyes and stared off through the chaparral. As he brought the stage up in his magnified field of vision

377

— a big Concord painted green with yellow doors on which GILA TRANSPORT CO., LAS CRUCES, NM. TERR. was stenciled in gold letters, Mateo said, "Frank, signal the others."

Skinner rose and walked out to the far edge of the scarp, keeping the mound of flat, black boulders between himself and the oncoming stage and its seven outriders. He held his rifle up high above his head and waved it three times. Cuno turned his field glasses on another scarp about a hundred yards north and west of his position, saw the return signal — a rifle waved three times above Mariano Azuelo's sombrero-clad head.

Azuelo was hunkered in the rocks on the side of that distant escarpment with Enrique Calderon and Franco Nervo. A good bit of loose rock clung to the scarp just beneath them, and when they received a second signal from Skinner, they were to kick the rocks down the incline to pile up in the trail below, sealing off the stage's trail to Diamondback, three miles north.

Skinner as well as Cuno and Camilla had convinced Mateo to effect the robbery out here, away from town, where there was more open ground and no danger of townsmen involving themselves. Cuno liked the idea, too, because there was was less chance of innocent people being killed. He wondered now if the old lawman, Spurr, had followed the gang out here with Sheriff Mason. In that regard, Cuno felt conflicting emotions.

On the one hand, he wanted to kill Mason. On the other hand, he didn't want to endanger the gang, which he had already done when he'd chosen not to inform Mateo of his run-in with the deputy U.S. marshal known as Spurr. He wasn't sure why he hadn't told them, as he felt a strong allegiance to Mateo, despite the man's obvious carelessness and cold-bloodedness.

But without Mateo and Camilla, Cuno would have been hanged that day that now seemed so long ago but was only a month or so back; he'd have been tossed without ceremony into a mass grave behind the Arkansas River Federal Penitentiary, where so many other prisoners had been discarded like food scraps from the dining hall tables.

He didn't know why he hadn't told Mateo about Spurr. Maybe his allegiance to the killer wasn't as strong as he thought. Maybe he didn't want to see the old lawman with the weak ticker killed, which Mateo would certainly have seen to if he'd known of the man's existence. He'd have had his men scour the town for him and show him no mercy. No mercy to anyone the lawman was holed up with.

Maybe Cuno's belly had rebelled at that possibility, and not wanting to face it, he'd merely kept his own counsel.

Now, wondering if Spurr and Mason had followed him and the gang out here, Cuno swept the surrounding terrain with the field glasses. Under the climbing sun, he saw nothing out here but sand-colored cliffs and spurs and broad stretches of gravelly flats bristling with bear grass, thickets of mesquite and catclaw, and some scrubby oaks.

"Why are you so interested in the east?"

Cuno lowered the glasses and looked at Mateo, who narrowed a suspicious eye at him. The outlaw leader rolled his bloodshot eyes toward the southwest, waving at the savage Green River. "The stage is that way, gringo. That way!"

"Doesn't hurt to look around," Cuno said. "Never know if someone might have followed us out of town."

"I kept an eye on our back trail," Mateo said. "I'm no fool. If anyone had followed us out of Diamondback, they would be dead by now and the coyotes would be tearing them apart and dragging them off. You just keep an eye on the stage, and when it is close to those rocks, you tell Skinner to send the final signal."

Cuno glanced at Camilla. Sitting with her back to the scarp, she looked at Cuno from beneath the brim of her straw sombrero skeptically. She had a .45 in her hand, absently, nervously turning the cylinder. Her eyes acquired a question she did not give voice to, but she and Cuno had become close enough that he knew what that question was: "What troubles you, gringo desperado?"

Yes, Cuno thought, *what troubles me?* He turned the glasses back on the stage that was a hundred and fifty yards away now and closing at a full gallop, the six-hitch team lunging deeply, dust broiling out behind them.

I've been waiting for this job. It not only means money and my ability to repay Camilla for all she's bought for me and to pay my own way into Mexico. But it means I've now accepted this new life I've decided is my only option. After all, I became a convicted killer nearly a year ago, when the judge hammered his gavel in Camp Collins, sentencing me to a life in the federal pen. I became a desperado as soon as I escaped, and a cold-blooded killer when I shot that local lawman not a mile from the penitentiary.

This is the only life I have left, and if I'm going to live at all, I have to accept it and show I can own up to it and live it despite what it means I've become.

He was watching the stage round a curve and move directly toward him, a hundred yards away and closing fast. There were four riders ahead, all holding rifles either straight up or resting across their saddle pommels, and three riders behind. Cuno stayed low and sheltered the field glass lenses with his hands, as the four riders were swinging their heads around this way and that — all big men in dusters, cartridges winking from bandoliers or cartridge belts wrapped around their waists.

The stage driver was a scrawny but tough-looking desert rat with a canvas hat and a big beard. He wore two pistols in shoulder holsters. The shotgun messenger held a sawed-off shotgun across his thighs; he had another barn blaster beneath the seat; Cuno could see it between his high-topped, mule-eared boots. Both men wore bandannas against the dust kicked up from behind the racing, thundering team.

Cuno lowered the field glasses, and, keeping his head low to the ground, turned to look past Camilla and Mateo to where Frank Skinner stood on the scarp's north end. "All right," Cuno said, handing the glasses back to Haines and absently running his sweaty palms on his denim-clad thighs.

He turned again to peer through the notch in the scarp just above his head. The first two riders galloped past the scarp, then the other two about ten seconds later. The stage came next, following the second set of lead riders about twenty yards behind.

Cuno lowered his head again, turned to see Skinner come running at a crouch behind the scarp, for the lead riders were now in position to see him. Skinner doffed his hat and dropped to one knee, glancing at Mateo while reaching for his Spencer carbine with one hand. With his other hand, he unsnapped the keeper thong from over the hammer of his Remington .44.

Cuno's heart thudded when he heard a muffled rumble and knew that Nervo, Azuelo, and Calderon had caused the rocks to begin tumbling down the opposite scarp. It was their job to take out the four lead riders. The last three were up to Cuno's bunch.

"All right, amigos," Mateo said with a desultory sigh, as if he'd rather still be whoring and drinking in Diamondback. He grabbed his Winchester and racked a live round in the chamber. "You know what to do, uh?"

Cuno drew a deep breath and looked at Camilla. She was standing now, glancing at him sidelong while running a hand down her Winchester's barrel — an oblique look, half inquisitive, half accusatory.

Cuno felt a ripple of annoyance as he grabbed his own rifle then followed Mateo, Skinner, and Haines out around the south end of the scarp, running at a crouch while the others took cover behind low boulders or barrel cactus. Camilla ran up behind Cuno, then dashed off to his right, taking cover behind a split, flat-topped rock.

The clatter of the boulders continued to Cuno's right as he dropped behind a gravelly shelf and a gnarled bit of catclaw.

The trail was forty yards straight out from him. The stage was about sixty yards to his right, and now he could hear the driver and shotgun rider shouting as rifles popped and horses whinnied. The first of the three trailing riders were just now passing in front of Cuno, riding side by side and trotting their mounts, holding their reins up close to their chests with one hand, rifles in their other hand.

The last pair of riders was about thirty yards to Cuno's left and obscured by the stage's broiling dust and cactus and shrubs.

To Cuno's left, Mateo's rifle cracked. The outlaw leader gave a high-pitched, ear-rending shriek as he ejected the spent cartridge, seated fresh, and took aim at a second rider through his own billow of powder smoke. Cuno held his finger taut against his own trigger as he saw the second rider, who'd just turned toward him, blown out of his saddle by Mateo's second shot.

"Two down, amigos!" Mateo bellowed, racking a fresh shell and turning to his left.

Haines had apparently already drawn a bead on one of the outriders, as a rifle barked in that direction. Out on the trail, a horse screamed shrilly.

Then Skinner, Mateo, and Camilla were opening up, as well, and Cuno realized that he was still staring straight ahead, at the trail where the first two shot riders' horses were fiddlefooting wildly, one apparently trying to rid itself of his own rider whose boot was hung up in his stirrup.

The horse buck-kicked and curveted, then finally, with another shrill cry, lunged left of the trail and galloped west across the desert.

Suddenly, the rifles stopping barking. The men to Cuno's left were whooping and shouting like lobos. Cuno turned to see Mateo, Skinner, and Haines running off across the desert, heading for the trail where a single man was screaming epithets.

Footsteps sounded to Cuno's right.

He turned to see Camilla running toward him on the trail of the others, gritting her teeth as she racked a cartridge into her Winchester's breech and glanced at Cuno, her eyes two brown saucers of yellow fire. "What're you waiting for? You want to rob a stage, but you don't want to do the work?"

Then she was gone, slamming her cocking lever home and sprinting off after her brother and the others.

29

Cuno jerked himself out of the quicksand-like trance he'd found himself in as soon as the ambush started, and pushed off his knees.

More rifles barked from the direction of the trail. Mateo and the others were finishing off the wounded outrider. The man wailed, and then two more rifles boomed, and the wails fell silent.

Mateo laughed loudly, and Skinner said something.

Cuno heard running footsteps and then he saw all four of the gang running toward the horses they'd tethered in a shallow wash east of the trail. His head still reeling and only half catching up to what had just happened, Cuno broke into a run after them, weaving around the rocks and grease-wood shrubs. He gained the wash a few seconds after the others. They were ripping their reins from branches and mounting their horses.

Mateo glanced at Cuno. "What the hell you doing, gringo? If that arm is slowing you down, I'll have to shoot you!"

His molasses-brown eyes blazed with the thrill of the chase and the kill. Whipping his reins against his horse's withers and gouging the mount's flanks with his savage spurs, he gave another raucous bellow and galloped off in the direction of the stage.

None of the others looked at Cuno as they booted their own mounts up out of the wash and took off after their leader. Cuno swung up onto Renegade's back and tried to clear his mind of the screams and the shooting, to replace them all with visions of a strongbox brimming with greenbacks. He booted the paint after the others, galloping off across the desert and onto the trail and then swinging northward to follow the trail behind the others until the stage came into view.

It looked tiny sitting there in the purple shade at the base of the high, shelving escarpment. Ahead of it, dust rose from the pile of boulders freshly tumbled off the incline.

The horses were blowing and stomping. There were three men on the ground, twisted and unmoving. Another was crawling into the brush off the right side of the trail. Female screams emanated from inside the stage, and they grew shriller and louder as Cuno pulled up behind the others, who'd stopped beside the coach.

Mariano Azuelo squatted atop the stage, his red neckerchief billowing. He grinned victoriously, eagerly, as he held his rifle across both shoulders, hooking it there behind his neck by his arms. The short, bandy-legged, Indian-dark Mexican, Franco Nervo, was strolling after the man who'd crawled off the trail.

"Leave him," Mateo told Nervo, then cast a hard look at Cuno. "Gringo, do some work for a change." He jerked his head toward the man whom Cuno could hear thrashing in the brush to his right, panting and wheezing desperately.

Cuno glanced at Camilla. She met his gaze with a faintly challenging, inquisitive one of her own.

"Sure."

Cuno swung his right boot over his saddle horn and dropped to the trail. Hefting his Yellowboy in both hands, he followed the scuff marks the crawling man had made in the trail out into the desert. He could hear the man sobbing and groaning, and when Cuno had walked several yards, he saw the

389

man half crawling and half running, dragging his bloody left leg.

He was a tall man in a powder-blue suit, with a string tie and a crisp white shirt. The back of his suit, just up from his right hip, glistened with fresh blood. Thick auburn hair curled over the collar of his jacket. As he glanced back toward Cuno striding after him, Cuno saw that he wore a dandy's pencil-thin mustache tight against his upper lip. He stretched his lips back, showing a full set of straight, white teeth.

He was one of the moneyed folks, likely a speculator of some sort, who frequently took the Gila Transport line to Snowflake and other burgeoning mining settlements in the mountains. The three Mexican gang members had done a job on him. He was leaving a red trail of bloody scuff marks in the sand and gravel behind him.

"Please," he begged as Cuno walked up beside him. He dropped to his right hip, and clutching his bloody leg with one hand, the bloody hole in his lower belly with the other, he stared horrifically up at his assailant. "Please . . ." He sobbed, tears running down from light brown eyes to streak the dust on his pale, fleshy, clean-shaven cheeks. "Oh, god — please don't kill me!"

Cuno felt his own chest rising and falling

sharply, heavily, as, boots spread, he stared down at the man. A girl's screams continued to emanate from the stage as did the occasional horse clomp and whinny. The morning was so quiet that Cuno could hear his fellow gang members talking amongst themselves.

He kept his eyes on the wounded man before him, who probably wasn't much older than Cuno himself, whose eyes showed such an animal horror that Cuno's spine shriveled at the sight of it.

Cuno glanced toward the stage. Mateo had climbed to the top of the carriage and he was standing there with his feet straddling the strongbox, fists on his hips, staring toward Cuno, his head tipped nearly down to his left shoulder. The shorter Azuelo flanked him, staring curiously over Mateo's shoulder.

Cuno turned his head back quickly toward the mustachioed dandy and raised his rifle. Blood oozed over both the man's hands. His eyes were desperate, pain-wracked, pleading.

"Oh, god. Oh, god. Don't do this."

Cuno swallowed against the nausea churning in his belly and threatening to jettison bile into his throat. The desert swayed around him. His hands inside his gloves were as soaked as if he'd dunked them in a rain barrel. Sweat dribbled down his forehead and into his eyes, stinging.

"Sorry, amigo."

He pressed the rifle's butt hard against his shoulder and lined up the sights on the dandy's forehead. He drew his right index finger taut against the eyelash trigger. He swallowed, paused to brush sweat from his right brow, then lined up the sights once more.

Why the hell was this so hard? He'd killed the town marshal of Sand Creek. He'd killed the bounty hunters who'd attacked the brothel. Why was killing one more man, a moneyed dandy who'd likely never give Cuno so much as a passing glance on a city street, so damn hard?

Cuno stared down the rifle barrel at the man, who stared back at him, sobbing and quivering and grinding one heel into the sand as though trying to push himself away from the cold-eyed killer bearing down on him. The rifle shook. Cuno gritted his teeth and tried to steady it. He'd just gotten it relatively settled when blood suddenly dribbled out from both corners of the dandy's mouth.

He made a choking sound, shoulders jerking, belly convulsing. Then his eyelids fluttered. His eyes rolled back into his head. The tension left his wounded leg, and he sagged back against the desert floor.

He gave a hard sigh. He lay silent and still.

Cuno narrowed an eye at him. Dead?

Keeping his cheek snugged against the Winchester's stock, feeling Mateo de Cava's eyes on him, lifting gooseflesh on the back of his neck, Cuno kicked the man's right foot. The foot jerked and fell still. The man's eyes were halfway open, sightless.

Cuno felt his hands steady. His heart quickened but also lightened with relief that he'd suddenly been relieved of his grisly task. He slid the rifle slightly to the right of the dead dandy's head and squeezed the trigger.

The slug tore up sand and grit, leaving a fist-sized hole. It blew gravel up against the dead man's left ear, peppered his face with red sand.

Cuno lowered the Winchester and ejected the spent cartridge. In the desert silence, the empty casing made a soft chinking sound in the gravel.

As he levered a fresh round into the rifle's breech, he glanced toward Mateo, who stood as he'd been standing before atop the stage. But now the outlaw leader gave a slight, expressionless nod, then turned toward Azuelo, and the two of them bent down to begin removing the chains that secured the strongbox to the stage.

"Hold it right there!"

Cuno frowned at the shouted command that seemed to come from somewhere north of the stage. It was a gravelly voice, an old smoker's voice. As Cuno turned to locate its origin, the man called again: "Any of you sons o' bitches so much as twitches, I'll pump you so full o' lead you'll be rattlin' when you take that long walk through the smokin' gates!"

Silence.

Cuno froze, holding the Winchester between his chest and his belly. He moved only his eyes until he'd picked out the two rifles protruding from the rocks at the top of the mound that the three Mexican desperadoes had tumbled onto the trail to stop the stage.

His heart had slowed after the dandy had died without Cuno's having to finish him, but now it thudded again in his ears. He turned his head toward the stage. The rest of the gang was looking toward the rifles, with Mateo and Azuelo still on their hands and knees atop the coach. Inside, the girl was crying more softly now.

"Now that we're all relaxed," the raspy

394

voice shouted from the rocks, "go ahead and drop your guns and knives — every last one — nice and slow-like!"

Turning back toward the rifles, Cuno's heart beat faster. The rifles were aimed toward the men and Camilla gathered around the stage. There was a chance the two lawmen — who else could the riflemen be but Spurr and Sheriff Mason? — could not see him. The brush and rocks were thick between Cuno and the rubble pile.

His heart beat faster, impulses rippling up and down his spine and making his fingers tingle. He licked his lips, unable to wet them. Suddenly, he raised the Winchester to his shoulder and began ripping out one shot after another.

The slugs hammered the rocks around the rifles, and then the rifles were pulled out of sight behind the rocks but not before both maws puffed smoke and geysered burned-orange fire. Cuno kept shooting to pin the two men down. Beneath the thunder of his leaping rifle, he heard Mateo shout. Camilla shouted then, as well, and then out the corner of his left eye, Cuno saw the gang members jerking to life and bringing their rifles to their shoulders.

Their return fire joined Cuno's own thunder a couple of seconds before the burly young freighter's firing pin dropped on an empty chamber. Cuno lowered the gun and began sprinting toward the stage. He leapt sage shrubs and rocks, breathing hard, hardly aware of the burning pain in his snakebit arm.

Ahead, Mateo and Azuelo rolled the strongbox off the stage roof just as a slug fired from the rubble pile ripped into the lip of the coach's roof. At the same time, Camilla, Skinner, and the others were all down on their knees in various positions around the stage, hammering the rubble pile with return fire, keeping the lawmen pinned down long enough for the gang to secure the strongbox and fog the trail southward. The gang's horses stood ground-reined around the stage's rear, but several were fiddlefooting as though about to run from the gunfire.

As Cuno leapt a last boulder and landed flat-footed on the trail, Mateo shouted something in Spanish. The others fired and levered their rifles as they scrambled for cover on either side of the trail around the stage.

Franco Nervo lowered his rifle and ran for one of the horses. Cuno dropped to one knee behind a barrel cactus, and began frantically thumbing shells from his cartridge belt and into his still-smoking Winchester.

As he did, he cast quick glances around the cactus toward the top of the rubble pile. Occasionally, one of the two lawmen managed to return a shot, but the gang was effectively keeping them pinned down. When Nervo was leading a dapple gray by its bridle back toward the carriage, a rifle poked out from the rocks atop the rubble pile.

Most of the gang members had emptied their weapons. Cuno slipped his ninth cartridge into his Winchester, racked the shell, raised the rifle to his shoulders, took quick aim, and fired.

His bullet ricocheted off the lawman's rifle barrel with a ripping clang, tearing up rock dust. Cuno heard the old marshal bellow a curse before pulling his rifle back into the little hole he was hunkered in. Camilla, still thumbing fresh shells into her carbine's loading gate, glanced over her shoulder at Cuno, one eyebrow arched.

Meanwhile, Nervo ran the dapple gray back to where Mateo and Azuelo were arranging ropes around it. Despite Cuno and the other gang members' return fire, one of the lawmen snapped off a shot from the rubble pile.

Nervo screamed.

Cuno turned to see the short man lunge forward as blood leapt from the back of his leather jacket between his shoulder blades. Mateo cast a wild look at Cuno, shouting something in Spanish that Cuno took to be a command to keep up the covering fire while the outlaw leader and Azuelo got the money out of the strongbox and secured on the dapple gray.

"What the hell you think I'm doin', god-damnit?" Cuno bit out under his breath as he snapped off another shot at the rubble pile, behind which both lawmen were now hunkered out of sight.

When after another two minutes of steady fire neither lawman showed a rifle, Cuno and the others held their fire.

Smoke wafted. The stage horses whinnied and stomped, wanting to run.

Nervo lay belly down in the middle of the trail a few yards from where Mateo now swung a bulging burlap sack over the pommel of the dapple gray's saddle. Azuelo had his head and shoulders inside the stage, and a girl screamed, "No! Leave me be! Leave me be, you greaser bastard!" Her voice broke on that last, and the carriage lurched violently, as though she'd tried to give her attacker a savage kick.

"Greaser bastard, huh?" Azuelo's indignant voice was muffled by the inside of the coach, which jostled and squawked on its thoroughbraces as he apparently tried to pull the female occupant out the front door.

Cuno looked at Mateo, who was tying the sack to the dapple's saddle horn with a long rope. Keeping an eye on the ominously silent rubble pile, he ran over to the dapple gray and spoke to Mateo standing on the other side of the horse.

"What the hell's going on?" He jerked his chin at the stage, out the front door of which Azuelo was wrestling a kicking, screaming blond in a spruce-green riding basque. "We're only here for the money, right?"

"That's all we were here for," Mateo snapped back.

He jerked his own chin to indicate the desert behind Cuno. Cuno swung around, casting his gaze westward. He bunched his cheeks when he saw the dark group of riders barreling toward him from a quarter mile away and closing at a hard gallop. Riding in a tight formation, they wore blue or tan hats and blue tunics, gold buttons flashing in the sunlight.

Cuno muttered, "Soldiers?"

He remembered what the old marshal had

said about Mason riding out to the cavalry outpost on Hackberry Creek, and he cursed under his breath. Maybe the old mossyhorn hadn't been lying.

Behind him the blond girl wailed.

"Security," Mateo said with a hard grin. "We're gonna need security, amigo."

30

Mateo took the girl away from Azuelo and gave her a vicious slap with the back of his hand. She fell silent and sagged in the outlaw leader's arms.

As he threw her onto the back of his black Arabian stallion, Cuno turned to stare again at the group of soldiers hammering toward the trail from the east, a guidon whipping in the breeze above the soldiers' blue- and tan-hatted heads.

They were within three hundred yards now and closing fast, the thuds of their horses gradually growing louder, building toward a rumble.

"Mateo!" Camilla shouted, thrusting an arm out toward the soldiers, whom she'd just now seen after raking her gaze from the rubble pile behind which the two lawmen were still hunkered down out of sight.

"Si, si, mi hermana hermosa!" Mateo swung up onto his horse's back while Azuelo

hopped around on one foot, trying to toe the left stirrup of his dapple gray, the money bag flopping down the mount's right wither. "Perhaps, if you're done fooling around here, we'd best head to Mexico finally, huh?"

The outlaw leader laughed and buried his spurs into the black's scarred flanks. The stallion leapt with a shrill whinny off its rear hooves and galloped south along the powdery stage trail, Azuelo following suit on the dapple gray.

Camilla cursed in Spanish, then backed away from her covering boulder, keeping her eyes on the rubble pile. Skinner, Haines, and Calderon, who'd been hunkered in the brush near the stage's team, all whipped around and made dashes toward their jittery mounts, casting cautious looks back toward the rubble pile as well as at the oncoming soldiers.

Cuno grabbed Renegade's reins as well as the reins of Camilla's chestnut. Skinner sidled up to the younger man as Cuno pulled his horse up close to him and turned the stirrup out.

"Where the hell you suppose them bluebellies came from?"

"How the hell should I know?"

Cuno heard the defensiveness in his tone

and felt his cheeks warm. Skinner cast him a quick, narrow-eyed glance as he swung up onto the back of his buckskin. Cuno turned away from the man and tossed Camilla her reins, which she caught one-handed and on the run, not looking at him.

Wondering what she was angry about but too concerned about the soldiers as well as the lawmen to dwell on it, Cuno swung up onto Renegade's back. He was about to boot the horse on up the trail when two rifles barked nearly simultaneously behind him. Enrique Calderon was blown sideways off his saddle and directly into Renegade's path, the wound in his head spewing goo in a long, thin line across the trail.

The paint reared with a start, giving a raucous whinny.

As Calderon's horse whipped around and into Renegade, nearly knocking Cuno from his saddle, Cuno glanced toward the rubble pile, a stone dropping in his gut when he saw the two lawmen — the man called Spurr as well as Dusty Mason — dashing out from the far eastern edge of the pile and into the scrub, firing their Winchesters on the run and from their hips.

"Mierda!" Camilla cried, propping her carbine on her left forearm and squeezing off a shot that sent Mason diving for cover

behind a half-buried rock.

The old marshal had dropped to a knee and was levering his Winchester. As he tried to get Renegade back under rein, Cuno heard the bullets screeching over and around him, several hammering the rocks and brush on the opposite side of the trail.

Skinner gave a yowl and thrust his head forward, as though one of the slugs had nipped the back of his neck, then kicked his piebald into a lunging gallop on up the trail.

"Get moving — I'll cover you!" Cuno yelled at Camilla as she racked another shell into her Winchester's breech, then fired another shot at the old lawman. The chestnut was already bounding forward, and her slug merely clipped a greasewood branch behind the man.

Spurr didn't so much as flinch but triggered two more quick rounds, evoking a yell from Haines, whose own horse had thrown him when the lead had started flying again. As Camilla hammered up the trail, casting an anxious glance behind at Cuno, Cuno jerked back hard on Renegade's reins and triggered a round at Spurr one-handed.

"Mount up!" he shouted at Haines.

Haines clutched his cream's reins in one hand and staggered toward the horse's stirrup. Cuno racked a fresh round and glanced at the man, about to shout at him again. But then he saw the blood on the outlaw's face. He appeared to have been shot through both cheeks. Blood oozed in a glistening, frothy torrent from between his grimacing lips.

"Fuck!" Haines shouted, the curse obscured by the blood.

"Mount up, Haines!" Cuno shouted again and raised his Winchester toward Spurr once more.

The old lawman had him dead to rights, but Cuno heard the lawman's hammer click on an empty round.

"Goddamnit!" he shouted, tossing the rifle aside. "Mason, where the hell — ?"

Another rifle barked twice, one slug drawing an icy line across Cuno's cheek, the other evoking another scream from Haines, who flew forward against his cream, throwing his arms up and out. The bullet that had taken the outlaw through the back must have gone all the way through him and into his horse, because the cream lurched sideways, then piled up on its right stirrup in a broiling swelter of adobe-colored dust.

Haines fell over the horse and lay writhing along with his mount.

Cuno reined Renegade hard right and rammed his boots into the paint's loins. As rifles thundered behind him, stitching the air around his head with screaming bullets, causing dust to puff along both sides of the trail and perilously close to the horse's scissoring hooves, he hunkered low and gave the beast its head.

He glanced to his left where the soldiers were now angling toward the trail, within a hundred yards now, dust puffing from raised pistols.

Spurr's raspy voice bellowed behind Cuno: "Goddamnit, Wilson, 'bout time you joined the party!"

Cuno kept Renegade several paces behind Camilla, who was riding behind Skinner, who in turn followed both Azuelo and Mateo, who held the girl on his saddle before him. Taking a hostage didn't set right with Cuno — especially a young girl. But he'd counted close to ten cavalry riders. Including the two lawmen, that made the odds twelve against five. Having the girl might slow down their pursuers or cause them to think twice before taking potshots at the outlaws.

When Cuno had galloped a quarter mile, he saw that Mateo was checking down his black, and the others were following suit. They were all curveting their mounts, looking down trail, as Cuno slowed Renegade and turned the skewbald paint, as well. He stared down the ribboning trail of cream-colored dirt, saw the soldiers led by two men in civilian garb — Spurr and Sheriff Mason — pounding toward him.

Mateo cursed and booted the black past the others, a savage look in his eyes. The girl was hunched before him. She appeared pale and delicate. Her blond hair had fallen from the bun atop her head. It was mussed and dusty, and her eyes were swollen and red, her cheeks wet from tears. The sight of the terrified girl in the clutches of such a savage as Mateo de Cava poked Cuno with guilt and revulsion.

He fought it off, swallowed it down. What could he do about the girl, anyway?

He was on a trail that could lead him in only one direction. There was no turning back. He wasn't fooling himself about the dandy in the powder-blue suit. He may not have had the stomach to kill the man in cold blood, but he was just as guilty of the man's murder as the man who'd dropped the hammer on him twice.

And the blond was likely the dandy's daughter.

Cuno watched as Mateo reined up the black about fifty yards back down the trail and held one of his silver-chased .45s to the girl's head. Spurr and Mason checked their own mounts down, followed by the cavalry men behind them, about fifty yards down trail from Mateo.

The outlaw leader shouted, "You follow us, amigos, and this pretty gringa gets a hole drilled in her head! *Muchacha bastante rubia!*" Mateo nuzzled the girl's neck, keeping the pistol taut against her temple. Then he laughed jeeringly. "Clear out, or she dies!"

Spurr and Mason shared a glance. Spurr looked back at Mateo and lifted his weathered, bearded face as he shouted over the head of his big roan, "You kill her, you die hard, amigo." He rose up in his saddle and pinched his eyes down hard beneath the brim of his battered tan hat. "I personally will see you hang slow!"

"I warned you!" Mateo shouted, then reined his black around hard. He galloped past Cuno, Camilla, and the others then angled off the right side of the trail and into the pinyons and mesquites carpeting a gradual rise amongst red rocks. The incline rolled up against a steep-walled, red sandstone mesa.

"Mateo, where are you going?" Camilla yelled, taking the words right out of Cuno's mouth.

"We're taking the high ground, *mi her-*

mana. We will rest our horses, wait for our pursuers to disperse, then head for Mejico!"

"That's tough terrain!" Cuno called after the man. "The horses are already winded!"

Mateo said nothing as he continued galloping up a low rise, his black charro jacket powdered with white trail dust, his black, silver-stitched sombrero flopping down his back. Skinner and Azuelo followed Mateo up the rise, Skinner casting a skeptical glance back at Cuno and Camilla.

Cuno looked down trail once more. Spurr, Mason, and the soldiers were milling around, the two lawmen conferring with a silver-bearded soldier with long gray hair wearing a tan kepi and yellow glove gauntlets.

Maybe the hostage would hold them. Maybe she wouldn't. If she didn't, Cuno knew Mateo well enough to know what would happen to her.

As he and Camilla followed the others up the rise, heading for the mesa wall, Cuno wondered how far they were from the Mexican line. They couldn't be more than an hour's ride. If they continued through this rough country beyond the trail, who knew how long it would take them to reach it?

It was clear why Mateo had chosen this

route, however. They could more easily be followed on the trail, and from this higher ground they could see if they were being shadowed.

As they climbed the ever-steepening rise to the base of the mesa wall and then rode alongside the formation, in its shadow most of the time, Cuno kept an eye on their back trail and saw no sign of their pursuers. They had a low stretch of open desert on their right. On their left was the mesa wall. The longer they rode with the wall beside them — it looked like a very long ridge — Cuno grew worried.

If they were attacked, they'd be trapped against the mesa.

When they'd ridden several miles from the looted stage, they stopped to rest and water their horses in a small stream that ran out from a narrow gorge cleaving the mesa from west to east. The gorge was rocky and lush with grama and bromegrass, small cottonwoods, and willows. A few yards beyond the gorge's mouth, the stream tumbled down a thirty-foot ledge — a pretty falls in a setting made for a picnic . . . if one were looking for a picnic rather than an escape route to Mexico.

They dismounted where the stream ran out of the canyon, loosened their saddle cinches to give the mounts a breather, and slipped their bits from their mouths. Renegade and the other mounts were sweat-lathered, the heat radiating off them and intensifying the pungent, leathery horse smell.

Mateo brusquely pulled the girl down off his stallion's back and threw her down hard beside the stream.

"Take it easy," Cuno told him. He'd removed his canteen from his saddle horn, and he was holding it now, ready to fill it from the creek. His voice was calm, but a burning rage at the outlaw leader made his pulse throb in his temples.

Mateo looked surprised. "Huh?"

"So we need her as a hostage. That's no reason to mistreat her."

"I didn't mistreat the little gringa *puta*."

"Yes, you did," Cuno said with a mildness that betrayed his eagerness to draw his .45 from its holster. He stared hard at the dark-bearded, dark-eyed man who stood a good two inches taller. "I'm sayin' don't do it again."

Mateo grinned maliciously. "Oh? And what if I do?"

"I'll kill you." The threat surprised even Cuno.

Mateo continued grinning as he glanced

at Azuelo, who'd just set the money pouch on a rock beside the creek. Azuelo returned Mateo's devious glance, then, straightening, slid his narrowing, incredulous gaze to Cuno while sliding his hand toward his belly gun. Mateo did the same with his own hand.

"Hold on, *pendejos!*" Camilla barked, shoving Cuno aside and moving up in front of her brother. "In case you lost count, we're down to five rider—"

A rifle bark cut her off. Mateo screamed and lurched forward, grimacing and squeezing his dark eyes closed while reaching around toward his lower back with one hand.

Camilla screamed, then, too, and threw both hands up toward her brother's chest as if to hold him upright but then she was crumpling beneath the tall Mexican's powerful frame.

Before Cuno's mind had caught up to what had just happened, Mateo was on the ground, on top of his writhing sister. Mateo cursed shrilly and lifted his head, gritting his teeth savagely and reaching for the Green River knife sheathed on his right thigh.

Cuno palmed his Colt and, bringing the gun up while clicking back the hammer, dropped to one knee to stare into the brush east of their makeshift day camp — the direction from which the shot had come.

"Hold your fire, goddamnit!" Spurr's raspy, enraged voice shouted from somewhere back in the rocks and brush growing up close to the stream, directed at his own men. "Goddamnit, Wilson — I didn't tell no one to shoot!"

Skinner and Azuelo had both spun around to face the brush, their bodies poised to return fire, their backs and necks taut as razor wire. Azuelo held an ivory-butted Remington while Skinner crouched over a carbine.

Cuno's mouth tasted like copper. He held his index finger taut against the Colt's trigger, waiting for another blast, frustrated because he couldn't see the men who'd been trailing them unseen and were now crouched just beyond the camp, ready to take him and the others down bloody.

Spurr was one wily old coyote to have tracked them so stealthily with a passel of tinhorn soldiers.

Mateo heaved himself up off his sister, leaving a patch of blood on the front of Camilla's calico blouse.

"Mateo!" she cried as the outlaw leader, red-faced with rage, went over and pulled the cowering blond girl up by her arm.

He dragged the sobbing girl to a rocky ledge that overlooked the brush and trees carpeting a gradual eastern slope. Cuno saw the bloody wound in the man's back, just up from his left kidney. It pasted his shirt tight against his body and quickly began to look like an outer layer of blood-sodden skin.

"You bastards!" Mateo shouted, holding the girl in front of him and raising the Green River knife to her neck. "You think I was joking you about killing this girl?" He laughed demonically. "What do you think now, bastards?"

Spurr shouted from somewhere down the brush-carpeted slope, "Don't do it, de Cava!"

The girl screamed as Mateo jerked her head back taut against his chest. Standing about ten feet directly behind the outlaw leader, Cuno raised his Colt straight out from his shoulder and fired.

31

Mateo's head jerked violently forward.

He dropped both arms and stumbled toward the lip of the ledge. The girl fell to her knees, shrieking. The knife fell from Mateo's hand and clattered onto the rocks at his high-heeled black boots.

As Camilla screamed and both Skinner and Azuelo shouted in horror, Mateo swung around toward Cuno and tried without success to palm one of his two fancy Colts. There was a gaping cavern in his saddle-brown forehead, leaking liver-colored blood and white chunks of bone and brains. The blood and brains had dribbled down to cover his right eye while the other eye rolled straight up into the man's head, showing only an egg-like white.

Cuno swung his smoking Colt toward Azuelo, who'd beat him to the mark. Yelling fiercely, the Mexican fired at Cuno a half second after a bullet flung from the brush-covered slope had plowed into his side beneath his outstretched arm and exited his body via his lower left rib cage, nudging his shot just wide enough that it kissed the slack of Cuno's left shirtsleeve before hammering into a pinyon pine behind him.

Frank Skinner was down on one knee, screaming as he triggered his carbine down the slope.

As the crackling of pistols and rifles rose from the brush, Cuno leapt forward, grabbed the blond girl beneath her arms, and dragged her back behind a boulder, out of harm's way. Bullets screeched through the air around him, riddling Skinner, who continued to scream and trigger his carbine as he flew backward into the stream with a splash. Cuno fired several shots to try to hold Spurr's men at bay, then turned to Camilla, who stood staring, mouth gaping, at her dead brother.

"We gotta go!" Cuno shouted, grabbing the girl around her waist and jerking her around toward her horse ground tied in the tall grass near the water. "We're heading up canyon!"

As a bullet slammed into a rock between Camilla and the creek, she jerked back to life with a start, then grabbed her chestnut's reins. Cuno emptied his Colt at Spurr,

Mason, and the cavalry riders before he grabbed the money pouch. He'd gone through too much to leave the cash behind. He'd take his chances without the girl, try to get shed of his pursuers another way, but he wasn't going anywhere without the money.

When he was sure that Camilla was following, crouching and triggering shots behind her, he headed up the canyon at a hard run, leading the fiddlefooting Renegade along a narrow game path along the creek.

Bullets hammered into the rocks and brush around them, but after they'd run a few yards, boulders closed around them, and the canyon swerved southward, the walls offering cover.

Behind, the shooting dwindled, and Cuno could hear Spurr shouting orders and arguing with another man, probably the commanding cavalry officer. That faded, too, the farther Cuno and Camilla led their horses on up the narrow, rocky canyon path, and soon all they could hear were the falls and the tinny rattle of the water of the stream dropping down its terraced bed, flowing over half-submerged rocks.

"Are you sure we can get out of here this way?" Camilla said when they'd both stopped to eye the falls looming before them.

Cuno shook his head. "No. We might be boxed in. At least there's a way around the falls." He started forward. "Let's see if the horses can make it."

He led Renegade across the creek that rose to Cuno's knees. On the other side there was a trail of sorts that snaked up the ledge, on the left side of the thirty-foot falls.

It was a tough, steep climb for both Cuno and the paint, both dropping to their knees several times, but they gained the ridge about fifteen minutes later. Camilla and her chestnut were right behind them, the girl's boots squawking, the horse blowing and shaking its head owlishly, as she came up to where Cuno stood watching the stream slide on over the ridge and down into the canyon below.

Farther down the canyon, there was no sign of Spurr and the others.

Cuno turned to Camilla. She said nothing as she stared down the canyon. Her eyes were glassy, stricken. Her breasts rose and fell heavily as she breathed. She hadn't yet comprehended what had happened to her brother.

"I'm sorry, Camilla."

She shook her head and continued to face

418

down the canyon.

Cuno sucked in a deep breath, his heart continuing to pound against his rib cage. Finally, he swung around and continued on up the canyon along the stream. "A little farther and then we'll rest."

A hundred yards up canyon, the walls began to open. Cuno and Camilla stopped here, where they could keep an eye on the narrower canyon up which they'd come and hold off any pursuers. They ground-reined their horses in the tall grass near the stream, fed them each a couple of handfuls of oats, and let them graze.

Then they collapsed side by side in the grass, in the shade of a tall willow, and Camilla doffed her hat and rested her head on Cuno's shoulder.

Cuno removed his own hat as well as his handkerchief. From here, to his right, he had a good view of the eastern canyon floor, the steep, rocky slopes on either side glowing nearly as white as flour in the sunlight, the floor of the canyon leafy, grassy, and shaded along the stream.

Cuno offered his canteen, which he'd just filled at the creek, to Camilla, who shook her head. He took a deep pull of the cool, refreshing liquid, then shoved the cork back into the mouth, and set the canteen beside his thigh. He wrapped an arm around Camilla's shoulders, drawing her tight against him.

"It's down to just us," she said, vacantly staring at the grass.

"You paid a high price, springing me from the prison."

"I was beginning to think so." She pressed her cheek more firmly against his arm, snuggling against him. "But now I'm not so sure."

"What changed your mind?" Cuno frowned at her. "I killed your brother back there."

"You saved the girl. She was innocent. She did not deserve to die so that we could make it to Mexico with a bag of stolen money."

"We likely won't make it now." Cuno cast another cautious glance down canyon, then ran a hand through his blond hair, squeezing the sweat out the feathery lengths of it curling down behind his shoulders. "You know that, don't you? They'll get around us, cut us off."

"*Si.*"

"We could give ourselves up, I reckon." The thought galled him, but he would have done it for her. That part was surprising, but it was a feeling of silk fingers caressing his heart. He'd lost that feeling for a time.

She raised her eyes to his and shook her head.

He pressed his lips against her forehead, held them there for a long while. Then he leaned his head back against the tree and closed his eyes. He tried to relax, let a shallow doze steal over him, give him the rest he so badly needed.

No, they likely wouldn't make it to Mexico. But he wasn't ready to unhitch his wagon. Not yet. He'd make a hard run for the border. He wouldn't go back to prison, and he wouldn't die. He'd fight, even if it meant killing more innocent men.

It just wasn't in him to give in, to stop fighting, or to relinquish his freedom after it had been stolen from him merely for his saving innocent lives.

He'd been screwed. And yes, he'd killed innocent men, and maybe his being screwed wasn't justification for those killings. Maybe he should give himself up. But he couldn't. Especially not when it meant that he'd be giving up Camilla, as well.

Calm resolve swept over him, light as hummingbird wings. The leaves rattled, caressing his sunburned cheeks with alternating hot sunshine and cool shade. The creek smelled sweet. The grass whispered.

Occasionally, a twig broke out of a branch and landed in the grass with a swishing sound.

Someone gave a clipped yell.

Cuno lifted his head, and so did Camilla, as rolling rocks clattered. They both reached for their rifles as the clattering rose, and Cuno turned toward the canyon's southern ridge to see a mini-rockslide. Close on the heels of the first rocks, a man slid down into view behind the screen of breeze-brushed branches. He slid boots first, on his butt, waving his arms as if to break his fall.

A Henry repeater tumbled down the steep ridge beside him.

Cuno bounded to his feet and ran through the brush as Sheriff Dusty Mason flopped over on his belly about halfway down the ridge and rolled violently, grunting and groaning, until he'd piled up on the loose rock mounded at the bottom.

Cuno splashed across the creek and stopped at the base of the ridge just as Mason flung his right hand out toward a walnut-gripped Colt Army that had fallen out of his holster and now lay propped against a fist-sized rock.

Cuno kicked the gun, sending it rolling wildly before landing several yards away. He loudly racked a shell into his Winchester's breech and aimed the long gun at the sheriff's head.

Mason was on his belly, limbs akimbo, staring at his gun. Slowly, he turned his mustached face toward Cuno, his eyelids and mustache covered in chalky sand and dirt. He stared at Cuno darkly, almost without expression except for a thin parting of his lips. The skin above the bridge of his nose wrinkled, as though he were bracing himself for a bullet. Blood stained some of the rocks around and above him.

Cuno stared tensely down at the man who had arrested him and forced him to stand trial for killing the territorial marshals. Cuno's heart thudded faster and faster, and he felt his finger drawing tighter and tighter against the Winchester's trigger.

All that he'd been through over the past year had been caused by one man who wouldn't accept his explanation for killing the badge-toting privy rats . . .

Footsteps sounded from the direction of the creek. Cuno glanced back to see Camilla walking up from the stream, looking around warily, scanning the ridge, as she held her cocked rifle in both hands across her blouse. She turned her head toward Cuno, dropped her eyes to the sheriff, then raised them again to Cuno and held them there.

Her gaze was cast with skepticism, expectance.

"Go ahead," she said softly, stopping six feet away from him and the sheriff. "This is what you have been waiting for."

Mason slid his frightened eyes between them.

Cuno looked down at the man once more. Then he lowered his rifle, walked over and grabbed the man's rifle out of the brush, and heaved it into the creek.

"Watch him. Make sure he doesn't have any more weapons on him."

He depressed his Winchester's trigger, then ran back across the stream and stopped beside a boulder. From here he could see more clearly down canyon, and just as he swept his gaze across it, he saw a man running out from behind one boulder to crouch behind another, smaller boulder along the base of the gorge's southern ridge.

Cuno triggered a shot that puffed rock dust from the ridge wall about two feet behind a man's shadow and a buckskin mocassin.

"That's far enough, marshal!" he shouted. "We have Sheriff Mason over here. You come another step farther, I'll drill him!"

Spurr poked his head out from behind the boulder, the brim of his hat casting a wedge

424

of shade over his forehead, just above his leathery eye sockets. He was holding a rifle, and he appeared to be breathing hard, crouched low, a hand on his knee, his eyes narrowed to slits.

He nodded, waved a hand in supplication. Then he dropped to one knee and stared anxiously up canyon toward Cuno, who shouted, "Throw that rifle out. A long ways out!"

Spurr held his gaze for a moment, as though he were considering the order. Finally, he threw his rifle about twenty yards out toward the middle of the canyon, where it piled up in a thick tuft of sage and bear grass. Too far away for the old lawman to make a run for it without Cuno's hearing and having time to grease him.

Cuno cast his gaze down canyon. No soldiers. Only rocks and the shimmering creek. Spurr and Mason must have followed Cuno and Camilla alone. The soldiers had likely ridden around the mesa, surrounding their quarry.

The young freighter turned to see Camilla leading Mason across the creek, water splashing up around their knees. Mason held his hands shoulder-high. Blood glistened low on his pin-striped shirt, just above his shell belt on his left side. It looked like a bullet wound. His long mustached face was dirty and sweat-streaked, and his dark brown hair hung in his eyes.

"If we're not going to kill him," Camilla said, canting her head toward the sheriff, whose large blue bandanna ruffled around his neck in the breeze, "what are we going to do with him?"

Cuno glared at the man. "Oh, I didn't say we weren't gonna kill him. But first he's gonna clear us a path to Mexico."

32

Cuno stopped Renegade at the edge of the mesa and stared down at the broken red rocks piled below, which were gathering elongated afternoon shadows.

Over the years, the rocks had tumbled down from the crest of the mesa wall, which was neither steep nor high on this western end of the formation, and now the fallen boulders offered good cover to the blue-clad cavalry soldiers hunkered behind them.

They waited there near the bottom of the game trail that angled down the ridge, knowing the trail was Cuno and Camilla's only way off the mesa. They'd circled around to cut off their quarry, and they'd probably been waiting there most of the hour it had taken the two remaining outlaws to make their way from east to west across the formation's table-flat top.

All Cuno could see of the federals were patches of blue tunic and the crowns of their tan or blue hats, the occasional yellow-gauntleted glove wrapped around the neck of a Spencer carbine, the barrel of which bristled above the boulders. A couple of the rifles were now angled up toward Cuno, though they dropped when Spurr yelled from east along the ridge, "Hold your fire! They have Mason!"

Cuno glanced at the sheriff, who sat his pinto only two feet ahead of him and on his right side. Cuno had a slipknotted noose around the man's neck. He'd also tied the end of his rifle barrel into the knot, so that Cuno's Winchester was snugged tight against the back of Mason's neck.

Cuno held both the end of the rope and the rifle in his right hand. The rifle had a live cartridge in the chamber; its hammer was cocked.

If anything happened to Cuno, the slightest jerk of his trigger finger would send a .44 round careening through the sheriff's head, killing him instantly.

Cuno glanced at Camilla sitting her chestnut bay about five yards directly behind him, her hair slicing across her forehead in the dry afternoon breeze. She slid her eyes from the waiting soldier to Cuno, a faint question there. Cuno looked east along the crest of the mesa. He could see neither

428

Spurr nor the lawman's horse. He hadn't detected the man on his trail, either, but he'd known the old marshal had been following, likely staying a good half mile back.

Now he didn't mind letting Cuno know he was there, likely within range of his old-model Winchester. Now he was here only to keep the nervous cavalry riders, most of whom were under twenty, from snapping off another impulsive shot and getting the sheriff drilled.

"Keep your rifles down and let him through!" Spurr ordered.

"What do you mean let him through?" This from a gray-haired gent down on one knee beside a flame-shaped escarpment about thirty yards out from the base of the mesa. He was staring up the ridge toward Spurr.

"You heard me, Wilson," Spurr shouted raspily, his voice pitched with frustration. "Let him through. Let him through clean." A pause, then Spurr's voice again, lower this time but still clear in the quiet desert afternoon and in the heavy silence welling up from below. "We're gonna let him and the senorita go."

Wilson stared up at Cuno. His face was like a raw block of copper with wooly tufts of silver-gray sideburns and a waterfall mustache and goatee. Slowly, he rose and held his Spencer carbine across the thighs of his blue wool trousers with the yellow stripe tumbling down the outside legs.

"All right," Cuno heard him say with the same grim note of frustration he'd heard in Spurr's voice. "Stand down, gentlemen. Uncock your rifles, hold them down." His chest rose sharply. "We'll let them pass."

There were ten or twelve men in the rocks around him, forming a semicircle around the area where the trail dropped down the ridge to the gravelly floor of a wash littered with driftwood chunks and dead Spanish bayonet leaves left by the recent heavy rains. Young, sun-browned faces, some sporting the down of attempted mustaches and beards, stared out from beneath shading hat brims.

The young soldiers all lowered their rifles and slackened their shoulders. Most remained crouched behind their covering rocks, peering over the tops or around the sides while two others, one a heavy, older man with sergeant's stripes on his sleeve, stepped out from behind their own covers, looking incredulously up the ridge at Cuno while holding their rifles straight down along their right legs.

"Nice and easy, now, Sheriff," Cuno said,

prodding the man with a gentle push on his rifle.

Mason held his own reins in his hands. Now, lowering the reins before him while sitting straight-backed and tense in his saddle, he tapped his heels against his pinto's ribs and started off down the trail. Cuno put Renegade down the slope, staying close enough to Mason, riding just off the man's left stirrup, in fact, to keep the Winchester barrel snugged against the back of the man's neck.

Cuno could hear Camilla's horse's slow hoof thuds behind him, following about five yards back. As Cuno rode, swaying easily in his saddle, he raked his gaze around the soldiers below and then to Spurr, whose craggy, chestnut face he could see peering over the top of a rock about fifty yards east along the rim of the mesa.

Renegade dropped gradually down the gentle grade, Cuno leaning slightly back in the saddle but keeping his right arm fully extended with the Winchester, holding the rope in the same hand against the rifle's neck. His arm was getting tired, but it kept him distracted from the continuing burn in his left forearm, a little worse now with all the tramping around.

Sweat trickled down his back. He was

relatively sure the soldiers wouldn't disobey Spurr's orders, but there was no telling with raw recruits, which was what several of the young soldiers appeared to be. He'd be glad to get clear, though he had little doubt the soldiers and Spurr would follow him clear to the border. What would he do with Mason?

Kill him?

The man deserved nothing less. Cuno had already killed one innocent lawman, and Mason wasn't really all that innocent, after all. Besides, if he was as close to the border as he thought he was, he could kill Mason and hightail it with Camilla on down into the cool, blue Mexican mountains and never be seen or heard from again, his bills collected.

He and the girl could live the rest of their lives quite comfortably with the money in the sack dangling from her saddle horn.

He followed Mason onto the second switchback in the trail. Down, down they dropped until they bottomed out on the gravelly wash. The sergeant, who had a knotted white scar on his blunt chin, regarded Cuno stoically, a nerve in his cheek fluttering along his jawline. Cuno pinched his hat to the man.

"Through there," he told Mason, nodding

toward a gap between two mounds of granite-laced limestone. A well-trammeled trail lay there, between clumps of brown bromegrass and jimsonweed, angling south down a narrower wash intersecting with the main one. A soldier stood to the left of the gap, sort of tucked into the rocks there. He stared defiantly up at Cuno, freckles sprayed across his deep red cheeks, a strip of snow-white skin showing just beneath his hat band.

He held his rifle up across his chest, and he was flexing his right hand around the Spencer's neck.

Cuno kept his eyes on him, and as he and Mason approached the lad, the private's taut cheeks slackened. He slowly lowered his rifle to his side and slid his blue gaze away.

Cuno could hear Camilla's horse plodding along behind him.

A horse whinnied shrilly. Cuno jerked with a start and drew back on Renegade's reins. Wincing and canting his head forward, away from the rifle barrel, Mason drew his own horse to a stop. There was another whinny, nearer and shriller, and he whipped his head around to see Camilla's chestnut shaking its head as it sent the last notes of the scream careening toward the mesa ridge behind them.

The chestnut tried to rear. Camilla cursed and held the reins taut, keeping the horse's forelegs on the ground while it snorted and blew.

Cuno's heart raced. He looked around to see what had startled the chestnut.

Then he saw the soldiers' horses tied to a picket line off the right side of the trail, in an alcove of sorts amongst the rocks. A rangy bay stood sideways to the trail, regarding Cuno and the others curiously, its bright eyes white-ringed.

"Shhh," Camilla told the chestnut, leaning forward to run a calming hand across the horse's left wither. "It's all right. He's just curious — that's all."

Cuno glanced around at the soldiers. He winced slightly at the pain in his right arm but kept the Winchester snugged taut against the sheriff's head. When he saw that none of the soldiers appeared to be raising a weapon, he put his head forward once more.

Mason had turned his own head sideways, looking back at Cuno. Side teeth shone beneath his slightly upturned lip. Fear shone in the sheriff's eyes.

Feeling a dull satisfaction, his heart slowing, Cuno said, "Ahead, Sheriff. Nice an' slow . . ."

Mason touched his heels to the pinto's flanks. Cuno did likewise to Renegade's flanks, and the three continued on up the draw, Cuno glancing back to see the wash dwindling behind Camilla, boulders crowding into his view from both sides, the soldiers walking out away from the rocks now to track the outlaws with their baleful gazes. The trail angled around a large chunk of sandstone and mica-flecked shale shouldering into the canyon from the left, and the soldiers and the main wash were out of sight.

Only the mesa loomed, glowing dark copper now as the sun continued angling westward.

The trail continued angling on up the draw, the walls of which lowered gradually until the canyon leveled out on a broad flat peppered with more sage, catclaw, and gnarled cedars. Here, Cuno finally removed his Winchester from Mason's neck, but kept the noose on the man. They all three broke into a gallop and held the hard, ground-consuming pace until they stopped to rest their horses at a spring lined with rocks and small willows.

Cuno scouted the area on foot. The northern distance stretching back toward the mesa was clear. The Diamondback range humped up beyond the mesa — rocky and pink and striped with salmon.

Cuno looked around with his field glasses. No, nothing out there. Even the breeze had died. But he knew Spurr was there. Somewhere. The old marshal was keeping pace. Bad ticker and all. The mossyhorned bastard was not accustomed to losing, would not give up the chase until Cuno and Camilla had reached the border.

"Get over here, Mason," he said as he headed back to the spring.

Camilla and the sheriff were sitting with their backs against a low, stone shelf on the far side of the spring. Camilla's rifle lay across her thighs, the barrel angled toward the sheriff, who sat with his hands tied behind his back, the noose still circling his neck. The bloodstain on his lower left side had grown. He and Camilla were both looking at Cuno.

"What for?"

"I said get over here."

The sheriff looked at Camilla. She kept her dark eyes on Cuno.

"I won't tell you again," Cuno warned.

Mason heaved himself to his feet and tramped heavy-footed over to where Cuno stood on the other side of the spring. He was breathing hard and sweating, his shirt basted against his chest and shoulders. He grunted softly, painfully, against the wound that had opened in his side.

"You gonna kill me now?"

Cuno shoved the man to his knees. "Put your head down."

"I'll take it from the front."

"Get your head down!"

Mason sighed and lowered his head to the ground. He felt a sharp pain against the back of his head, and he figured it must have been the bullet. He was dead. But then the pain awakened him. That and the thud of shod hooves growing louder. He heard a horse blowing nearby and the squawk of saddle leather.

"Good Christ." Spurr's voice.

There was the soft crunch of moccasins in the gravel near Mason. Someone shook his shoulder.

"Sheriff?" Spurr's labored breath whistled in his nostrils. "You with us, Sheriff?"

Mason groaned, lifted his head, felt goat heads and gravel sticking to it. He blinked. Spurr reached up and brushed the gravel and burrs from the sheriff's forehead with a gloved hand.

Mason looked around, frowning. "What . . . ?"

No sign of the firebrand and the Mex girl. No sign of their horses, either. Nor of Mason's, which had been tethered to a cedar to the left of the stone shelf.

Mason brought his gaze closer in, saw the money sack sitting beside him, two feet away, just as Spurr picked it up and untied the rope around its neck with one hand. The old marshal looked inside the bag and frowned. He couldn't quite believe what he was seeing. Spurr had thought maybe they'd left him a couple of angry rattlesnakes.

He shoved a hand into the sack, pulled up a fistful of greenbacks, small bundles of twenty and hundred dollar bills wrapped in heavy brown paper bands.

"All of it there?" Rubbing the sack of his head where Massey had tattooed him, Mason looked incredulous.

"Looks like it. Won't know for sure till we count it."

"Where's Wilson?"

"Worthless bastard's waitin' for us a mile north. I told him to stay put, wait for me to send a mirror message. He done sent a few of his boys back to Diamondback with the girl."

Spurr returned the several bundles of greenbacks to the bag and dropped it to the ground. He tramped around the spring and climbed atop the stone shelf, staring south-ward across a broad expanse of desert painted with the reds and pinks of a fast-approaching sunset and rolling away toward low, violet mountains that marked the Mexican border.

Vaguely, he saw two riders and one rider-less horse galloping off across the flat toward the mountains. They were little larger than pinheads from this distance of nearly a mile.

Spurr shook his head, cursed under his breath.

Captain Wilson hadn't made it to Dia-mondback until early that morning. He said he'd been running down renegade Apaches before getting caught out in the storm, but Spurr had smelled hooch on the man's breath. If the man had gotten his soldiers to town just an hour sooner, Spurr would have had Massey in custody now.

Now, it looked like the gringo desperado had gotten plum away. Scot-fuckin'-free. No telling if he'd ever show his face north of the border again. Spurr didn't want to go after him — not really, for he felt the kid was in a situation he had little control over — but he had to. Running down despera-does was his job.

"Forget it, Spurr."

The old marshal wheeled in surprise. Mason was standing just on the other side of the springs that was turning lavender now in the late afternoon's tender rays. He was dusty, dirty, sweaty, and crestfallen.

"I don't forget nothin', Sheriff," he heard himself say with a passion he no longer felt. "You local boys don't understand us federals."

"Didn't you say we got some slavers who need runnin' down in the Nations?"

Spurr stared at the sheriff.

"Shit," Mason said. "Massey and the girl'll be in Mexico by sundown."

"You think 'cause he didn't kill you and left the money, we should let him go? I don't know why he did that — maybe he has *some* good in him. So do a lot of 'em. But he's a convicted murderer and an escaped convict from a federal penitentiary. That there's the sorta thing I don't never let go."

"Let it go, Spurr." Mason turned away, stared back toward Diamondback unseen across the vast, rolling desert.

"Why?"

"Because, goddamnit . . . !" Mason turned to glower at Spurr over his right shoulder. Lowering his voice, his features turning pensive, dropping his gaze to the grass around him as though searching for something he'd lost, he said, "I just been realizin' lately . . . I . . . I think I mighta made a mistake." He paused. "You ever do that?"

Spurr looked around uncertainly. He puffed his chest out, tramped heavily on down the shelf toward Mason. "Of course I ain't never made a mistake. And I'm insulted that you'd suggest I ever had!"

"Christ, Spurr."

"Come on, goddamnit," Spurr said, poking his hat brim low against the falling sun as he tramped on back to Cochise. He hoped Mason didn't see the relief in his eyes. "Let's get you back to Diamondback. Get you back in June's bed and on the mend again. And then maybe, *just maybe,* I'll let you pound the trail o' them consarned slave traders with me up in the Nations. I'll be goddamned if I let a winter come without runnin' *them* wolves to ground!"

Mason felt his lips quirk a reluctant smile as he walked toward Spurr and the big, waiting roan. "Spurr, about you an' June . . ."

"That's none of your business."

"Was that you an' her I heard the other night — ?"

"I told you, Sheriff, that is none of your

goddamned business. Another word out of you, and I'm gonna leave your sorry ass out here to fend for yourself against the bobcats and rattlesnakes. Lord knows me and Cochise could get to town on the lee side of supper if we didn't have to tote your rancid hide!"

"Ah, shit, Spurr." Mason chuckled.

When Mason had climbed up behind the old marshal, Spurr heeled Cochise north toward Diamondback. He glanced once more over his shoulder, saw nothing but the darkling desert behind him.

The riders were gone, swallowed by the shadows of the far mountains.

Spurr glanced at Mason, narrowing a speculative eye.

A mistake, huh? One hell of a damn mistake.

He remembered the eyes of Cuno Massey staring down at him over the kid's Winchester. He'd had Spurr cold. He could have killed him, and he hadn't.

Had those been the eyes of a killer? No. More like the eyes of a young bobcat only wanting to be left alone.

Alone in Mexico with his girl.

Well, at least Spurr would get to spend more time with June in the days ahead while the sheriff healed. Quite a woman, June Dickinson. If they made the mattress sing again like it sang the other night, her skills as a doctor might come in handy . . .

Spurr snorted to himself.

He urged the big roan toward Diamond-back, which seemed way too far away just now.